A DESTINY UNLOCKED

A DESTINY UNLOCKED

CHRONICLES OF AN URBAN DRUID™ BOOK 12

AUBURN TEMPEST
MICHAEL ANDERLE

DISRUPTIVE IMAGINATION®

Copyright © 2021 LMBPN Publishing
Cover by Fantasy Book Design
Cover copyright © LMBPN Publishing
A Michael Anderle Production

LMBPN Publishing
PMB 196, 2540 South Maryland Pkwy
Las Vegas, NV 89109

Version 1.00, December 2021
eBook ISBN: 978-1-68500-563-4
Print ISBN: 978-1-68500-564-1

THE A DESTINY UNLOCKED TEAM

Thanks to our JIT Team:

Rachel Beckford
Thomas Ogden
Deb Mader
Jim Caplan
Dave Hicks
Kelly O'Donnell
Paul Westman
Dorothy Lloyd
John Ashmore
Larry Omans
Debi Sateren
Diane L. Smith

Editor
SkyHunter Editing Team

CHAPTER ONE

"Let's do the time warp again!" Dancing in the front hall with Emmet, I've got my arms up and am rocking my pink dress and white sweater. He looks hilariously awesome in fishnets, a black leather bodice, and navy eyeshadow.

"Come on, Irish," he shouts up the stairs. "Stop stalling. Let's see your costume."

Ciara runs up the basement steps, her Magenta costume slightly more French maid than the original but hey, if you've got it, flaunt it.

"How cute." I point from her to him and back again. "You're both wearing thigh highs and garters. It's a marital bonding moment."

Ciara laughs. "And killing it. Look at those legs. I never thought I'd say it, but my hubby looks as good in heels and leather lingerie as I do."

Emmet lifts his arms and gives us a runway turn right as the back door opens.

Dillan walks in with his plus one, and I back up to check out their costumes. "Riff Raff and Columbia. Noice."

"Looking good, bro." Dillan escorts Evangeline inside our

back hall and closes the door behind her. "See, angel, I told you Emmet makes a fine-looking female."

"Oh, stop." Emmet bats his sparkly gold eyelashes and rolls his shoulders forward to make cleavage.

Evangeline's laughter rings through the air and makes everyone smile. It's like hearing a happy little songbird on a sunny summer morning.

The full-figured blonde with corkscrew curls emits a loveliness that radiates from her. I've resisted the urge to ask Dillan flat-out which of the many magical sects she belongs to, but it hasn't been easy.

I don't want to be rude...but I'm crazy curious.

We've only spent time with Eva twice before tonight. The night of the FUR Ball when everything went to shit and at Kevin's and Calum's wedding when my attention was all over the place.

What do I really know about this girl?

Nada.

Dillan calls her "angel," so I think that's a clue, but I had a chat with Myra about the hierarchy of angels. There are many kinds with many different purposes within the heavenly choir.

Or maybe she's not an angel, and he only calls her that.

She flashes a full-dimple smile and gestures at our costumes. "Dillan said it was an all-out *Rocky Horror* night, and he was right. You all look wonderful."

I curtsy and hold out my skirt. "We try. Come in. We're predrinking before we leave for the club. What can we get you? FYI, we've stocked our bar, and we've all spent time as bartenders in our aunt's pub—"

"Stepmother's pub," Emmet corrects.

I make a face at him. "I'm still not used to that. Anyway, my point is you can pretty much ask for anything, and we'll get you set up."

"A Cosmo would be lovely."

"Oh, yummy choice."

Emmet checks with Ciara, and when she nods, he winks and gestures for us to head toward the living room. "You ladies get comfy, and I'll play the part of bartender tonight."

I lead the way toward the front of the house as Sloan jogs down the stairs. He's dressed in a plain blue dress shirt, slacks, and a beige jacket. For other people, this might be a normal outfit. For Sloan Mackenzie, it's probably the strangest costume of the group.

He jogs down the stairs and frowns at me.

"You don't like it?"

He pulls at the pants and scowls at the jacket. "It feels awful. What is this made of?"

I giggle and look at Eva. "Sloan is used to the finer things in life. He's a clothes whore and has likely never had a poly-blend touch his beautiful skin in all his life."

Sloan frowns at me and smiles at Dillan's date. "It's wonderful to see you again, Eva. You mustn't let Dillan keep you to himself so much. We'd love to have you drop in more often."

"Yes, we would," I add.

The flush on Dillan's face is unfamiliar.

Honestly, this whole scenario is unfamiliar. Since when is Dillan not the cockiest guy in the room?

"Call me greedy," he says, "but I wanted Eva to myself before foisting the entire family on her. Clan Cumhaill tends to be a bit much. I didn't want any of you to scare her off."

I laugh. "Pot-kettle much? You're the worst of us. If we should cordon off anyone to keep from spooking new people, it's you."

Emmet slides three cosmopolitans in short-stemmed martini glasses across the island's counter and looks at Sloan and Dillan. "Guinness or whiskey, boys?"

"Whiskey," they say in unison.

"Jinx," Dillan shouts, punching Sloan in the shoulder. "Geez, Irish. It's like you don't even try."

Sloan rubs his shoulder and looks at me bewildered.

I chuckle. "No siblings, remember? Give him a break and remember what you said about making non-Cumhaills feel welcome."

Dillan snorts. "Sloan's been a Cumhaill since the beginning. He's our late bloomer."

I'm glad he remembers it like that. In truth, Dillan didn't take to Sloan in the beginning because of how he first tested me and my druid skills. He traumatized Kady while pretending to mug me, and that didn't go over well.

I thought Kady might've been the one for Dillan.

Nope.

Even with Kady, Dillan was only ever surly, saucy, and protective. He was never twisted up or lost in the emotions of dating her. Eva might well have done what no woman before has managed.

She's truly turned his head.

I hide my smile behind my drink and sip the fruity delight. "So, Eva, tell us, are we as bad as Dillan makes us seem? Do you have siblings to compare us to?"

Dillan frowns at me and tips back his tumbler, emptying the glass with three large swallows. "You don't have to answer that."

"I don't mind."

Dillan gives me the stink eye, and I shrug. "What? That's not prying. That's making conversation."

Eva chuckles at my brother. "Yes, I have many brothers and sisters—hundreds actually." I'm not sure what she sees in my reaction, but she's laughing again. "While they get rambunctious and sometimes spark a lively conversation, no, my relationship with them is nothing like you share."

"Hundreds of siblings," I repeat.

"Can you imagine?" Emmet asks.

I look from Em to Dillan and shake my head. "Nope. I can't wrap my head around that."

"How can you have hundreds of siblings?" Emmet asks. "Were your parents part of some empowered love-in commune or something?"

Dillan's scowl deepens. "What kind of a question is that, fucktard?"

Emmet shrugs. "Sorry. Just curious."

"No offense taken, Emmet." She chuckles again. "It's perfectly understandable that you'd be curious about the woman your brother is spending time with. I'm an angel, so immortality tends to increase our numbers."

So, I was right.

"No wonder I didn't recognize your particular energy signature when we first shook hands. I don't know that I've ever encountered another angel."

She sips her drink and smiles. "Then, I'm happy to be your first."

I gulp down my drink and slide my glass back to Emmet to go again. Then I pause and look back at Eva. "Is it okay if we get our buzz on? I don't know angel protocol."

Dillan groans and runs a hand over his face. "Don't make this weird, Fi."

"I'm not." I look around at the group and frown. "Was that weird?"

"No, it's fine," Evangeline says. "It's fine," she repeats to Dillan. "Please don't go out of your way to change anything because of me. I'm happy to be here and very hard to offend."

I laugh. "The hard to offend thing is a relief. I tend to offend people often. Just know I don't mean to. I simply don't filter well."

"There's nothing wrong with that. And no." She downs her Cosmo and sets the empty glass on the counter next to mine. "Getting a buzz started is a great idea. I'll warn you though, getting an angel tipsy is a different kind of experience."

Dillan grins, and it's the first glimpse I've seen of the brother I know and love. "No complaints there."

I'm not sure I'm ready for the story behind their shared smile.

"So, the two of you met at Dionysus's housewarming party," Ciara says. "Is that right?"

Dillan nods. "Andromeda arrived late and brought a few friends. Evangeline was part of the late arrivals."

The next morning was when he first told me he was leading the "got laid parade." "I remember."

Emmet sets Evangeline and me up for round two, tops up Ciara, and sets Dillan up with a two-fingered dram this time around. "Okay, can I ask all the awkward questions so we can get them out of the way?"

Eva blinks. "Sure. Go ahead."

Emmet grins, and I'm almost afraid to—"Do you have wings? Can you fly? Do you live in the heavens and sleep on a cloud? Do you really have four faces—and if so, what do they look like? Most importantly, why are you dating Dillan?"

Dillan flashes Emmet a middle-fingered salute. "You have to excuse my eejit brother. He's suffering from stage five stupid. You don't have to answer any of those questions."

"I'm fine, sweetie. Stop worrying." Eva lifts her chin as if trying to recall the rapid-fire questions. "Yes, I have wings. Yes, I can fly. No, I live in a condo and sleep on a memory foam mattress. Yes, I have several faces, but that's hard to explain and more ethereal so I can't show you without burning your eyes out of your skull. Most importantly, I'm dating Dillan for the sextastic orgasms."

Dillan chokes on his whiskey and bends over sputtering and red in the face.

Hilarious.

"I love this girl." I step beside D and pound his back as he spits and sputters. "All righty then. Great answers."

Dillan accepts the napkin Sloan offers him and pats his face dry. "Fi isn't the only one who lacks a filter."

Eva grins and side hugs him, sliding her arms around his waist to rest on his opposite hip. "You said just to be me."

"Absolutely." I take my glass to the sink to rinse and leave for later. "Always be yourself. I doubt there's anything you could say or do that would faze us."

"On that note," Emmet says, "should we go and act foolishly in a drag club for the night? This corset is killing me."

I burst out laughing. "Sounds perfect."

———

Sloan *poofs* us to the back room of Dora's drag club, Queens on Queen, and we file into the club and find our hostess with the mostess. It's been an odd month of transition with Dora and with all the time Merlin has spent in Iceland with the dragons, I've barely had the chance to check in and find out how life without his empressness is going.

Merlin told me he loved performing in drag and his life in the club, so that much hasn't changed. He also told me to go with the pronoun of the person I see in front of me, so that's what I've been doing.

Tonight, she's one hundy percent Pan Dora, club owner and drag queen entertainer extraordinaire.

I wave as we file in, and she shuffles over to meet up with us. "Brad and Janet, the couple of the evening." She leans in for a double kiss before moving on to Sloan. When she steps back, she winks at Emmet. "Handfasting agrees with you, Em. You're looking more fabulous than ever."

Emmet laughs. "Thanks. Not too many men can say their wife did their makeup before they went out."

Ciara laughs. "It was strangely sexy."

Calum laughs, joining us with Kevin. "The two of you think

everything is strangely sexy."

"Do the words strange and sexy go together?" I ask.

Sloan shakes his head. "I don't think so, no."

Calum waggles his brows. "That's why you two are such a perfect Brad and Janet."

I grab Calum's thigh garter and snap it.

"Ow. Damn it, Janet."

That gets a round of chuckles from the fam jam, and our last two guests arrive.

"Ohmygoodness, look at you two." My mouth drops open, and I pull out my camera to take pictures of Nikon as Frank N Furter and Dionysus as Columbia.

"Respect." Kevin raises his fist to bump the two of them. "Dionysus, you're crushing the red metallic lips, my friend."

"Thank you." He flashes us a toothy grin and tips his gold sequined hat. "I admit, I love wearing cheetah prints and boas. I think I need to fill out my wardrobe with much more of it."

"Hells yes you do." Dora holds out her arms and gives us a full view of her cat print bodice. "Now, all you fabulous people take your seats. I'm going to go kick us off."

"Are we dancing in the theater?" Emmet asks.

"Oh, cookie. Looking like that, you can do whatever you want. Damn, Cumhaill, you make drag look good."

Emmet grins, and Calum and Dillan laugh at him.

When Dora sashays off toward the stage, Dillan shakes his head. "I don't know why you look so proud of yourself, Em. She said you look good dressed up as an over-the-top guy in drag."

Emmet shrugs. "The important part of that compliment was that I look gooood."

I giggle and point at our row of seats. "Everyone. Let's get ready to have some fun. We have first-timers here, so we gotta represent."

"Represent!" my brothers repeat, pumping their fists in the air as we hustle our butts to take our seats.

CHAPTER TWO

"**A**m I the only one who thinks it's a mystery of the universe how Dillan ended up in love with an angel?" I stick my fork into the stack of raspberry chocolate chip pancakes and fan three out on my puddle of syrup.

Emmet snorts while holding out his hand, and once I've poured a top layer of maple goodness on, I pass him the bottle. "The bigger mystery is how she fell in love with him. I'd think Dillan violates everything in the angel handbook."

Calum and Kevin dig into the back bacon and pass it along. "Dillan's not that bad," Calum says. "He's just grouchy and opinionated."

"And swears the most out of all of us and sleeps around more and holds grudges longer," I add.

"And is the first to start a fight and the least remorseful for his actions."

Calum chuckles. "Okay, on paper he doesn't test well, but maybe as an angel, Evangeline can gauge his soul or something. He's a loyal, solid guy who lives by a code. He's protective of others and would give his life for any one of us."

I lift my glass of juice. "True story."

"Or maybe he really is a superhero in the sack, and she's in it for the orgasms," Ciara adds.

I laugh and almost spit pancake. "Or that."

The six of us are still chuckling about that when my phone rings and the African tribal call of the Lion King tells me Garnet is on the line. After patting my mouth with my napkin, I get up from the table and grab my phone from the island.

"Good morning, boss man. How's life living on the wild side?"

"It could be better. I'm calling an emergency meeting at ten o'clock."

"Team Trouble or Lakeshore Guild?"

"It's a Guild of Governors meeting. Will you be in the country and able to attend?"

I check the clock. "So far, so good, but that's forty-five minutes away. You never can tell what the world might throw at me."

"I'd laugh if that was funny. Fine. Barring any mass murder or mayhem, I'll see you there."

"Agreed. It should be fine." I end the call and text Nikon.

If you're going to the meeting at ten. Swing by and I'll go with you. If you don't mind the company.

I lurve your company, Red. You know that.

K. See you soon.

I set the phone on the counter and rejoin the family breakfast. "Sorry."

"Ye mentioned forty-five minutes. Does Garnet need us fer somethin'?"

"Only me this time around. He's calling an emergency Guild of Governors meeting."

"Why? What's gone wrong now?" Calum asks.

"He didn't say. He requested my presence and went on to call the others, I suppose." I reclaim my cutlery and get back to enjoying my breakfast. "I texted Nikon to see if he wants to go together. He'll be here soon to pick me up."

"Och, good." Sloan sips from his coffee mug.

I swallow and cast a sideways glance at him. "You realize I don't need an escort. I'm perfectly capable of getting to and from a meeting without anything crazy happening."

Cue the arched brows and crooked smiles around the table.

"Shut up, you guys. It's not like I'm a total disaster. I still have the odd moment of normalcy."

"Odd is right," Sloan says. "While none of us would ever argue yer not capable of takin' care of yerself, the truth is when ye have one of us with ye, we all feel a little better."

Emmet nods. "It cuts down on the response time."

Calum snorts. "That's true. Then we know when you've been attacked or kidnapped or sucked back in time from the moment it happens instead of hours later. It gives us a chance to rally."

"Har-har, you guys are hilarious."

"Are ye sayin' we're wrong, *a ghra?*"

"Well, no, but you don't have to think it's so amusing that my life is a centrifuge of whacked and weird."

"Och, we might make light of it, luv, but none of us find it amusin'. I think it's safe to say we'd all prefer ye not have to deal with such things."

They all nod.

"But, knowing that's not likely," Calum says and snags a raspberry off Kev's plate, "making fun of you is the next best thing."

I ignore the snickers and go back to eating my breakfast. "You guys suck. Have I mentioned that lately? No? Well, you do."

Cue a round of belly laughs at my expense.

Yeah, you gotta love family.

When I first learned the Lakeshore Guild of Empowered Ones held regular meetings, I envisioned a Hogwarts head table kind of gathering. Reality rarely lives up to my imagination. Garnet would never be confused with Dumbledore, and none of the others remotely resembled their on-screen counterpart.

Except maybe some Snape-like creepers.

That was back in October of last year, and a lot can change in a short time.

Not everyone turned out to be horrible. Suede, Zxata, Nikon, and Garnet have grown to be some of my closest friends.

Nikon especially.

The Greek and I hit it off from minute one, but what I didn't know was he'd been waiting to meet me for centuries after his grandfather told him we'd be the best of friends. Time travel is trippy.

When Nikon snaps into my living room at a quarter to ten, I start the dishwasher and hug him. "Hey, that was super fun last night. Thanks for joining."

"It was a blast. An evening out with your clan is guaranteed to be a good time."

"Dionysus had fun?"

"He seemed to. I think he's still a little cautious after the whole Loki thing, but he's bouncing back."

I make a mental note to check in with him and meddle with his sex life. I know, that's not something a friend normally plans on doing, but Dionysus is a special case. Loki undermined his manly mojo. I want to make sure he's getting back on that horse.

And when I say horse, I mean—

"Earth to Fi." Nikon waves in front of my face and grins. "Are you ready to roll?"

"Yep. Sorry. Give me two." I hold up my finger and shuffle to the top of the basement steps. "Bruin, we're ready to roll. You coming?"

"On my way."

I wait the beat it takes before the air around me swirls and I feel the increased pressure in my chest as my bear companion takes his place.

Grabbing my purse off the wall hook, I loop it over my head and settle it on my hip. Next, I come back to the living room and lean up the stairs. "Okay, Nikon's here. We're going to go."

"Good luck," Kevin calls from their room. "Let us know if the city is about to be invaded by dark fae forces and we should evacuate."

"Will do."

Sloan *poofs* down and holds his fist up to bump. "Good morning, Greek. How are ye feelin' after last night?"

"Good. It was a great time."

"It was indeed." Sloan chucks my chin and gives me a soft kiss goodbye. "Be good, *a ghra*. Try not to get into too much trouble. Keep an eye on her, Greek."

"Always."

I roll my eyes at both of them, but they mean well, and they're not wrong. It never hurts to expect the unexpected when I leave the house.

Or even when I stay in the house.

Before we leave, Nikon raises a finger to catch Sloan's attention. "Hey, Irish, can I ask you a favor?"

"Of course. What is it?"

"A friend of mine had an item of great value and importance stolen from him, but he can't admit it or there will be widespread repercussions. Do you think you could help me help him find it?"

I smack his shoulder. "Hello? What about me? Didn't you hear how I scried for Ireland's pacifier and solved the case of the skunk stolen sou-sou?"

Nikon grins. "This item is a magical antiquity. It falls squarely in Sloan's wheelhouse. Considering he's been mentoring you on all things druid, I figured he was the go-to guy on this."

"Och, don't look so dejected, luv. Yer not the perfect fit fer every disaster, just most of them."

I chuckle. "I suppose that's true."

"It's also true that Irish is the emperor of empowered objects," Nikon says. "The three of us will likely work together on this, but I think Sloan is the man to take the lead."

Sloan lowers his chin. "Thanks, fer the vote of confidence. What's the stolen item and when would ye like to get started trackin' it down?"

"The item is Eros' bow, and we need to find it last week if possible."

Sloan chuckles. "Well, I don't have time travel on demand, so I'm not sure how I'll do on last week, but I can get started right away."

"Eros' bow?" I release my initial panic. "You had me worried for a sec. So what if someone shoots love arrows indiscriminately into the crowd? Big whoop. The next thing we know we'll be facing world peace."

Nikon runs his fingers through the shaggy blond hair hanging over his eyes. "That's if the people shot are unattached and a good match. Imagine if someone shot Myra with one of Eros' arrows and she left Garnet and Imari to be in love with say…the Toronto Chief of Police. How do you think that would go?"

Oh, that would be ugly. "Garnet would likely go full killer kitty, murder him, expose the empowered world, and cause a citywide manhunt."

"Exactly. Love is an incredible gift in the right situation, but in the wrong hands, it's as dangerous a weapon as a ballistic missile or a bomb."

"Gotcha. Okay, so who does he think stole it?"

"I'll take you two to see him after this meeting, but for now, we gotta go. We don't want Garnet to go killer kitty on us."

Sloan bends down to give me a chaste peck on the cheek. "In the meantime, I'll learn what I can about the bow and put some subtle feelers out into the empowered circles to see if anyone is talking about taking it or possibly selling it."

"Thanks, Irish," Nikon says. "Again, please play it close to the vest. The members of the Greek Pantheon aren't the nicest bunch and the gods and goddesses who fall within its purview try not to draw the attention of the others."

"I promise the utmost discretion."

I squeeze Sloan's hand and hook my arm around Nikon's for transport. "Speaking of not wanting to draw the attention of a nasty bunch, we need to go, or we'll be late for a meeting."

While the monthly meetings for the Lakeshore Guild of the Empowered Ones are often at different restaurants or locales around Toronto, when someone calls an emergency meeting, it's Guild Governors only, and it's always in the conference room at Garnet's downtown office.

Before we enter the room, we grab the last two robes hanging on the hooks and shuck them on. "Oh, goody, we're last."

"Everyone knows cool kids are fashionably late."

"Does the man who turns into a lion know that?"

"Oh, yeah. He'd be late too if he could."

"Would you two jackasses like to stop jabbering in the hall and come take your seats?" Garnet sounds pissy, but that was only his exasperated pissy voice. His irate pissy voice has a lot more growl.

Nikon makes a face at me, and I stifle a laugh. I fix his lapel, and he looks me over and gives me a thumbs-up. The two of us walk in like scolded children and Suede lifts her hand across the table and points at the two empty chairs beside her.

Glancing down, I confirm we are—in fact—exactly on time but decide not to make a point of it. Obvi, something has our not-so-benevolent leader wound up. We take our seats and give Garnet our undivided attention.

"Now that we're all here and seated, let's get right to it. This morning I got word there's a mass gathering of reapers in town."

Eyes widen around the table, and I get a distinct impression that this is very bad news.

"If any of your sects are gearing up for something, I want to know now. This is the only time I'll accept your confession with full amnesty."

Conspiratorial gazes bounce around the table, and I finally give in to curiosity. "Sorry, could you 101 that for me? What does a mass gathering of reapers mean?" When eyes start to roll, I raise my hand and expand on my question.

"Obviously, I understand what a mass gathering is and am familiar with the concept of the grim reaper, but I mean in the context where you all look like you're regretting not wearing brown undies today."

Garnet stands at the head of the table and leans on his knuckles. "Reapers are warriors who serve Death. They're neutrally aligned and tasked with escorting souls of the recently departed to their final destination regardless of where that destination might be."

"Up or down, got it."

Garnet arches an ebony brow. "It's a little more complicated than that."

Suede shifts in her seat beside me. "Many sects have their versions of the afterlife: the Elysium Fields, Valhalla, Zion, Eden, Shangri-la, or conversely, Dystopia, Hell, Pandemonium, and Hades. Then there are the in-betweens like purgatory, limbo, or the Neitherlands."

Zxata nods across the table. "Reapers are the beings who escort all of us to our appropriate resting place."

"Death Ubers, got it. So, does a mass gathering have to be bad? Maybe they hold ruination conventions or get together to discuss tips on extermination etiquette or coaching classes on, 'You're dead... what to do now.'"

"Not likely, I'm afraid."

"But if they're neutrally aligned, maybe them being here isn't a panic button moment."

Garnet's scowl softens, and he relaxes onto his palms. "I'm afraid that's not likely. Before any mass death, there's a mass gathering of reapers. They're here for a reason. If we don't figure out why and stop whatever event is pending, a lot of people will die."

"Well, crappers. This is such a Monday morning problem. No wonder it gets a bum rap." I sigh and look around the table. "Okay, so who's planning something stupid?"

Nobody seems inclined to fess up.

"So, what then, should we go around to all the local diners and see if guys are handing out Post-its with peoples' names on them? Or to the big box builder stores to search for goofballs with a red Dust Buster?"

When everyone stares, I shake my head. *"Dead Like Me? Reaper?* Hello? Sometimes it's like talking to the walls in here."

"On that note," Garnet says, "if any of you would like to speak to me privately, I'll be in my office until two o'clock. You have until then to tell me what I need to know. After that, I'll hold you responsible if we end up with a demon released from hell or dark fae collapsing buildings in the downtown core."

"How much time do you think we have until we can't turn this around?" Zxata asks.

"For a natural disaster, they tend to gather earlier because there's nothing to be done but prepare. For an intentional event of mass destruction, their arrival usually signifies the beginning of the end."

"So, either way, we're screwed?" I say.

"Now you're getting it, little girl."

I frown down the table at Andreas Markdale, High Priest of

AUBURN TEMPEST & MICHAEL ANDERLE

the West Village Wizards. The guy is a lanky man with a dark skull-trim buzz cut and a new tattoo of a serpent wrapping around his throat.

I thought we were cool, him and I.

Huh…guess not.

Andreas was originally anti-Fi because I killed his cousin Salem when the dumbass tried to release a greater demon. Then we patched it up when I took out Horacio Baynes as his opponent to replace him.

It seems wizards are fickle folk because by the scowl he's sending my way, I'm guessing he's no longer wearing his half of our best friends necklace.

"What? Are you mad because we caught a murderous thief in the West Village a couple of weeks ago? Dude, pick your battles. That French douche canoe used you in hopes of avoiding Team Trouble extradition."

"You and your team had no right to pursue a wizard guest into my territory."

"Except that he broke into our office, tried to steal from my boyfriend's vault, and managed to steal from an event we were running security for. Any of those things give us the right to pursue him."

"Not the issue we're here to discuss," Garnet growls. "Back on track here, people. Reapers. Fess up. Let's stop this before we're looking at mass casualties."

"Fair point. Well, my ideas of how to track things down got pooh-poohed, so what do you want us to do?"

CHAPTER THREE

Nikon holds the door to STOA open for me, and I head into Sloan's antiquities shrine. The last time I was here, I was in my saber-tooth panther form, and Bruin, Doc, Manx, and I were chasing the Duchess d'Aboville around in her ghostly mandagot form.

Good times.

"How was yer meeting, luv?" Sloan comes out of the back hall. He closes the vault door behind him and locks things up. "What's the emergency? Or is that privileged information?"

I check with Nikon, and he shrugs. "Garnet didn't say anything about keeping it a secret."

No, he didn't, and honestly, I feel better when we bounce everything off Sloan. He has a breadth of understanding that boggles me, and that genius has saved my bacon a dozen times.

"We have it on good authority there's a mass gathering of reapers in the city. Garnet's freaking out because that only happens when large numbers of deaths are about to occur."

Sloan nods. "Aye. I studied the mass gathering of Pompeii in university. Sad but very interesting."

"Well, we don't have any active volcanos close by, so I think it's safe to cross that possibility off the list. Now, we need to work through every other potential source of mass death and stop it from happening."

"Oh, is that all?"

I nod. "Garnet is giving all the Guild Governors until mid-afternoon today to check in with our sects and report back if there's a potential of being behind the pending disaster."

Sloan chuckles. "The druid sect isn't much of a presence in the city. That's a very short list."

"Right? Lucky me. There's Merlin and us. I called him before coming over, and we're heading there now. Then Nikon needs to check in with his sect."

"Which is even smaller."

Nikon grins. "Me, my sisters, Dionysus, and currently added to that, Eros. Wanna join?"

"I do. I want to speak with him about his bow."

"Have you found anything?" I ask.

He grabs his leather jacket off the back of the guest chair and shrugs it on. "In the hour ye were gone? No, luv. I'm good, but I'm not that good. There are, however, things we need to know to help us narrow the search."

Nikon nods. "I told him you two would probably need to retrace his steps and ask him some questions."

When Sloan holds out his hand, I link our fingers. "All righty then, mass death first, then mass love."

Nikon chuckles and takes my other hand. "That's fine. We can fit both into our schedules."

Nikon snaps the three of us to the back office of the soup kitchen that shares the building with Queens on Queen. Dora has been a pillar of support for the homeless and hungry in the city for years. Whether empowered or no-magic humans, it doesn't matter.

Everyone is welcome.

Part of our agreement for her to take us on as our druid ink master in the beginning was that we'd volunteer and give her a hand.

It works out for all involved.

My brothers and I are happy to help, and it gives us a chance to keep our fingers on the pulse of what's happening on the streets.

"Oh, good timing, gentlemen," Dora says as the three of us make our way out of the office. "Come flex your muscles for me, would you?"

She's in bell-bottom jeans, a zebra print midriff sweater, and her long, black Cher braid is swinging down past her booty.

"Are you single-handedly unloading a supply truck of donations?"

She hands her load to Nikon and wipes her brow with a leopard print towel. "The driver delivers. It's not his job to help me unload them and put them away."

Sloan shrugs off his leather jacket, and he and Nikon get straight to work. After taking a moment to admire the scenery, I rush forward to grab a box too. "Wow, this is a lot of donated goods."

"It is at that," Dora says. "It's from a local poker club. Twice a year they have an in-house tournament, and the ante is forty dollars' worth of non-perishables. Multiply that by seventy or eighty players, and you get a very welcome donation."

"That's amazing."

"Angels come in all shapes and sizes, cookie."

That makes me think of Evangeline.

Man, spending time with her and Dillan last night was such a pleasure. Being around the two of them together makes me smile. "Yes, they do."

"So, on the phone, you said you needed to talk to me in an official capacity?"

"It's a formality. Garnet called in the governors this morning. There's a mass gathering of reapers in the city. We've all been tasked with speaking to our sect to find out if anyone is doing anything or planning to do anything dangerous."

"Reapers? Oh, that's not good."

"That's what Garnet said."

"Well, I'm afraid the search goes on for the source of the danger, girlfriend. The only thing I've got on my calendar is a Merry Queens and Scots bachelorette next weekend. Then I'm off to Iceland to spend a week with my other family."

"Oh, send Cazzie and the others my love."

"I will. Will Dart be joining me?"

"I'll ask him. I'm sure if there's an offer, he'll accept. He loves spending time with them and learning, and of course, spending time with Saxa."

Dora's grin broadens. "Oh, that boy is smitten."

"I know. Please tell me it's not one-sided."

"It's not, though Saxa is keeping things simple for now. Dartamont has a lot of life ahead of him and falling for the first female he spends time with is like a fourteen-year-old boy saying he's going to marry his homeroom teacher. He has more growing up to do before she'll allow their relationship to become anything beyond a special friendship."

"But she is fond of him?"

"Oh, yes. She adores him. Her hesitation is completely for his benefit."

"That's good." I release a heavy sigh. "I'd hate for him to have his heart broken."

"Hearts, plural." Dora holds up her fingers. "Westerns have three."

"What? Why didn't I know that?"

Dora chuckles. "Two primary pumps and a third that only

comes into play to offer increased blood flow during times of exertion in battle."

"Good to know."

Sloan finishes unloading the last boxes and hands them to Nikon to stack on the pile Dora had started inside the back hall.

"Are ye finished helpin', *a ghra?*" he asks, chuckling as he takes the one box I started to move.

I chuckle and surrender my load. "Yeah. Whew, that was a workout."

The boys laugh.

"Speaking of working out," Dora says. "I wanted to ask if I could start sparring with your lot at the Acropolis to get back into fighting form. I've spent the last centuries denying who and what I am. I need to get back into the swing of things."

"You're always welcome. We can add you to the chatroom, and you can come over whether we're there or not. Our Badass Bootcamp is your Badass Bootcamp."

Nikon nods. "Your rusty and out of touch is still stronger and better than most of us, so I wouldn't be too hard on yourself."

Dora chuckles. "That's kind of you to say, Greek, but when I was at my best, there was nothing and no one I couldn't take on."

Sloan grabs his jacket and shrugs it on. "Merlin of old isn't gone, my friend, only hibernatin'. We'll help ye as much as we can."

"Thank you. I look forward to getting back in shape both physically and magically."

I hug Dora. "Okay, off to speak to others about the reaper problem. If you think of anything you might be doing to cause a mass homicide or natural disaster, be sure to give me a call."

"I can safely say I won't be calling."

"Excellent. After all the trouble I cause in the eyes of the other guild members, I'll be glad if this disaster has nothing to do with me."

"That would be a refreshing surprise, wouldn't it?" Nikon asks.

"Sure would."

The four of us finish our goodbyes and snap off to Dionysus to speak to the Greeks.

The past few weeks have been tough on my favorite Greek god. First, he lost his ability to be sexually fabulous. Then he learned that Loki was targeting him for a perceived offense against his daughter, Hel, and the trickster god took him prisoner, tortured, and humiliated him.

That's a lot to come back from.

Although his bachelor apartment is back to normal and Dionysus is once again wearing his easy grin, I feel the hurt in him, and it breaks my heart.

"Hey, Tarzan. Looking good, my friend." I hug him for longer than necessary, but he needs it, so I let him absorb all the love I can send him.

My attention swings over to the Mediterranean man with shoulder-length ebony hair and swirling silver eyes. He's lounging on Dionysus's couch with his ankle crossed over the knee of his black jeans, and his drink pressed to his full, perfect lips.

Man, hanging out with gods is tough on the ego.

"So, what have you and Eros been up to today?"

"More importantly," Nikon adds, "might it have led to the arrival of a mass gathering of reapers?"

Eros arches a brow and pulls his glass from his lips. "When I find the fiend who stole from me there will be bloodshed. I can't imagine it being an all-out massacre, but I won't rule it out."

Nikon scowls. "Not good enough, *adelphos*. I need to vouch

for my sect, and as long as you're in the city, that includes you. We need to be clear on this."

Eros abandons his drink on the coffee table and stands. Whiskey sloshes over the rim of his glass as if it couldn't contain his contempt.

As he stalks closer, the rush of his power signature hits us like a bursting gale force wind.

Sloan and I both take a step back as the air pressure forces us off-balance. Nikon doesn't suffer the same effect. Then again, he's been dealing with gods and their fury for centuries longer than we have.

Eros finishes his approach directly in front of Nikon, and the hostility he's emitting makes my spear hand twitchy to call for Birga.

"Will I take an oath not to smite a room full of people if they're behind the theft of my most precious belonging? No. Human life is inconsequential."

"No, it's not," I snap. "If you really think so, why are you here, living among us? Don't let the portal door hit you on the way out."

Eros casts me a disdainful look and a fake smile. "To those of us who have stood long before this generation and who will stand long after, humans are nothing but bones and ash waiting to happen."

"We have to mean more to you than that. You're the god of love, for shit's sake."

"No. You're right. They also offer an outlet for my base urges as a male with needs. Other than that, they're weak and offer me nothing."

I scoff. "We offer more than an opportunity to wet Willy Wonka in Wonderland. Isn't it an occupational necessity for you to care about us?"

Eros snaps forward. He's inches before me, running my hair between his finger and thumb. The change in his position is

AUBURN TEMPEST & MICHAEL ANDERLE

jarring and sudden. The thrumming of my girl parts is even more alarming.

Sloan moves to intercept, but I swallow and hold up my hand to stop him from escalating this.

The rush of attraction I feel for Eros is wholly unnatural, and I fight it with everything I have. The warmth of his body against mine and the scent of his skin call something dark and hungry within me...

The raven-haired god brushes the back of his finger against my cheek and the sensations it releases are utterly indecent. I lock myself down and meet his gaze, showing him nothing.

I swallow, my nipples tight and tingly under my t-shirt. "I get that you're a god of attraction and I'm a measly human, but whatever you're doing, it's not going to work. Was threatening to smite the puny mortals foreplay? Do you really think I'll fall panting at your feet and beg for it? Think again. You are *so* not my type."

"Eros, stop," Dionysus snaps. "Fiona is my friend. She could be your friend too if you don't fuck it up. Friends don't try to seduce friends. That's a rule."

Eros holds me in his thrall for a moment more and releases me. "You're either very headstrong or very powerful to defy me like that."

"Both." Nikon flashes me an apologetic smile. "So, if you've finished making an ass of yourself, how about we get back to the problem at hand and talk about your missing bow?"

I groan, trying to rein in the waves of wanton overwhelming me. "That doesn't work for me at the moment. Sloan, I think I left the iron on. Could you please *poof* me home? Like...right now. Straight to our room if you don't mind."

Sloan frowns, but I don't want to get into it.

I toe off my shoes and am reaching for the button of my pants unbidden. Yes, I realize I'm standing in the middle of Dionysus's loft, but Eros's magic is gaining on me. "Like, right now, please."

"Do as she asks, Irish." Dionysus pushes him toward me. "We'll be here when you get back. I'm sorry, Fi. I didn't realize what he was doing until it happened. Don't worry. Distance and a few releases will ease the effects of his seduction. Now go."

Thankfully, Sloan doesn't argue, and a moment later we're in our master bedroom at home.

"*Gale Force*." I sweep a hand toward the door, and it slams shut. I cross my arms and yank my t-shirt over my head, tossing it as I go for my zipper. "Pants off, Mackenzie. I'm dying here."

Sloan seems stuck between fury and confusion, but thankfully, he doesn't hesitate. That's my guy. Always ready to pitch in where he's needed.

Stupid Eros. I really don't like that guy.

It's close to four when I'm back in control of myself and ready to return to Dionysus' loft. When we materialize, the three stop their conversation, and Eros stands and holds out his hands. "Nikon and Dionysus tell me I owe you one free strike by way of apology—"

Storming forward, I pull my arm back, call *Bestial Strength* to top me up, and swing with all my might. As Da taught me, I follow through as if I'm punching straight through the back of his head.

Eros assplants hard and slides across the polished floor with a look of surprise I'll never forget.

I shake out my fist and hiss as my knuckles protest the violence. I don't care. There's no way I'll regret giving his face everything I've got.

"That was me being friendly about being wronged and settling it the Irish way, dickwad. One free shot, now you buy me a drink and apologize for stepping *way* outside the friend zone."

Eros sits up and probes his cheekbone and the split in his lip. "This is you being friendly about it?"

Nikon is grinning ear to ear, his chest bouncing with amusement. "I told you she'd be pissed."

"Wow, my face hurts."

I step away from him, gaining some much-needed distance. "You're lucky I went for your face. Try something like that again, and I'm going lower...and it won't be my fist either." I flex my hand and call Birga to my palm. "Imagine her ripping through your scrotum and kebabbing your balls. Are you looking forward to that?"

"I am," Sloan says.

"Put Birga away, Red." Nikon holds up his hands as he approaches me. "You don't need to elaborate. He gets it. He fucked up."

Dionysus comes over, brings my throbbing knuckles to his lips, and kisses them better. The moment his mouth touches my skin, the pain ebbs away, and the redness from the impact subsides. "Are you okay, Jane? Everything ironed out?"

His touch soothes all the rough edges away, and there's no way it's a coincidence. I accept the Zen boost and release Birga to return to the tattoo on my forearm.

"Thanks, yeah. I'll be fine."

"The more important question is if Irish is okay." Nikon casts him a sideways glance. "You still have the strength to stand, do you, my friend?"

Sloan doesn't laugh.

He's locked in an aggressive stance, glaring at the god of love. If he could call a weapon to his palm as I can, he'd be moving in to draw blood. "I'm waitin' for *my* free shot. Stand up, asshole."

Eros chuffs and makes his way to his feet. "Your female defended herself against the slight well enough. Your request is denied."

Sadly, Eros's god healing has already kicked in, and his lip has sealed and stopped bleeding.

"How about this?" he says. "I offer you *both* the heartfelt apology owed. I've been in a foul mood since my bow was stolen and behaved poorly. While it doesn't excuse what I did, I assure you I'm not normally such a *dickwad*, as Fiona put it."

"That's true." Nikon sobers. "Eros can be spoiled, entitled, and often insensitive, but he's not usually such a tool."

Eros casts him a sideways smirk. "Thank you?"

Nikon sends us both an apologetic smile. "He's worth getting to know, guys. That's all I'm saying. This was an anomaly, I assure you."

"It better be," Sloan snaps. "Fi gets side-swiped enough by enemies. I won't have her fucked with by people who are supposed to be friends, even if they're friends of friends."

Nikon nods. "Trust me. I know Eros well enough to vouch for him. We have a long history. We grew up getting drunk together and crashing our chariots."

"And getting eaten by crocodiles," Eros adds.

Nikon smiles. "He's not even kidding about that."

I'm not sure what to do with that mental image, but it doesn't matter. I move next to Sloan and rub a hand over his shoulders. "It's fine. If Eros steps out of line again, you're up next and can practice your Oscar De La Hoya moves on him."

"With pleasure."

"In the meantime," I continue, "let's go over the facts of how the bow theft occurred and who might have wanted to steal it."

Eros's silver swirling eyes are quite unnerving when bearing down on you with full impact. "Everyone wants to steal it. My bow is one of the most coveted objects in the empowered world."

Dionysus nods. "A great many beings, immortal and not, covet his bow. Perhaps if we start with what happened, Fi and Sloan can help us narrow down a list of suspects. Fiona's entire family has trained to apprehend those who pillage and plunder."

Nikon points at the couches. "Let's sit."

Eros takes his seat and sighs. "No offense, but I still don't understand why you believe they'll be any more successful in finding my bow than we will? They're humans, flawed, mortal, ordinary humans."

I huff. "We *are* humans, but I wouldn't say we're ordinary. Sloan happens to be the smartest guy I know, and he's brilliant with antiquities and those who covet them."

Eros studies Sloan and doesn't seem impressed. "Brilliant, you say."

"Absolutely. While most guys grow up sneaking off to watch porn, Sloan was watching Google Earth."

Sloan frowns at me. "When you hear words like that come out of your mouth, do you still think you're complimentin' me?"

I chuckle. "My point is that you're exceptional and smart, and you know everything you need to know about lots of things to figure out how to find out about other things you don't know... You know?"

Nikon rakes his fingers through his hair. "Did that make sense to anyone, or did I just have a stroke?"

"It wasn't just you," Dionysus says, his face screwed up. "Jane, come sit with me before you hurt yourself. I think you overexerted this afternoon. Maybe you're dehydrated. Here, we can eat those little chicken pockets you like so much."

He gestures at the coffee table, and a ceramic platter of buttered chicken samosas appears next to the bottle of whiskey and five glasses. "There we are...all the comforts of home. Sit, and we'll get to the bottom of things."

Dionysus produces two spotted bean bag chairs. One is hot pink with black spots, and the other is bright gold with brown. Both of them have fuzzy little ears and the face of a leopard.

I take a seat, and as my butt shifts deeper into the little balls of the stuffing, the leopards make me think of another jungle cat. "Crap. I totally missed the deadline to check in with Garnet."

I'm wriggling to get to my back pocket when Nikon holds up his hand. "I RSVP'd for the both of us. You're good. I didn't think reporting about reaper issues would be high on your list."

"No, it wasn't. Thanks. But what did you tell him? Can we be sure that Eros's bow won't be the cause of the mass death hanging over the city?"

"Sure? No. I don't *think* that's what's happening, but I gave him a heads up. Without another sect to blame, I'm in the hot seat. I'm supposed to keep him in the loop as things progress, and he wants us focused on finding the bow and eliminating it as the potential catalyst of death and destruction."

I giggle and grab a snack plate, stacking it high with a pile of warm samosas.

Nikon's golden brow arches beneath the floppy shag of his bangs, and he smiles. "You seem very pleased with my situation."

"I am. For once, the disaster is falling at someone else's feet. I love it."

He chuckles. "Honestly, that's fair. You face more than your fair share of shit-hitting moments. I'm happy to take the heat off you for a bit."

I raise my drink in salute. "To the Greeks. May your chaos be short-lived and easy to plunder."

Eros sends Nikon and Dionysus a questioning glance. "My confidence is not inspired."

Nikon chuckles and waves that away. "Start at the beginning and explain to Fi and Sloan how someone made off with your magical bow. If you're lucky, they'll help despite your sexual supercharge powerplay."

I sigh and swallow a mouthful of sweet and spicy splendor. "Yeah. We're big like that. The lives of the many outweigh the sexploitation of the few. Go ahead, give us the lowdown."

CHAPTER FOUR

After hearing Eros's story, I call a family meeting at our place. I haven't filled them in on the gathering of reapers and what that means. With the addition of Eros's missing bow and what it means, I figure it's a good time for us to all brainstorm.

I release Bruin when we materialize at the back door and free him to catch up with the companions downstairs.

"Oh good, you're here." Kevin comes into the hallway at the far end of the house. "We have a visitor."

"Oh yeah? Who's here?"

Kevin steps back as I join him at the front of the house. Tad McNiff and his animal companion Aurora are sitting at the table.

"Hey, this is a nice surprise. It's good to see you. How are things?"

Sloan comes in behind me and extends his hand. "You're a welcome face to come home to. To what do we owe the pleasure?"

I study Tad as he shakes Sloan's hand and I'm relieved by what I see. McNiff's been going through a hard time since his father merged with the evil essence of Mingin and tried to kill him.

He looks good, though. Solid.

"I have news. Good news, I hope."

"Excellent." I turn as Dillan and Aiden come in from next door. "We love good news, don't we?"

"Although it doesn't seem like we get it very often," Dillan says. "Hey, McNiff, good to see you."

Tad rounds the table and commences the appropriate greetings for Clan Cumhaill. Those include handshakes, knuckle bumps, and backslapping hugs.

By the time all that is taken care of, Emmet and Ciara are jogging down the stairs, and Calum is unlacing his boots at the back door.

"The gang's all here," I say.

It's a good thing Sloan enjoys a busy house because with my family around there's always someone coming and going.

We give Calum a moment to come in and lock his sidearm in the gun safe, then show him we have a guest. "McNiff. Good to see you, my man. What brings you to our side of the pond?"

"Good news," I say, catching him up, "but we haven't heard what it is yet."

The general buzz of nine people in one room quiets down, and we all give Tad the floor.

"Well, as ye know, Lugh helped me settle things with Da's estate in the murder of my step-monster. The solicitor friend of his is a witch out of Cork, and she used a bit of his magic to help smooth the optics of things."

"That's really great," Aiden says. "We're all so relieved you didn't get jammed up in the mess of everything."

"For the most part, that's true, at least in the legal circles. It's a different story altogether with the neighbors and people in town. They all look at me like the poor little rich boy went psycho and offed his family."

"Fuck 'em," Dillan snaps, flicking his hand in the air. "Your friends know the truth."

"Exactly right," I say. "And your friends are one hundy percent behind you."

Tad grins. "That brings me to the good news."

Aurora lets out a shrill squawk and ruffles her wings. Her feathers fluff up, and it doesn't take a falconer to realize she disagrees.

Tad frowns. "It is *so* good news, girl. Ye'll see."

Now my curiosity is piqued. "Okay, spill it. What's the news?"

"Well, I came into a bunch of money and wanted new neighbors, so I bought the house down the street to try city life for a while."

"The Party Palace?" Dillan asks. "Mrs. Graham said someone bought it, but we were all still wondering who."

"Mystery solved." Tad pulls a set of keys from his designer jeans and jingles them in the air. "Anyone want to go over and check it out? I haven't started working on it yet. It's a bit of a dump, but I figured in this case, it was all about location, location, location."

The boys turn to me with the question hanging.

"Of course." I give it the green light. "We'd love to check it out. Family meeting about upcoming death and doom is postponed twenty minutes."

"Ominous." Kevin makes a face.

"Do I have a second to take off my uniform and throw on some sweats?" Calum asks.

"Yeah, you do that." I point at the bar in the living room. "We'll line up the celebratory toast and order pizzas, so we don't have to figure out dinner when we get back."

"Excellent. Be right back." Calum takes off toward the stairs, jogging up two at a time.

Kevin and Emmet launch into action, grabbing the glasses and getting us set up.

"This is really great news." I side-hug Tad and pat his shoulder. "We're happy to have you on the street."

"Thanks, guys. It means a lot."

"Of course. So, what do you think you want to do here? Are you looking for a job, taking it easy, or do you want me to hook you up with Team Trouble?"

Tad grins. "I'll take door number three, Monte. If I can help to take down the evil bullshit building in this world, I'm in. If my bastard father is ramping up for the Culling, I'll do anything I can to help fuck up his plans."

Emmet pours the first few drams of whiskey and frowns. "None of us blames you for what Riordan did. You know that, right? You have nothing to prove to anyone, least of all, us."

Tad accepts the glass and swigs it down in one gulp. "I tell myself that but there's this little voice in the back of my head that says different. Fighting this uprising is the only way I can think of to fight my demons."

"Then we'll fight them together." Aiden holds up his glass.

Calum jogs back down the stairs, and I hand him his tumbler while Emmet refills Tad's.

"To good friends becoming good neighbors." I raise my glass. *Slainte Mhath.*

"Slainte Mhath."

The Party Palace is a Victorian century home like all the other houses on our street. The only difference is this one has been rented out to university students since an absentee owner bought it almost ten years ago.

Prior to now, it's been the bane of our serenity, the blight on an otherwise perfect street.

I'm excited that's about to change.

Having Tad diagonally across the road will be great. We already started taking bets on whether it would be Aiden or Sloan who'd fill Da's shoes as the fun police.

Da's annual shakedown of drunken students has been a source of great amusement for everyone on the block for years.

It seems that tradition has ended.

"Wow." Emmet crinkles his nose. "I hate to say it, dude, but you were right. This place is a dump."

Aurora squawks, seemingly to agree.

Tad waves away the concern. "The current condition brought the price down a couple of hundred grand, so I can't complain. What I saved on the purchase price, I can invest in renovations."

"We'll be happy to help you paint and spruce things up," Kevin says. "If you want a mural or something fancy, Nikon and I have been working on some cool techniques."

While they talk *trompe l'oeil*, I saunter over to Tad's companion standing stiffly and gripping her perch. Aurora is a beautiful, red-tailed kite—similar to a hawk—and has been with Tad since he was a kid.

"May I offer you a few words of consolation? It's a lovely neighborhood, and once you get to know Bruin, Manx, Doc, and Daisy, I think you'll like it here. We're close to the Don Valley green space and have enough mice and bunnies to keep you busy most of the year."

Since she's only been squawking and not talking, I take that to mean she isn't interested in making friends quite yet, so I leave her to her thoughts.

"She'll come around," Tad says. "She was the same way when I went to university. Once she gets to know the other companions and adjusts to our new life, she'll thaw out."

The heavy footsteps on the hardwood stairs bring the touring group back down to the main floor.

"Okay, we've got our work cut out fer us." Ciara grins. "Kevin and I just so happen to be in the market fer a new passion project. The restoration of a badly neglected home is exactly what we need."

"Exactly." Kevin grins. "If you're game, we'll bring over warm cinnamon buns in the morning. You're in charge of the coffee."

Tad nods. "How do ye say no to an offer of home décor and warm cinnamon rolls? I'll be ready. Thanks, guys. This means a lot to me."

"You're welcome." I give him a big hug and point at the front door. "Now, everyone back home, we have a meeting to hold and a disaster to stop. Tad, if you want to get sucked into the chaos, come along. If you'd rather take one night to settle in, no one will blame you for sitting this one out."

"Och, no. Gettin' sucked into the chaos is why I'm here. I'm in."

We get everyone back to our place before the pizzas arrive and have enough time to get squared away with drinks before the doorbell rings.

Sloan answers the door while I pull out the plates and Emmet grabs the napkins from the drawer.

"Okay, so end the suspense." Dillan bites off the tip of his first slice. "We know you got called in by Garnet this morning and had some kind of sex marathon this afternoon—no judgment—but so you know, the companion animals are scarred."

I rub my hand across my face and sigh. "That wasn't my fault. Eros was being a dick and whammied me with sexual mojo. It happened. It's over. It will be filed among the topics never to be spoken of again."

"Consider it filed," Aiden says. "Let us not speak of sexual marathons and our little sister in the same sentence ever again."

Okay, that makes me laugh. As embarrassed and uncomfortable as I am, they are too.

I open a garlic ranch dip and dump some onto my plate next to my honey garlic wings. "So, let's go chronologically through my day. Garnet's meeting was about a mass gathering of reapers in Toronto. These supernaturals work for Death and deliver people to their final resting place: good, bad, or in between. When a bunch of them get together, it signifies the coming of mass death."

"Couldn't they be on vacation?" Emmet asks.

"Right? I suggested something similar and got the Garnet 'you're an idiot' look."

"Maybe it's about the Culling," Calum suggests. "If they know what's coming, they might be preparing."

Sloan shakes his head at that one. "The Culling isn't until the Winter Solstice—that's five months away. No. Whatever is happening, it'll be within days to weeks."

"The Culling is a global event," I add. "That wouldn't explain why reapers are gathering in Toronto."

"How many are too many?" Calum asks. "When they say a gathering, how many are we talking about?"

"Maybe a gathering means a group," Emmet says. "Like a gaggle of geese or a murder of crows."

Dillan pauses with his pizza at his mouth and gives Emmet a look. "I'll be sure to tell Grim and his friends your theory when men with sickles surround us."

I continue. "Garnet had each of the Guild Governors contact the people within our sects to gauge where the danger might lie. For right now, the biggest lead we have falls at Nikon's feet."

"Nikon?" Calum almost chokes on his pizza. "The Greek is planning a mass murder?"

"I did not see that coming," Emmet says.

"It's always the ones you least expect," Dillan says.

Sloan rolls his eyes and I wave that away and try to keep everyone on topic. "Of course not, but Eros is staying with Dionysus, and he's having a bit of a crisis at the moment. It might be related or not. That's what we need to figure out."

"Eros?" Calum repeats. "What happened to make love, not war? Since when does Cupid kill people?"

"He doesn't, but someone stole his enchanted bow. He's concerned that whoever took it might cause a major upset if they start shooting it at the wrong people."

"So, we need to know who stole the bow," Aiden says. "We find that out, and maybe we can stop this mass death before it happens."

"That's the plan."

"Who does he think took it?"

"That's the problem. Dionysus held a post-Loki celebration orgy. Cue the drinking, the sex, the losing track of what's going on. Then Eros wakes up the next morning, and his bow is gone."

Dillan snorts while drinking his beer. "So, we get to interview the attendees of one of Dionysus's orgies? I'm in."

I roll my eyes. "You're in a committed relationship with an angel. Behave."

Dillan laughs. "Shall I remind you I met Evangeline at one of Dionysus's orgies? Don't put her in a box, Fi. She won't stay there."

"Back to the point of our story," Aiden says. "Do you have a list of who was at the party? More specifically, who Eros slept with or was near him when he fell asleep?"

"What I don't get," Emmet says, "is how anyone could walk out of Dionysus's loft carrying an enchanted bow and not get noticed. The thing is pretty freaking noticeable."

"I thought the same thing," Sloan says, "but when it's not in use the bow shrinks down, and he wears it as a pendant on a chain around his neck."

"Handy," Emmet says, "but not as secure as our weapons inked into our tattoos. It's a wonder the gods haven't figured out a better system."

"They likely didn't expect anyone to be stupid enough to steal from them."

"Good point."

Sloan finishes with his slice of meat lovers and hands me his crust. I take a bite and point it at them as I think. "Eros is fairly certain that it has to be one of four people he sexed at the end of the night. Before that, he didn't fall asleep."

"Okay, four's doable." Emmet hears his words and starts laughing. "And also doable."

Calum and Kevin get a kick out of that.

Herding cats, most days. Seriously.

I continue. "So, Eros remembers one of the women touching the pendant not long before they went to bed and when he woke up, it was gone."

"Do we know who the four people are?" Dillan asks.

"Nikon and Dionysus are working on that. Tomorrow we'll start tracking them down."

"So, what do you need us to do?" Aiden asks.

"For right now, keep an eye out when you're at work for anything that might trigger or set up a mass death event. We're not sure what's coming is an empowered issue. The reapers gather for any disaster, magical, natural, or otherwise."

"Then we keep our eyes and ears open." Aiden grabs another slice as he stands. "We report back if anything strikes us as a potential for disaster."

Emmet snorts. "In Fi's life, that could be just about anything."

"Har-har." I toss the crust at him.

He laughs, plucks it out of the air, and takes a bite. "Just keeping it real, sista."

The sad thing is…he's right.

CHAPTER FIVE

"Are you sure we're in the right place?" I cast Nikon and Dionysus a wary glance and focus on the mansion in front of us. The home is a four-story stone monstrosity surrounded by more trees than you would expect in the city. The manicured lawn stretches off into the distance and probably takes up as much land as my entire street.

The three of us are standing in the center of the arrival loop in front of the house, and I feel like an ant about to be squashed.

"You're sure one of the one night stand girls lives here? This place looks really big and powerful. If we misstep here, Garnet will get big backlash."

Nikon grips my elbow and gets us moving toward the door. "What happened to justice is blind, Red? I didn't expect you to back down from chatting with a potential witness to a crime because her daddy has money."

"I'm not backing down. I'm questioning our conviction before we go stir up trouble."

Dionysus laughs. "Since when do you worry about stirring up trouble?"

I throw him a look. "Maybe I'm maturing."

Nikon taps my nose and chuckles. "It'll be fine, I promise. Sloan trusts us enough to take you out for the day. You need to trust us too."

"I do trust you. That's not the problem."

"Then what is the problem?" Dionysus asks. "Yes, the people who come to my parties are often gods, and kings, and daughters of powerful families steeped in wealth and influence, but take their clothes off, and they're only naked people."

Nikon laughs. "You're not afraid of nakey people, are you, Red?"

"I suppose not, no."

Nikon chuckles and presses the doorbell. "Besides, we're starting here because this one-night stand girl is a friend. Relax. Everything is fine."

When the loud chiming of pipe organs ends, the door opens, and we're facing an alarmingly skinny man with black hair standing up like a startled sea urchin on the top of his head. "Yes?"

Nikon lowers his chin. "Good morning. We're here to speak with the young miss—"

"I've got it, Tig. I'm expecting them."

I recognize the voice, but it's out of context until I see Suede skipping down the grand staircase toward us. "Come in. Come in."

She waves us in, and Tig closes the door behind us.

I admit I'm a little nervous for him. Instead of Tig, I'm pretty sure his name should be Twig. "Do you need anything, Miss? A tea tray, perhaps?"

"That would be lovely, thank you. Would you ask Leola to add some honeyed bear cookies?"

"Of course, Miss."

Tig strides away with far more speed than seems advisable. If he bumps into something, I'm pretty sure he'll snap a leg. "Your butler is—"

"Too skinny, I know. I keep telling him if he doesn't eat something and fatten up, I'll put a plaid shirt on him and set him out in the garden to startle crows."

I chuckle. "Funny but not funny. Is he sick?"

"No. Just really old. Elves get like that sometimes. He still lives to serve though, and has been with my family for centuries."

"Suede, I'm on a call." The loud voice booms from above and echoes off the marble and glass of the grand entrance.

"Sorry, Papa." She points toward a receiving room opposite the entrance and waves for us to follow. Once we're inside, she closes the door and relaxes. "Sorry about him. I'd say he's in a bad mood, but he's not. That's the way he is. He's a yeller."

"Not a problem." I'm awed by the room's gold-gilded opulence. "Wow, you live here?"

"Against my wishes some days, but yes. Honestly, the house is big enough that if I want to pretend I live alone, it's fairly easy."

A knock on the door brings the return of Tig. This time, he's carrying a silver tea tray that looks like it weighs as much as he does. "Shall I wait for it to steep, then pour, Miss?"

"No, thanks. We're fine, thank you."

When we have the room to ourselves again, I shake my head. "I'm dazzled. For some reason, I pictured an elven Guild Governor's home to be a lot more..."

"Like Bilbo Baggins' house in the Shire?"

"Yeah, more like that."

She gestures at the leather seating area and moves the tray from the buffet to the glass coffee table. "I get that a lot. Honestly, most of my life is breaking people's expectations."

"Mine too," Dionysus says. "The first person to get me was Fi."

I make a heart with my curled fingers and press it against my chest. "I heart you too, Tarzan."

"Does everyone want tea?" Suede asks.

That's a yes.

Suede pours four cups, and we all reach forward from our

seats to fix it the way we want. Once it's ready, we sip and nibble on the little bear cookies baked in honey.

"So, Nikon mentioned that he needed to talk to me about something that happened at Dionysus' celebration party last week."

I finish my cookie and swallow. "That's right. At some point that night or in the morning, someone walked away with Eros's enchanted bow. He said when he's not using it, it shrinks into a silver pendant."

Suede nods. "I remember seeing the pendant. I didn't realize that was his bow."

"It's not common knowledge," Dionysus says. "Gods tend to keep stuff like that quiet."

"So, you're saying someone stole it that night?"

"Yeah," I sip my tea and reach for another cookie. Man. These are addictive. "So, what we're trying to do is figure out who could've taken it and why."

"You're not seriously looking at me for this?" She suddenly looks much less friendly.

"No, not you." Nikon holds up his hand and waves away her worry. "You spent time with Eros during the night. We thought you might remember who else was there at that time."

"Doesn't he remember?"

I roll my eyes. "No. Eros doesn't commit himself to remembering people who are beneath him."

Suede is still studying the three of us as if she's gauging how sincere we are.

"This honestly has nothing to do with you," I say, biting off the next bear's little head. "We know you, and we trust you. It so happens that you were in the right place at the wrong time and can help us."

Suede runs her fingers down the long silver braid plaited by her ear. "The last I remember of Eros's night is when he paired off with an ebony-haired woman with a thick accent, the selkie girl, and Pan's friend with that weird earring."

"That's Maros," Dionysus says. "He's on our list to speak to as well."

"What kind of accent did the woman have?" I ask.

Suede finishes her tea and sets the cup on the delicate china saucer. "European. Russian maybe. When I left, they were playing a sex game with a bottle of vodka—drinking it, not using it."

My mind didn't go there because I'm stuck on her description. The hair on my arms stands on end as I consider that.

I'm sure there are a lot of attractive Russian women with ebony hair but linked with the trouble of Eros's missing pendant and mass death on the horizon...

"Why do you look sick all of a sudden, Red?"

I meet Nikon's concerned gaze and swallow the last of the honey bears, my head spinning. "Just haunted by a ghost of disaster past. It could be nothing, but that description reminds me of Baba Yaga."

"That's a terrible idea."

I shrug. "I didn't want my mind to go there. It just did. Dionysus, have you ever met Baba Yaga? I mean would you know her if she was in your loft?"

Dionysus shakes his head. "No. We don't run in the same circles at all. Isn't she the one who eats children in the forest?"

"Her and her two sisters were a collective nightmare. Now there's only one left."

"Thankfully."

I draw a deep breath and get over the sense of dread weighing me down. It could be paranoia, and I don't want to take our investigation off on a tangent, so I get back to actual questions. "You never saw anyone admire or touch Eros's pendant?"

"No. When the vodka started flowing down naked body parts, I opted not to get sticky and left them to do their thing. I joined Dionysus in the other room."

"Yeah, you did." Dionysus grins.

I rub my hand over my forehead and close my eyes. "As relieved as I am that you got your mojo back, do you have to sleep with all my friends?"

Dionysus sits up straighter. "You have a lot of friends, Jane. I haven't slept with a quarter of them. Suede joined me and a few others of her own will. Grown-ups get to do grown-up things in private."

I grab another bear and bite his head off. "Didn't the trouble with Hel make you think twice about resuming sexcapades that don't mean anything? Whether you realize it or not, emotions get tied up when people are intimate."

Suede flashes me a patient grin. "It's sweet you believe in monogamy and loving one soulmate for the rest of your life, but that's a human concept. In the fae world and pagan pantheons, that's not a thing."

"Besides." Dionysus grabs a cookie for himself. "After what happened with Loki and my months of missile malfunctions, my party was about more than getting naked with a lot of people. It was a randy reset."

"A reset?"

"Exactly. If I plan on developing feelings and relationships going forward, I want to ensure everything is working properly. Consider me having sex with Suede as a penile palate cleanse... like a sexual sorbet."

Nikon bursts out laughing. "I love that."

Despite how cray-cray that sounds, I'm sure it makes sense to Dionysus.

I unzip my hoodie and peel it off. The tea is heating me from the inside, and the room is starting to swim. "We're veering off-topic. Let's get back to Eros and the bow. Who brought the woman with the thick accent?"

Dionysus makes a face, holds his hand out, and a phone appears. With his thumbs tapping over the screen like he's done it all his life, he starts texting his friends. "Talk among yourselves. I'll see who claims her."

Nikon chuckles and tilts his head toward him. "He seems to be adjusting to modern life, don't you think?"

"I do. Maybe a little too much." Nikon's haircut shows off his pretty eyes and makes him look older than he did when we first met.

"Why are you looking at me like that, Red?"

"I like your face."

Nikon chuckles. "Thanks. I like your face too."

I finish my tea and set it down on the delicate china saucer. My hands must be a little unsteady because the teacup rattles until it's securely on the table.

Weird.

Since I unlocked my druidness, my hands have been rock solid. I hold them up in the air in front of me. "Do my hands look weird to you guys? Have I got the right amount of fingers?"

"The right amount of fingers?" Nikon leans closer and is looking at my face and not my fingers. "What the hell is in these honey bears, Suede?"

"Nothing mind-altering. They're only cookies. It's a recipe my mother's maid makes. She used to sneak them to me when I was a kid. I love them."

"Those little suckers are good." I reach forward for the last one. "I could eat these all day long."

"How about you don't." Nikon grabs it before me and pops it in his mouth.

Dionysus finishes with his call and puts his phone away. "Pan says he met Anca a month or two ago. She works at an empowered bar off the Queensway."

"The Queensway…the Queensway…uh-huh, uh-huh," I sing, bobbing my head. "Lots of Russians on the Queensway."

"Did he mention which bar?" Nikon asks.

I point at Nikon and touch my nose. "Oh, good question, Sherlock. Point to you. Yes, what bar?"

"It was the Tuatha De."

Before we leave Suede's mansion, Nikon looks up the location of the Tuatha De and gets the Google Earth street view. Then, when he knows where we're going, he snaps us to the alleyway behind the pub.

I check the time on my phone, surprised it's only eleven a.m. "I'm starving. Are you guys hungry? Do you think we can eat in the pub?"

Nikon blinks at me. "Are you asking if I think there's food in the pub or whether I want to eat it?"

"Both?"

Dionysus chuckles. "Let's go in and see what we find out about Anca. If it's a short visit, we'll go home and get you food. If it looks like it'll take a while, we'll order here."

"Okeedoodle. Are you guys hungry? I'm starving. Why am I so starving?"

Nikon takes my hand and sets it on the crook of his elbow as he guides me out of the alley and toward the street in front of the restaurant. "I think you have the munchies, Red."

"I know that. I told *you* that. I just don't know why. I had breakfast."

Dionysus laughs. "No, Jane. Nikon is saying you have *the* munchies. The aftereffects of being high on honey bears."

I scrunch up my face and look from one of them to the other. There's something I want to say, but then my mental hamster does a somersault, and I'm thinking of taking up the banjo...but I've heard it's a very difficult instrument. Maybe the harmonica, then.

"So pretty," I say, grinning at them. "You boys are *sooo* pretty. Inside and out."

Dionysus chuckles. "How are you feeling, Jane?"

"I feel... sunshiny, and my fingers are tingly, and I can't feel my cheeks. Do you want to feel my cheeks?"

"I do." Dionysus reaches forward to poke my face.

"Do you feel them?"

"Yes, I feel them."

Nikon kisses the top of my head and pulls me to the side as someone comes out of the pub. "I think we should drop you home, then Dionysus and I will come back and see what we can find out about Anca."

I smack my hand against my chest and gasp. "You want to be private dicks without me? But I'm one of the three musketeers. I'm D'Artagnan. Dionysus, you are Aramis sexing up all the lads and ladies, and Nikon can pick between Porthos and Athos."

Dionysus narrows his gaze. "If it's three musketeers, why the four choices?"

I blink, and my mouth falls open. "That is an *amazing* question. Ten points to you, Tarzan."

My phone rings and I start digging for it and singing. It's Garnet and the Lion King song is playing...and I'm still digging in my purse.

"It's the circle of liiiife," I sing, searching the depths of my seemingly empty purse.

"Here you go, Fi." Nikon brushes a hand across my butt and hands my phone to me.

"Nikon, are you a magician? How did you do that?"

"A magician never exposes his secrets. How about we answer the phone?"

I swipe green to accept the call. "Hello, Garnet Grant. This is Fiona's phone."

"Are you drunk? Fuck, Fi, it's eleven a.m.."

"I'm not drunk. I had tea. But now that you mention it, I do feel funny." I smile up at Dionysus and Nikon. "Can we get something to eat? I'm hungry."

"Hey, I have an idea, Red." Nikon holds out his hand. "Why don't you let me talk to Garnet for a minute? Then, after that, Dionysus and I will get you something to eat."

"Deal."

Nikon takes my phone and starts talking to Garnet while I hug Dionysus. "I'm really glad you're having all the sex again. It made me sad that Loki was mean to you and your mojo. I'm sorry you got cockblocked."

"Thanks, Jane. That means a lot."

A car stops at the lights at the corner. It's playing Phil Collins loud with the windows down and the sunroof open. The bass is so high that I can feel the drumbeats in my chest.

In the Air Tonight...great song.

I sway with Dionysus on the sidewalk. "You're a great dancer."

"Thanks, although I don't think you can tell how good I am by swaying on the sidewalk. I used to love to dance. Maybe when you're sober, and no one is targeting us for death, we'll go dancing."

"It's a date. Although I don't know when that will be. Someone is almost always targeting me for death."

"Yeah, I know."

"*A ghra*? Are ye all right?"

I stop the easy sway of sidewalk dancing and smile at Sloan. "Hi, McKenzie. I didn't know you were in the pub. We would've come in to join you. Did you see Anca? Is she Baba Yaga? I can't imagine her as a waitress, but she was a luggage girl, so who knows, amirite?"

Sloan is looking at me and making a frowny face. "I, uh...I don't know about that, luv. Nikon gave me a call and said I should probably join ye."

I give the Greek a solid thumbs-up. "Good call, Nikon. Everything is always better when Sloan's around. He's amazing." I step back from Dionysus and curtsy. "Thank you for the dance, sir."

Dionysus bows and sweeps his hand to the side. "It was my pleasure, ma'am."

Sloan's smile is funny when he looks at me. "What exactly is she on?"

"Elf bear cookies," Nikon says. "Suede says they're not a drug and shouldn't have affected her. We all had them, but it seems Fi is having a whack-a-doodle reaction to them."

"She did eat the most," Dionysus adds.

I giggle. "I totes did. I ate a lot of those little honey bears, but you know what's crazy?"

"What's that, luv?"

"I'm hungrier than ever."

Nikon and Sloan start whispering about something. When they fall quiet and glance over at me, the worry in their eyes makes my chest ache. "Sad face. What's wrong, you guys?"

"Nothing ye need to worry about in yer current state, *a ghra*. Let's talk about it later." Sloan wraps an arm around my back and turns me the way we came.

I cast a glance over my shoulder at Nikon and Dionysus. They aren't coming. Why aren't they coming?

"No, hotness. We were already in this alley. We need to go to the pub. Maybe Baba Yaga is in there."

"Dionysus and Nikon are going into the pub. I'm taking you home to make you lunch. Ye'd like that, wouldn't ye? I'll heat ye some of that yummy broccoli soup ye love so much."

"*Yes*. Can we have cheddar cheese on it, too?"

"Of course. Whatever ye like."

With that, I snuggle into Sloan's side and close my eyes. Soup. Soup. Soup.

CHAPTER SIX

"Did anyone catch the license plate of the car that ran over my head?" I'm lying on my side on our living room sofa and blink, shading my eyes. "Better question. Am I still high on honey bears or is my favorite Man o' Green sitting in our living room?"

"Och, I'm here, Fi." Patty lounges sideways in the oversized club chair opposite me. "Sloan explained yer situation and I came straight away."

I force myself to sit up and gather the throw blanket into my lap. After I hang my head for a moment while the slosh in my brain slows down, I meet his sparkling gaze. "Which situation is that? I think the needle on my record might've skipped a few times this morning."

"Sloan said ye've got a gatherin' of reapers in the city, someone stole Cupid's bow, and there's a possibility the Russian witch is in the muck of things."

"Oh, yeah, that situation."

"There's more, I'm afraid." Sloan brings me a mug of something hot. "Garnet called ye earlier when ye were out of sorts. He

52

said yer friend Laurel went missin'. Xavier and Benjamin have been out lookin' but had no luck findin' her. He was hopin' ye could tell them some of Laurel's old haunts."

"What? You should've told me."

Sloan gives me a knowing smile and sits on the chair to my right. "At the time, ye were flyin' high. Ye'd have been no use to Garnet, and I wasn't about to put ye in front of emotionally distraught vampires when ye were liable to set them off. Yer not the most PC girl when yer at the top of yer game. This mornin' ye were far from that."

"Okay, yeah, I get that. What exactly happened, anyway? Do elven cookies normally send people loopy?"

"No," Patty says. "Then again, when have ye ever been normal?"

I chuckle. "I was perfectly normal before Sloan activated the Fianna shield on my back. Boring really. He tipped the scales on me."

Sloan rolls his eyes. "Ye know full well I did no such thing. We've been over it a thousand times."

I grin. "It still riles you up when I say it. You gotta learn to take a ribbing, hotness."

He points at the mug. "Drink yer tea. It'll clear the effects of the cookies from yer system. It seems to work almost instantly."

"Oh? How do you know that?"

Patty points at the mountain of brown fur sleeping on the living room floor. "Because it turns out yer bear is allergic to rugach root, which is a common ingredient in elven baked goods. Yer reaction was his reaction."

"Is he all right?"

Sloan nods. "I gave him the remedy, and now he's sleepin' off the worst of it. Yer turn."

I sip the tea and fight to swallow. "Blech. My bear's allergic so the remedy is to poison me?"

AUBURN TEMPEST & MICHAEL ANDERLE

"It's a wee bit bitter, I know, but it'll fix ye right up, so drink, luv."

I plug my nose and take three quick gulps. The tea burns my tongue and stings my throat, but it's worth the rush to get the drinking over with.

When that's down, I abandon my mug and make my way over to my bear. "You're sure he'll be okay?"

"I am, luv. He said he was feeling much better after he drank the remedy and from what I know about his allergy, he should be fine."

That makes me feel loads better.

As often as I end up with some strange and unusual thing happening to me, I much prefer that over having anyone I love suffering.

"Okay, first things first. We need to talk to Garnet about Laurel. Finding her is the most pressing. Then we'll follow up with Nikon and Dionysus about what they found at the pub. We'll continue to work on the gathering of reapers."

Sloan takes my empty mug over to the sink to rinse it and put it in the dishwasher. "Patty? Where did ye want to begin?"

"Och, don't let me be a worry. I'm happy to tag along and see if I can help. I have a few ideas about Eros's bow, but yer right, the missing friend is most important."

"Should I wake Bruin or let him sleep?" I ask. "I know I'm not supposed to leave the house without him, but if he was the one who had the allergy, he must be feeling pretty rough."

Sloan nods. "He likened it to being run over by a farm plow and getting mulched into bits."

My poor boy.

"Okay, let's leave him to sleep it off. What's the worst that can happen?"

Sloan winces. "Why do ye say things like that? Ye know you're temptin' fate."

I giggle and pat his arm. "Mostly I say it to see the look on your face when I do. You make the best faces, Mackenzie."

"Besides that," Patty says, "I'll come with the two of ye fer the afternoon. I might not be eight feet tall and have razor-sharp claws, but I can protect ye well enough should the unexpected occur."

I grin and blow Patty a kiss. "I have no doubt. Okay, give me two minutes to pee and get ready to roll."

"So, what can I expect and when should I step in?" Patty tugs down the hem of his green and gold vest and buttons his emerald coat. He's got his everyday wool cap today, and when he pulls it on, it makes the fluffy white tufts of his hair expand out the sides by his ears.

"You shouldn't need to step in at all. Xavier and I have a bit of a volatile history, but we've come to understand one another."

"Aye," Sloan snaps. "The man feels guilty because he lost control, attacked, and almost killed Fi."

"Bygones, hotness." I wave that away and grab my purse off the end of the couch. "Xavier will come off like a ruthless asshole, but he's an onion."

Sloan curses under his breath. "An onion, is he? I think that's generous on yer part."

The three of us are ready to *poof* to the carriage house of Casa Loma, but I'm not taking Sloan there until he gets this out of his system.

"When I first learned there were seethes of bloodsucking undead living in my city, I wasn't keen on it. Then I met Xavier, and I hated it."

"I can see why," Patty says. "Though we don't get many on the Emerald Isle, throughout my life, I have had a few nasty run-ins with their ilk."

I suppose any empowered creatures living lives of longevity will cross paths eventually. "Xavier is a man born of another era. He looks like a cold-hearted control freak in a three thousand dollar suit, but that's where the onion part comes in."

Patty chuckles and grabs his walking stick. "Oh, good, I was looking forward to the onion part."

"Yes, he's the king of vampires, but I learned recently that not all vampires are created equally. He holds his seethe to a higher standard."

"Fi, the man is a drug dealer."

"True story. I was glossing over that part in my mind. Okay, let's say a higher standard when it comes to feeding."

"How so?" Patty asks.

"Well, instead of stalking humans in the shadowed streets at night, Xavier established a symbiotic arrangement between the vampires in his seethe and members of the community who'd run out of options. My friend Laurel is one of them."

"What does that mean?"

"Her family was murdered when we were in high school after her father got in with some bad people. All we knew was that there was a house fire, and no one else survived. Laurel did, but she had no one and nothing so one of Xavier's family took her as his companion feeder."

"What does *that* mean?"

"We've never gotten into the logistics. From what I understand, they have an exclusive arrangement where Benjamin feeds off Laurel, and in return, she is protected and given a home and money and education and options she wouldn't have had otherwise."

Patty looks surprised. I don't blame him. I was quite surprised when I first heard this is how they handled their feeding requirements. "As I said, Xavier is an onion. Peeling back the layers might make your eyes water, but if you don't, you'll miss what's going on beneath the surface."

Sloan seems less than impressed with this entire conversation. I don't blame him. I've grown up with protective men surrounding me. It comes from a place of love, and I'm grateful that he cares so much.

"All right, enough chatter. Let's go see if we can help find Laurel."

The three of us step apart and take in the surroundings as we materialize across town. "Och, what a lovely castle ye have here." Patty leans out of the carriage house shadows to look at the stone architecture of Casa Loma. "I didn't realize ye have castles in yer city."

"I guess you can teach an old dog new tricks."

Patty arches a snowy brow at me and snorts. "Who are ye callin' an old dog, Red? I'll have ye know I'm as spry today as I was when I was a boy of two hundred."

Huh, I've never wondered how old leprechauns get.

If two hundred is a boy, I wonder how old Patty is. A second thought hits me then. Maybe he's more than a roommate of the Queen of Wyrms. Maybe they're bound, and his longevity extended as mine has with Dart.

That's a question for another day.

I tilt my head toward the interior of the carriage house and the stables beyond. "Follow me to the super-secret vampire lair."

When we get to the far end of the stables, I stop at the second stall from the end. Nothing about a ten-by-twelve wooden horse stall screams entrance to a vampire lair, which is likely how it remains super-secret.

I try to remember what Garnet did the day he first brought me here. It takes me a minute to put all the pieces together.

I take a wooden-handled hoof-cleaning tool hanging on the sidewall and stick the metal point into a hole in the old, rusty box on the floor. With a twist, the top of the box unlatches. I put my face in front of a security screen.

When the screen activates, I smile at the camera. "Fi and friends to see Xavier and Benjamin. I believe they expect us."

The three of us wait, but there's no *click* beneath our feet like there was the last time I was here.

"Maybe we need to stand off the platform before they unlock the floor section," Sloan suggests.

Giving that a try, the three of us move to the side and stare at the straw-covered floor.

Nothing happens.

The floor doesn't move. It doesn't expose the set of stairs. And it doesn't allow us entry into the lair below.

"Well, this is anticlimactic," I say. "I guess I'll text Xavier. Maybe he's out, and the person on the screen doesn't recognize me."

"That's likely all it is," Sloan says. "Send Xavier a message and see what he says."

I pull out my phone, scroll through my contacts, and send Xavier a quick message to let him know we're here.

Almost instantly, Garnet appears in the corridor outside the stall. By the look on his face, I know before he says the words.

Nonononono... "You found her, didn't you?"

Garnet nods. "I'm sorry, Fi. I know she was your friend."

I swallow past the lump of emotions pushing at the base of my throat and blink fast to fight back the hot sting of tears welling in my eyes. Drawing a deep breath, I force myself to look at this as a professional here to help. "How was she killed?"

"By all accounts, it appears to be a vampire attack. Xavier is exploring the possibility of a rival seethe trying to make a point. If it's not vampire, whoever did it took great pains to stage the scene."

"Do you think me looking over the scene will help?"

Garnet shakes his head. "Not this time, Fi. You don't need to see her like that. Xavier and I will handle the scene. I'd like you to speak to Benjamin and begin the investigation."

I nod and turn back to Sloan and Patty. "Do you guys want to go home? I can meet you there later."

"Och, no, Red." Patty shifts in beside me to wrap his arm across my hip. "We'll see ye through this. If there's a killer in yer streets, ye'll not be trackin' him down on yer own—especially if it's a vampire."

I set my arm across Patty's shoulder and nod. "Thanks. I appreciate the company."

Sloan moves in beside me and takes my hand. "I'm sorry, *a ghra*. I know how fond you were of Laurel and how happy ye were to reconnect."

I can't look at Sloan. If I do, the tears trying to escape will break loose. It's not time for that because as upset as I am, Benjamin's world has just been altered.

"Garnet, if you'll do the honors and take us where we need to go."

Garnet looks me over, his gaze not that of my cranky pants authoritarian boss but of the sweet man few people get to see. "Are you sure you're up for this? You weren't feeling well this morning."

"That was an allergic reaction to some bad elf root. I'm good. Laurel was a great girl and a friend. If I can help find who did this, I want to be involved."

"I figured you would."

"So, where are we going?"

"Anyx took Benjamin to the Batcave. He's understandably distraught, and Xavier thought it best that he be isolated for a few hours while we handle the scene."

"Did Benjamin find her?"

Garnet shakes his head. "No. Local PD found her and Maxwell flagged us to intercede. Your dad is handling the case transfer to SITFU, and I inserted our man in the coroner's office to handle the examiner's report. There shouldn't be any exposure."

Good. That's good.

With Patty's arm still around me, I glance at Sloan then away. "To the Batcave, hotness. Let's start the hunt for Laurel's killer."

CHAPTER SEVEN

S loan *poofs* us to the outer entrance on the tenth floor of the Acropolis. He and I always wear our team trouble pendants, so I let him take care of the scanner and open our way.

Benjamin is pacing the main room looking as devastated as I anticipated. His clothes are rumpled as if he's worn them for days and his sandy blond hair is sticking up like it can't decide which way it's supposed to go.

The two or three times I've seen Laurel's companion before today, I never got a dangerous vibe from him. Nothing about him screamed vampire.

That's not the case today.

Even approaching him wakes my Fianna shield and my back tingles with a warning.

As I draw closer, Anyx subtly shifts his body from facing Zuzanna to keep me in his view. The lion might pretend he's all growls, but he's quite sweet.

It must be a lion thing.

I stop six feet from the vampire and swallow. "Benjamin, I'm so sorry for your loss. How can I help?"

"Don't you know? Garnet and Xavier stuck me in this office

under house arrest and told me you would come and help me find out who did this. If you don't know how to help, what am I doing here?"

"I'm sorry. Of course, I can help you. Can we sit?" I gesture at the chairs surrounding the long conference table and take a few leading steps. When he doesn't follow, I stop to gauge his intentions.

Honestly, I don't think he's making conscious decisions at all.

He's in shock, hurting, and obviously very angry.

"Let's start by you telling me what you do know. When did you realize Laurel was missing and where was she before that?"

Benjamin clasps his hands and hooks them against the back of his head. I recognize the action for exactly what it is. He's fighting his most aggressive impulses.

I stand my ground and casually widen my stance. In no way do I want to take an offensive position against a vampire, but I also don't want to be caught off-balance if he loses his battle of control.

"Benjamin," I say, calling forward *Persuasion*. "You and I need to go through this, so we can find out what happened to Laurel. You want that, right?"

I didn't know that vampires growl.

His gaze narrows on me, and my fingers itch to call Birga to the fore.

"Why are we standing around when we could be doing something? Xavier and Garnet have an idea of who did this. They're just blocking me."

At this point, I don't blame them.

It suddenly dawns on me maybe the mass death the reapers are here for has something to do with Benjamin going on a vampire vengeance rage through the city.

"I'm sure Garnet and Xavier will be here soon to get us all caught up. Let's have something worthwhile to tell them. When did you realize Laurel was missing?"

There's that growl again.

As Benjamin locks his glare on me, his eyes darken from chestnut brown to black.

"Come here to me, *a ghra*," Sloan says, his voice low and calm.

I'm known in my family for being headstrong and not listening, but I'm also well-attuned to when I need to listen without question.

I don't know what a vampire's eyes turning black means, but Sloan is much more educated in the ways of the empowered species and probably does. When my shield ramps from a tingle to a burn, I realize it's not good.

I take a slow step backward, but Benjamin comes with me.

It's like something draws his body to follow, his agitation heightened.

I raise my palms, hoping it seems submissive. In actuality, I want my hands up to call Birga and cast. "I know you're upset, Benjamin, but what would Laurel want you to do right now? She'd want you to calm down and help me find the person responsible for this, wouldn't she?"

"Back off, vamp." Anyx stalks forward. "Fiona's not your enemy here."

"No one's your enemy here." I make it very clear that Benjamin doesn't need to be on the offensive. "Laurel was a special girl. Of course, you're very upset. We all are."

As he fights his violent nature, my mind whirls and my mouth prattles off every soothing thought I can think of. I give the guy credit...he's trying to hold it together.

There's no question when he loses the battle.

I've been attacked by a vampire before.

The look in their eyes before they launch isn't something you forget.

The air *snaps* with violent energy and I call my body armor forward. At the same moment, something *cracks* hard behind me.

Benjamin is thrown twenty feet backward and pinned against the wall.

Not understanding what's happening in front of me, I pivot to see what that noise was.

Patty is standing with his feet spread apart, and his walking stick gripped in both hands in front of him. The gold-encased end is embedded in the floor between his boots, and the tiles are cracked in a four-foot radius.

I've seen Patty use magic a few times, but I have no sense of how powerful he is. "Thanks for the save." I retreat to stand next to them.

Sloan puts an arm around me and kisses my cheek before the three of us address the vampire writhing against the wall like a feral cat.

"I don't think he's calming down," I say.

Anyx finishes sending a text and edges Zuzanna and himself closer to our side of the room. "How long can you hold him, little man? I told Garnet to bring Xavier back here immediately but if we need to evacuate, now's the time."

Patty shakes his head. "Och, no. I've got the wee lad. He's not puttin' up much of a fuss. He's just worked up and out of sorts."

Out of sorts.

I suppose that's one way to look at it.

Garnet and Xavier appear beside the elevators a moment later. The two look like they're racing into a battlefield and pull up short when they find us all standing there watching Benjamin.

I hike my thumb over my shoulder and point at Patty. "Man o' Green to the rescue. S'all good."

"Remind me not to piss you off." Garnet casts Patty an approving smile.

Xavier rushes straight to Benjamin and pushes his palms against his shoulders. "You may release him now. He won't cause you any more trouble."

Patty checks with me, and I nod. "Yeah, go ahead. Xavier's got him."

When Patty releases his hold on the vampire, the energy in the air dissipates, and my shield stops stinging. "Well, that was fun."

Garnet arches an ebony brow at me and shakes his head. "Did you get anywhere with him before this happened?"

"Nope. He felt a little frustrated being here with me instead of out in the real world tracking down Laurel's killer."

"That was for an excellent reason." He points at where Xavier is struggling to calm Benjamin down. "I was getting mass death vibes off him and thought we'd try to prevent that."

I nod. "The thought occurred to me too."

The struggle between Xavier and Benjamin seems to be escalating. We all turn, ready for the next event.

"Sleep." Xavier catches Benjamin as his body goes limp in his arms. The vampire king bends to scoop the young man against his chest and straightens.

"We have a holding cell that will contain a vampire in a rage." Garnet points toward the back rooms.

Xavier shakes his head. "Benjamin is a gentle soul. His anger is isolated. If I can get an escort home, I will secure him in the bunker until we know more and can give him the answers he needs to calm down."

Garnet looks at Anyx and nods. "Take them back to Casa Loma and wait until they're both below ground and seal the exit."

Xavier scowls. "Do you doubt my ability to take care of my people?"

"No, but there is a gathering of reapers in the city, and I'm not taking chances while there's a distraught vampire in a murderous rage."

Xavier doesn't seem to appreciate Garnet's theory. "Keep searching for another answer for the reapers. Benjamin isn't your man."

AUBURN TEMPEST & MICHAEL ANDERLE

"I hope you're right."

Xavier holds a tight rein on his fury and frustrations as he moves to stand closer to Anyx. "Do your job, Garnet. Find out who did this to Laurel and there won't be any trouble from my family."

Garnet looks like he wants to reply but then thinks better of it. "Get him out of here."

When Anyx flashes out, the tension eases.

"Is this a normal day in the life of Fi?" Patty glances around. "Reapers, angry gods, being drugged, an innocent woman murdered, and bein' attacked by an out-of-control vampire?"

I exhale a heavy breath. "Pretty much. Hey, it's only Monday afternoon. There's still lots of week left. Who knows what's up next?"

"Glad your sense of humor is still working," Garnet says. "Let's go over what we know."

In the end, we don't know much. Laurel was out with Xavier's companion, Karuna, and several other women dedicated as feeding sources to the male vampires in Xavier's family. The ladies went shopping at the Eaton Centre along with three male guards.

"It's a regular outing they take once a month, and nothing seemed out of the ordinary."

"Except Laurel going missing and ending up dead."

Garnet rubs his fingers over his eyes and sighs. "Yes, except for that."

"Where was the body found?" Sloan asks. "Was it near the shopping center? Benjamin said Toronto PD found her."

"Private security found her when the security alarm went off at Karuna's home here in the city. They found her, called the cops, and here we are."

"Karuna's house," I say.

"That's right. Someone left Laurel's body in the front foyer for us to find."

A shiver runs down my spine as I think of that house. As beautiful as the old, Georgian-styled mansion is, the last time I was there was when Xavier lost control and attacked me.

"Her murder was a message," Sloan says.

I nod. "Obvi. Whoever is behind it wants Xavier to know that not only can they get to one of the companions, but they know about the private residence of *his* companion."

"That's how we interpreted it, yes."

"Huh, once again, someone is gunning for Xavier, and innocent humans are getting killed as collateral damage. That's becoming a disturbing pattern."

Garnet frowns. "I'm sorry about your friend, Fi, but this isn't Xavier's fault. He does his best with the hand life dealt him. Another vampire king likely wouldn't go to such lengths to keep his flock reined in."

I sigh and run my fingers through my hair. "I get that. While I agree it's not his fault, I'm worried it's not the only message his enemy will send."

"What about Galina Romanov?" Sloan looks at Garnet.

Garnet frowns. "What about her? She's dead and burned. I took care of the body myself."

Sloan holds a finger to his lips and taps his mouth as he thinks. "Fi? What if Suede got it wrong, and it wasn't a Russian accent the woman spoke with but a Romanian one? I find it suspect that someone is aggressively targeting Xavier again and the message ties back to that house."

A shiver runs up my spine. "You think the dark-haired woman with the accent we think stole Eros's bow has something to do with kidnapping and killing Laurel? How do those two rando events line up?"

He lifts a shoulder. "Just throwing it out there. Galina was an attractive, dark-haired woman with a thick accent. It's plausible anyone sent by her family or from within the family might have similar characteristics."

"But what does the murder of a vampire's feeder companion have to do with the god of love's enchanted bow?" Garnet asks.

"I don't know and possibly nothing. I was simply wondering if there was a connection. Perhaps the mass death on the horizon has something to do with the vampire war in our streets and the Romanovs plan to use the bow in some way to secure their position."

"Och, that seems like a lot of speculation, lad," Patty says. "The three events might have no connection at all."

Sloan nods. "Aye, fair point."

Garnet growls and points at the blank monitor wall. "It's time for some investigation and evidence. See what you can find. Maybe try Galina's properties and known places of interest to see if you can come up with anything that suggests the Romanovs are moving to town to avenge her."

The idea of the Romanian crime family coming back to Toronto presses hard on my heart. They're bad people on the human side of things. If any of them followed Galina's lead and chose to become vampires, things will get very bloody.

I turn to Patty as I set my purse on the conference table. "You don't have to stay if you don't want to. If you have other things to do, don't feel obligated to hang."

"No. I won't. Is there any chance Sloan can start yer investigation of the vampire syndicate while we speak to Eros about his bow?"

"Do you have an idea of how to find it?"

Patty nods. "My people are drawn to rare treasures. Unless whoever has it expects a wee Man o' Green to come lookin', I don't think they would've warded against me finding it."

I check in with Sloan, and he nods. "I'll get started here. Emmet is off today, and he and Ciara are helping Tad across the road. I'll pop back to get him, and the two of us will work on the computer searches."

"Excellent. With any luck, maybe we can divide and conquer and be done with this whole mess by dinner."

Sloan chuckles. "Are ye still high, *a ghra*? Nothin' ever works out that well fer us."

I shrug and extend my hand to Patty. "There's a first time for everything."

Eros is alone in Dionysus's loft when we *poof* upstairs. He's magicked himself a bed in the corner and is lounging on his side watching TikTok videos.

"Hey there. Just you? Are Nikon and Dionysus not back from the pub yet?"

Eros holds up a finger for us to give him one minute and bursts out laughing. "Have you ever seen the TikTok Made Me Do It? They're insane. I love how humans celebrate being total jackasses."

"Yeah. TikTok brings out all kinds of kinds."

Patty points his walking stick at the lounging god. "I hear ye lost a treasure ye wish to reclaim as soon as possible."

Eros notices Patty then and sits up. "What business is it of yours, leprechaun?"

I cringe at the use of the L-word. I might think it sometimes in my head, but I'm always very careful not to say it aloud. Patty and his people don't like the term and take it very personally.

"Patty prefers Man o' Green." I put it out there as a friendly public service in case he didn't know. "He mentioned it because he thinks he can help us find your bow."

Eros scoffs and stands. "I'm sure that's it. What might he want in return, I wonder?"

I don't like his tone or the insinuation that Patty would only help if there were something in it for him. "Patty is a dear friend of mine, and we've got some serious warnings going off in the city. He's a good guy, here to help."

"Don't get yerself worked up, Red," Patty says. "There are those of my kind who are known to be self-serving when it comes to acquiring treasures. It's not how I do business, but I'm familiar with the prejudice."

"Still, I'm certainly not gonna let anyone berate you when you're here out of the goodness of your heart. Nothing says we have to help Eros find his bow. In fact, I'm beginning to think being without his divine purpose might teach him a little humility."

Eros frowns at me. "Are you still upset about earlier? I told you I was sorry."

"And yet, I'm not feeling the sincerity on that."

"What happened earlier, Red?"

I know how protective Patty can be. As much fun as it would be to unload and watch the chaos ensue, there's the matter of reclaiming the bow and eliminating it as the source of trouble bringing the reapers to town.

"It was nothing. Eros was a jerk. I punched him in the face. End. Of. Let's focus on getting that bow back."

Nikon and Dionysus materialize in the center of the loft. "Patty!" Nikon breaks into a grin. "It's great to see you, my friend."

The two of them come over and give me a good once-over.

"How are you feeling, Jane?" Dionysus asks.

"It's been a rough couple of days."

"I'm sorry about your friend." Nikon moves in for a hug. "I know how jazzed you were about connecting with her. Has Garnet figured out what happened?"

I fill the two of them in on what we found out and Sloan's theory about how that might tie in with the Romanovs coming to town and starting a vampire war.

"That would explain a mass death," Nikon says. "I spent

enough time in Europe to know the Romanov name. They're a dangerous bunch over there as humans. Having them here and branching out in the vampire world is a scary thought."

"It's still too early to know if that's what we're dealing with. Sloan and Emmet are downstairs trying to track down anything to support the theory. What did you guys find out at the Tuatha De?"

Nikon pulls out his phone and opens a picture of a picture hanging on a wall. "Anca doesn't work today, but they had pictures of the staff members with customers, and Dionysus recognized her."

I study the picture. "Okay, I've got good news and bad news."

"Oh, I love this game," Dionysus says. "Let's start with good and go downhill."

Nikon chuckles. "You sound so excited about that."

Dionysus shrugs. "I love surprises. Go ahead, Jane. Lay it on us."

I love Dionysus's enthusiasm. "In the good news column, I see no resemblance between this woman and the woman I know is Baba Yaga."

"Winner!" Dionysus raises his fist in the air.

"And the bad news?"

"She bears a striking resemblance to the very dead Galina Romanov. I mean...almost a dead ringer. I think the theory of the Romanov vampire war just moved to the top of the shit pile."

Dionysus grins. "Big finish, Jane. You're right. That's very bad news."

CHAPTER EIGHT

The Greeks, Patty, and I move downstairs and join Sloan and Emmet in the research. Nikon uploads the picture of Anca, the waitress we believe stole Eros's bow pendant, and once it's on the Team Trouble server, we open it onto the monitor wall. Looking at it side-by-side with images of Galina, it's no stretch to see the resemblance.

"Sisters?" I ask.

"That would be my guess." Sloan frowns.

Emmet's fingers dance over the flat touchscreen of the computer table. Information and other images pop up.

"The Romanov family business is run by twin brothers, Andrei and Anton. Andrei is considered to be the more dangerous of the two and also the head of the family. He had four sons, and Galina was his only daughter. Anton has three daughters and one son, although Interpol doesn't believe Anton's girls are in the family business."

"Are there any images of Galina's cousins?" Dionysus asks. "With their fathers being twins, the genetics are close enough they might end up looking like sisters."

While Emmet searches news articles and web images, I scan

through social media, looking for any events in Brasov, Romania that might spark picture-taking, parties, weddings, vacations...

"Romania seems like a lovely and peaceful country." I scroll through the beautiful images of the people in the countryside.

Nikon leans in to look over my shoulder. "It is. Often when there is a heavy criminal presence in a place like that, the crime rate is very low."

Sloan chuffs. "Everyone knows to behave because they also know what will happen if they don't."

"Skunks don't stink up their burrow," Dionysus says.

I laugh and give him my full attention. "Come again, Tarzan? What's that now?"

"People are always worried about a skunk living under their porch, but it's the neighbors that should be worried. Unless you scare a skunk, he won't spray in his own home."

"Unless he had epilepsy," Nikon says.

I chuckle. "Daisy has medication now. She's good."

"She is. She's an angel."

She is. I consider Dionysus's analogy. "So, you're saying the Romanovs don't do business in the little town where they live. Their crime dealings would be farther from home."

Dionysus nods. "That's what I'm saying, yes."

It's strange, but it makes sense. When we first looked into Galina and the Romanov presence here in Toronto, we considered the possibility she was importing women kidnapped from villages in Europe to be sold into the sex trade in North America.

Whatever the reason they're here, it's not good.

"All right, Sloan and Emmet, you keep working on that. Eros? Have you decided whether or not we're helping you find the bow?"

"Why wouldn't we help him?" Nikon asks.

I shrug. "Patty offered to help, and the god of love got all dickwad again. I know you said he's a good guy and you vouch for him, but so far, I'm not impressed."

"You realize I'm standing right here," Eros says.

I grin wide. "Oh, I realize it. One thing you should know about me is I never say something behind someone's back that I wouldn't say right in front of them."

Eros scowls at Nikon. "Why are you hanging around mortals? They're so touchy."

Nikon sighs. "You have to stop pissing off people trying to help you. Why can't you just say thank you?"

"Because I'm the fucking god of love. I don't need help from people beneath me, and I definitely don't need to placate them for offering it."

I throw up my hands. "Okay, we're out. Find your bow yourself, dickwad. Patty, thanks for the offer, my friend, but we're free to go home and have a pint."

"Lovely. Even better." Patty pinches the brim of his hat and nods at the group. "Gentlemen. I wish I could say it's been a pleasure. It hasn't. May the bird of paradise fly up yer nose, Cupid. And while she's up there, may she shit in your skull."

I laugh, hold out my hand, and a moment later, the two of us are standing in my living room. "I loved that bit about the bird of paradise."

Patty tips his head, removes his hat, and unleashes the wispy white tufts of his dandelion hair. "Are we truly givin' up the search, Red? That bow is a danger out in the world."

I stride over to the bar and grab a Guinness and two frosted glasses out of the mini-fridge. Opening the bottle, I pour us each half. "Oh, no. We'll find the bow, but Eros doesn't need to know that. Let him stew. You're right. That bow is much too powerful to be out in the world and the hands of ne'er-do-wells."

"Now there's a word worth bringing back into modern use." Dillan strides in from the back door. "What ne'er-do-wells are we tracking down today? More importantly, can I come and wear my cloak?"

I grin. "Yes, and yes. Let me see if Bruin's feeling better and ready to join us."

The extra few hours of allergy recovery have done Bruin good, and he's up and ready to catch a thief. Patty and I finish our shared beer and get ready to leave. All we need now is Dillan.

"How long does it take for him to run home and grab his cloak?" Patty taps the tip of his walking stick against the floor.

I'm not going to complain because I'm usually the one who makes everyone else wait, but yeah, he's been gone for a while.

The back door opens, and we straighten and get ready to— "Oh, hi, Eva."

Dillan escorts her in, and she beams at us with a sunshiny smile. "Dillan says we're off to catch a thief."

We? "Uh...you want to come?"

"If I'm welcome. I mean, I don't have to."

"Of course, you're welcome." Dillan glares at me. "Isn't she, Fi?"

"Absolutely. I just...the thief might be from a vampire crime family that murdered a friend of mine. It could be dangerous."

"I live for danger." She beams.

She's so sincere that I don't know how to respond.

"She'll be fine, Fi." Dillan scowls at me. "She's immortal and can take care of herself. I told you before not to put her in a box."

I glance over at Patty and Bruin, and they look as stymied as me. "Then sure. It's fine. If murderous vampires don't faze you, and Dillan's not concerned about your safety, welcome aboard."

"Excellent." Eva's blonde curls bob next to her cheeks as she bounces on the balls of her feet. "I'm Evangeline, by the way. I'm with Dillan."

Patty gives her a polite nod, and I snap to it and complete the appropriate introductions. When that's taken care of, I pat my chest to welcome Bruin home.

"Okeedoodle, it's time to find the enchanted bow of Eros... AKA dickwad Cupid. Where do we start?"

Patty stands and holds up his walking stick. It's a beautiful old relic. It looks like a gnarled piece of weathered teak with a gold-dipped tip and a gold ball handle. "We start with my talking stick."

"Don't you mean walking stick?" Dillan asks.

"Yeah, like that's all I'm good for, you judgy little shit. How about you zip it and let the grown-ups talk."

I blink, my focus locked on the gold grip at the top of his walking stick. What I mistook for a ball is the bald head of a grouchy gargoyle face.

Correction, a grouchy talking gargoyle face.

"A talking stick," Patty repeats. "Everyone, this is Cain. I apologize now fer anythin' and everythin' he says to offend. I'm afraid he tends to be a little brusque."

"Brusque?" the face snaps, scrunching up its...well, its face. "There's nothing wrong with speaking the truth, Pattycakes. Maybe I wouldn't be so brusque if you took me out of the godforsaken lair more than once every other century."

Patty casts him a dismissive glance. "Weel, maybe I'd take ye out of the lair more often if ye weren't such a feckin' pain in the ass. Remember the scene ye caused the last time?"

"Oh, you're not still bitching about that, are you? It was an honest mistake."

"Ye called the pixie queen a whore and nearly got me killed, ye mouthy git."

"No, I said she was *dressed* like a whore, and it needed to be said because she was and no one wanted to see her show-and-tell."

"It certainly didn't need to be said. I'm still not welcome behind the faery glass to this day. I swear ye live to make my life more difficult. Yer a right pain in my arse."

"Maybe I wouldn't be such a pain in that fat arse of yours if you took me for a walk now and then. A little exercise would do you good, old man."

"Maybe I'd take ye fer a walk if I didn't think I'd end up with a tribe of orcs tryin' to chop me to bits."

"One time. Stop your boohooing, Nancy-girl. I swear, you're worse than a wee girlie in piggy tails."

I hold my hands up between them to stop the insanity. "As amusing as this is, we have an enchanted treasure to find and a mass murder to stop."

Patty shakes himself back to the present. He pushes his rimless spectacles up his nose and nods. "Aye, yer right, Red. Sorry about that. Cain tends to push my buttons."

"Of course, blame it on the talking stick," Cain snaps, glaring. "So why are we here, Padraig?"

"Someone took Cupid's bow, and we fear they'll use it in the plot of a group of malcontents."

Cain grins, and the expression looks odd on him. "I do love to spoil the plot of malcontents."

"Aye, I know ye do, sham." Patty grins. "So we're lookin' for a highly valuable treasure, powered by Greek gods, and likely in the hands of someone who doesn't truly know what they've got."

I wonder about that statement, but Patty and Cain are finally on the same page, so I don't want to disturb the flow of conversation. Does Eros' bow do more than inspire insta-love in those he shoots?

If so, could there be another reason—other than making a calamitous couple fall in love—why someone stole it? Does Nikon know, and he didn't tell me?

If Dionysus didn't tell me, it's likely because he honestly didn't care or think it was important, but Nikon knows how my mind works. If there were more to the bow, he would've told me, wouldn't he?

As much as I don't want to think badly about Nikon, I fear his friendship with Eros has clouded his judgment on a few things.

He swears the guy is solid. So far, I've only seen a self-righteous dick.

Patty holds the talking stick out in front of himself and gives Cain a slow three-sixty turn. "Anything?"

"No."

Patty looks at me and shrugs. "Road trip. Have ye got a sunroof on yer car, Red?"

"Uh...no."

"Well, we need one. Hope ye don't mind. Grab yer keys. We're takin' this show on the road."

Before I can respond, Patty shuffles his short little legs toward the back door. Dillan is giggling and grabs Eva's hand, tugging her along behind him.

I follow, grabbing my keys off the hook by the door, and wondering how a sunroof fits Patty's plans.

The backyard of our home has a back deck, a little postage stamp patch of grass, and a lot of sacred grove. Since we merged the property with my childhood home next door, we decided to use as much of the land as possible for our druid forest. That means I park my Dodge Hellcat SUV in the backyard spots next door.

"Patty, I thought I sensed you." Dart rushes out to greet us.

My dragon companion, AKA my blue boy, is growing in both size and skill every day.

He amazes me.

"Aye, ye did. Sloan gave me a call earlier to ask if my particular skillset could help Fi locate Cupid's stolen bow. We're headin' out. Would ye care to stretch your wings?"

Dart looks at me, and the hopeful spark in his eyes cleaves me in two. Sometimes my life gets so busy, I get pulled in a million different directions and neglect his need to be a dragon.

I need to do better.

"That's a great idea. We don't know where we're going yet but having aerial support can't hurt. You'll have to stay glamored though."

Dart rolls his eyes and gives me a "well duh" look I've given my father a million times. He always said that one day my kids would return the favor.

Payback is a bitch.

I raise my hand. "I know you knew that. Sorry."

Dart has moved on, finding interest in Dillan's girlfriend.

As Patty continues toward the cars, I introduce them. "Evangeline, this is my dragon companion and a beloved member of this family, Dartamont. Dart, this is Eva, Dillan's girlfriend."

Dart tucked his wings back and lowers his chin close to the ground. "It's a pleasure to meet you, Evangeline."

Eva smiles. "A pleasure to meet you too, Dart. If you don't mind, perhaps I'll fly with you while Fi and Patty figure out where we're going."

Dillan grins. "*Noice.* I finally get to see you fly?"

Eva giggles. "It's not as exciting as you think. I'm much more excited about flying with Dartamont. I haven't seen a dragon in the air in centuries. It truly is my honor to share the sky with you."

"Are we doing this or not?" A terse voice calls from the parking spots behind the house.

The four of us strike off and find Patty sitting on the roof of my SUV with his feet dangling through my new sunroof. He has Cain in his hand and is holding him out like a knight with his raised jousting lance. "A little less conversation, a little more action, please."

I take the hint and slide into the driver's seat. "All righty then. Saddle up. The game is afoot."

CHAPTER NINE

"D, could you please hold onto his ankle? I don't want my favorite Man o' Green rolling off the back of my truck and becoming fae roadkill. Who knows what might happen if he gets squashed? He might explode into a rainbow of red hearts, green clovers, and purple horseshoes."

"Ye know I can hear ye, right?"

I chuckle and hit my indicator to turn right onto Wellesley. "Grumble at me all you like. You're more than a pretty hood ornament to me."

"Ye think I'm pretty, do ye?"

"For sure. Mind of a scholar and face of an angel."

"Speaking of an angel." Dillan leans forward and looks up at the sky outside the front windshield. "She's pretty spectacular right?"

Stopped at the light, I take the opportunity to glance up at the plump white dove soaring in the sky above. It might be my imagination, but I swear there's a streaming golden glow of heaven's light radiating off her.

"Definitely spectacular," I say. "I'm happy for you, D. She really made an impression on you, eh? Worked her way right under your crusty outer shell and into the chocolatey goodness inside."

"Are you comparing me to a cracked M&M?"

I chuckle and slow down to wait for the car ahead of me to turn. "Maybe."

"Red, this is taking too long to cover distance. Let's try the freeway."

I blink at Dillan and make a face. "Are you sure you want me to go on the highway while you're sitting on the roof of my truck?"

"Why so worried? I'm the one that will be eatin' bugs, aren't I?"

"True. Okay, we can give it a try, but if it's too fast and you want me to take the exit, let me know."

"Too fast," he grumbles. "I'll have ye know I used to race ostriches in my youth. I can handle playing the part of the ornamental figurehead on the front of yer ship."

The image in my head of a young Patty riding an ostrich becomes him throwing his stubby arms out to the side as Leonardo DiCaprio hugs him at the front of the *Titanic*.

Okay, that's weird.

Following Patty's request, I make my way down to the Lakeshore and up the ramp to access the Gardener Expressway. As I merge into the first lane, Dillan twists in the passenger's seat to hold both of his ankles.

I step on the gas, more than a little relieved my brother has a good hold on him. "Anything?"

"It's not an exact science, Red. Patience is a virtue, and all that."

"Yeah, not one of my best events."

"I might've noticed that."

Booking it along the westbound Gardener, we go over Sherborne, Jarvis, and Yonge. Once we cross over York Street, I'm beginning to wonder if this is a good idea. Maybe going fast makes it harder for Cain to pick up the magic vibes of Eros's bow.

Patty says something I don't catch. The whistle coming through my new sunroof and the sounds of highway driving drown out his voice.

I turn to Dillan, and by his headshake, he missed it too.

"Come again? Did you say something, Patty?"

He leans to the side and sticks his head into the truck. "Get off on the next exit. Cain's got something."

I hit my indicator and exit at Spadina. "You want me to stay on the Lakeshore or head north into the core?"

"Stay along the lake fer now."

I do as instructed and continue westbound. As we drive along, I glance to my left and smile at all the boats and beachgoers along the lakefront. "We should organize a volleyball match this weekend and see who wants to play. Then we can go to the pub for dinner."

Dillan nods. "It'll be good for Tad to learn what the city offers. Maybe Aurora might even enjoy it."

"I asked Doc to go over and invite her to spend the day in the grove with the others. Hopefully, they can convince her."

"Turn right, here," Patty calls.

I slow to squeeze into an opening between cars, hit my blinker, and turn right to go into Exhibition Place.

Established in 1879, this section of Toronto's Harbourfront is more than a vast span of land where we host the yearly Canadian National Exhibition and Royal Winter Fair. It's also home to BMO Field, Medieval Times Dinner and Tournament, one of Toronto's top-rated hotels, and a bunch of massive event centers.

"In here, eh?" Dillan says.

"That doesn't make me feel good."

"Me either." Dillan pulls out his phone. "Okay, let's see what events we have going on right now."

"Hopefully none. If we're engaging vampires in a battle over

Eros's bow, I'd rather not do that in the middle of a ten-thou-sand-person event."

"It wouldn't be ideal, no."

I weave through the private laneways between the buildings, scanning the scene for which event centers have something going on.

Unfortunately, there's more than one.

"What's at the Queen Elizabeth building?"

"A summer *Better Homes and Gardens* Show."

"And at the Enercare Centre?"

"Everything To Do With Sex Show."

"You're kidding."

"Would I kid about that?" He waggles his ebony brows. "Hon-estly, I might take Eva and stop in if we zero out on the Cupid's arrow mission." His gaze glosses over, and it's obvious I've lost him to the lure of lewd.

"Try to stay focused. We don't have the luxury of zeroing out on recovering that bow."

"Oh, and there's also a Toronto FC game this afternoon. That should be good for another fifteen thousand people in the area."

"Awesomesauce."

"Okay, Red. Find us somewhere to park. Cain says we're gettin' close."

I stop at the gate for the pay parking, and the guy working the booth frowns at Patty. "Never mind him." I call on *Persuasion*. "How much for an hour?"

"It's twenty bucks whether it's for five minutes or five hours."

I reach behind the seat to grab my purse, but Dillan beats me to it. He stretches in front of me and taps his phone to the guy's hand-held payment machine.

After the *beep* signals we're all paid up, the attendant rips off our receipt and points at the dash. "Keep this in the front window where we can see it."

"Will do."

I hand it to Dillan to place it on the dash while I enter the lot and search for a spot to park. Instead of going close to the buildings and getting stuck in the congestion, I take one of the dozens of empty spaces close to the exit.

We're all about the getaway these days.

Once that's taken care of, Dillan helps Patty down, and I lock up. "Dart? Are you here, buddy?"

A gust of wind blows my hair, and I pull it out of my face. "I'll take that as a yes."

Eva's songbird laughter makes me smile a moment before she steps out of Dart's glamor and appears five feet in front of us. "That was super fun. I've always wanted to fly with a dragon."

"Another thing to check off your list." Dillan hugs her and shifts her to stand at his hip. "Eva has a long list of things she wants to experience in her life. Today, we helped her mark off another one."

"Glad to help." I scan the three closest buildings. "I don't suppose 'recover Eros's enchanted bow' is on there? We could go for a twofer."

"No, but that's fine. I'm excited to be included in the hunting party. Dillan says you do this kind of stuff all the time. How thrilling."

"In the past year, yes. Before that, I was just the girl next door. I worked part-time at Shenanigans and sold bracelets on Etsy. Boring."

"I doubt very much ye've ever been boring, Red." Patty is turning a three-hundred-and-sixty-degree circle with Cain's gold sour puss scowl glaring out at the unsuspecting world.

"Warmer," he shouts.

Patty shifts a bit more to the right.

"Warmer."

He shifts again.

"Colder."

Patty corrects and twists back again.

"Warmer."

Patty looks at me and nods. "And so, it goes. Come along, kids. We have a treasure to find."

I should've known when Dillan read out the list of events taking place we'd be heading straight for the Enercare Centre.

"Everything To Do With Sex Show," Eva says. "That sounds both fun and informative."

Dillan grins. "A win-win. We can hunt down a stolen bow and also educate ourselves on some of the fringe nuances of the show."

I don't even want to think about what the fringe nuances are at the sex show. Despite Suede's insinuation earlier that prudish ideals somehow bind me, I know how to have fun in the bedroom.

My brothers are more adventurous than I am, but there's nothing wrong with keeping the private life of two people private and behind closed doors.

"Four, please," Dillan says when we arrive at the ticket booth. "Oh, and can the two of us have re-entry stamps in case we have to leave in a hurry?"

He sticks his hand into the booth and waves Eva over to do the same.

"Do you really think going in there is necessary?" I peg him with a look. "Why would members of the Romanian syndicate be at this trade show? More likely, they're in a different part of the building somewhere. The place is over a million square feet. They could be anywhere."

Dillan looks at me and frowns. "Didn't you say the Romanovs are involved in smuggling women to Toronto to sell into the sex trade?"

"Yeah. So?"

He sweeps a hand toward the entrance. "It's not such a stretch to get from sex trade to sex trade show, is it? Maybe there's a front business or a shell company they use to get the women here or to vet clients. I have no idea, but Cain brought us here, so here we are. Investigate all possibilities, amirite?"

I look from him to Eva and wonder if it occurs to him that he's taking an angel into this trade show.

It doesn't seem to, no.

"Okay, let's get in and out."

"That's what he said," Dillan says.

I roll my eyes and stride off into the show. "You're enjoying this too much. I suppose you're planning to torment me the whole time we're here?"

"You know me so well."

I stop and let Patty lead the way. "What are you picking up, Cain?"

"Cold," he says as Patty points the talking stick to our left and starts a slow swing through the space. "Cold. Cold. Warmer. Warmer."

We take the aisle on our right and start weaving our way through dildos and leather lingerie. Thankfully, being mid-day and during the week, there aren't large crowds. The people who are here, however, are very interesting. "Oh, goody, cosplay. Wasn't it fun to dress up for *Rocky Horror*?"

Dillan chuckles behind me as we pass a man in a full neoprene bodysuit. "I don't think that's cosplay, Fi. I think that's him getting his groove on."

I don't even want to imagine that.

Shutting my brain off, I keep my eyes down and focus solely on my leprechaun and his verbally abrasive talking walking stick.

Dillan and Eva fall to the back and cover the rear. Other than pointing at a few booths and sharing a few private conversations, the two of them remain remarkably on task.

"Feelin' hot, hot, hot." Cain suddenly takes on a reggae rhythm.

The couple closest to us glances over. I'm not sure what it says about our society when people don't question the end of a walking stick playing Hot-Cold.

"He's like the sorting hat in *Harry Potter*." The woman leans closer. "How cute."

"Cute?" Cain's face screws up.

Before he can finish whatever is about to come out of his mouth, I usher Patty quickly down the next aisle.

"You look like a fit young lady," a man says, trying to coax me toward his display. "Have you ever thought about having a dancing pole in your home? They're great exercise, and we've got some great show specials right now."

I blink. "Have I ever wanted to have a stripper pole in my living room? No. Can't say that I have. Sorry, dude, you're barking up the wrong pole."

"It's for exercise," his voice trails off behind me.

Dillan's snorting and I roll my eyes. "Can you seriously imagine Sloan's face if I came home with a brass pole and told him I wanted to put it up in the house?"

Dillan shakes his head. "Fi. Seriously, you're overthinking. I think if you came home with that pole, Sloan would have his tools out and be securing it in place before you got your coat off. Irish might be uptight, but he's still a guy."

Whatevs.

I'm about to tell Dillan off when my shield wakes up, and my back starts to burn. I hold up my hand to stop the chatter. "Alarm bells are ringing, folks. Look alive."

The four of us stop, and I scan the booths close by.

There's a hedonist resort kiosk with travel brochures, next to that is a glass dildo company, across the aisle is a woman who makes corsets, beside her is a fleshlight company…ew, and—

There!

Slipping behind a curtain dividing the space from the adult to XXX section is the woman from the picture Nikon showed me.

"Anca Romanov," I whisper. "Follow me."

I take the lead and duck behind the curtain.

The cordoned-off area is draped with cloth walls and houses ten-foot booth areas on the left and right to demonstrate bondage techniques. Knot tying, hair-pulling, flogging, clamps, restraints, and a bunch of things I don't have time to figure out.

"There." Dillan points at the far end of the space where Anca is slipping through the back curtain. "We're losing her."

The four of us pick up our pace and beat feet to the exit. My shield is burning hot now, and my adrenaline is pumping.

"Watch your backs. I've got a feeling—" The moment I step through the back curtain, I glimpse a door closing on the far wall —only it's not a door.

At least from this side of the wall.

It's a panel system that opens from the other side.

"*Open Sesame.*" I press my hands on the flat panel. "D. Help me get this open."

Dillan pulls the hood of his cloak up, and I feel the surge of magic as it activates. He grins over at me and smiles. "It's important to successorize."

With a cocky grin, he swings the door open, and the four of us rush through—

Crack!

The concrete pillar beside my head explodes and chunks of stone fly at my face. I turn back fast, shielding my eyes, and call my body armor. "Take cover!"

Gunfire rattles off at regular intervals, mulching the concrete beside me. The only plus in the situation is that the shooters have silencers so we aren't causing a panic.

"I'm pinned." I check that the others are locked down, and everyone is whole. "We need to get a better vantage point."

"I'm not pinned." Eva smiles as she skips out into the open.

"No. Eva…"

But it's too late. Dillan's girlfriend bursts into the fray and the three of us are left to wait. I glance over at my brother and yep, he looks as freaked and pissed as I expected he would.

"D, move when the shooter stops to reload and stay behind me. My armor will keep us both safe."

When the shooting stops, I launch. Rushing out from behind the pillar, I'm twenty feet across the vastly open event space when I realize the shooter isn't reloading—she's engaged in a battle.

Hubba—wha?

I blink and look at Dillan. "Did you know about this? If you did, I'm seriously going to kick your ass."

CHAPTER TEN

Holy-crapamoly... Evangeline is a reaper.

Patty, Dillan, and I stand there gobsmacked, watching Dillan's girlfriend locked in battle. She's swinging her scythe with a smile on her face and beating the ever-loving snot out of two highly skilled fighters.

When she said she was an angel, I assumed she meant a cherub. How can she be a reaper? She's sunshine in a jar. Wow... she's also a damned good fighter.

Eva slices the air with her scythe, spinning as she battles, attacking with her weapon and her feet.

"Hokeedoodle, she could be a freaking Rockette with a kick like that."

"She is very bendy." Dillan takes in the show.

Movement in the background draws my attention to a woman who can be none other than a member of the Romanov family. She's the spitting image of Galina except maybe without the cruel glint in her eyes.

Is she a vampire like her cousin, or not?

It's impossible to tell from this distance.

The three of us move in, searching for a way around the battle between Eva and the bodyguards without disrupting Eva's flow. There isn't one.

That's fine. We're in no rush. Anca's backed into a corner. She's not going anywhere, and neither are we.

"We need her alive if possible," I shout, unsure what Eva's intentions are once she fights her way through those bodyguards.

My words are still ringing in the air when a dozen more men shouting in Romanian rush in to join the fun.

Shit on a stick.

Outnumbered much?

Gripping my Team Trouble pendant, I press it hard between my fingers and signal for backup. With that taken care of, I flex my palm and run toward the insurgence of testosterone, Birga in hand.

I meet three of the Romanov goons head-on and dig in. Sloan, Garnet, Nikon, and the others will get here as soon as they can. In the meantime, we'll hold them off so Anca doesn't get away.

"Any sign of the bow?"

"Workin' on that, Red." I hear the strain in Patty's voice and shift my footing so I can take a quick peek at what's up with him.

He's fighting off two guys with Cain and has his arm extended toward the battle between Eva and Anca's bodyguards. I see it then. The silver pendant around Anca's neck is hovering in the air and stretching to answer Patty's call. He's a treasure whisperer, and the bow wants to obey.

One of Patty's opponents throws himself into a punch and grunts as his fist hits an invisible barrier. The *crunch* of knucklebone makes me wince, and I focus on my guys again.

Red? Do ye need me?

I'd like nothing better than to release Bruin to make quick work of this fight so we can reclaim that bow, but I'm not sure if these people are human or not and we're in proximity to thousands of innocents.

Releasing a battle beast into this fight is exposure waiting to happen.

Need you, yes. Can I release you, no.

Och. Why? I can be subtle.

I snort as I raise Birga in both hands and brace against an overhead strike. *You're an eight-foot-tall, massive grizzly bear. Nothing subtle about that.*

I tense as the skylights sixty feet above us blow out in an explosion of glass. Shattered window panes rain down on us, and I have a bad feeling I know why.

Fuckety-fuck. There's nothing subtle about a glamored dragon crashing through the ceiling and fighting either.

The two guys Patty is struggling with are suddenly torn off their feet, tossed into the air like jellybeans, and disappear. It looks like they vanished, but the truth is, Dart has snapped them up and is chomping them behind his glamor.

The veil of invisibility is amazing at keeping us from seeing what's happening, but it does nothing to keep us from hearing it.

Ugh...gross. I hate the sound of crunching people.

Patty, now free of his opponents, swings the gold head of his walking stick from left to right and back again, pulling at the silver chain.

Anca is holding onto the chain with both hands, fumbling to grab the pendant.

The air *snaps* with a magic signature I recognize, and I exhale a heavy breath. Garnet, Anyx, Sloan, and Emmet arrive in a flash of energy, and I dial down my adrenaline.

The cavalry has arrived.

A projectile catches me in the shoulder and knocks me spinning to the concrete floor. Nothing penetrates my body armor, but it's a rude awakening.

I'm distracted.

Well, yeah. Dillan's girlfriend is a reaper. My dragon is actively eating civilians. Anca now has Eros' bow in hand and is firing into the crowd.

Awesomesauce.

I glance over and pick up the spent arrow that nailed me in the shoulder. The surge of magic from the arrow tingles over my skin, but it didn't penetrate, so I think I'm safe from its effects.

I roll to my feet, my adrenaline red-lining once again. "Cupid's bow is in play. Watch yourselves."

Emmet shifts into his kangaroo form, and I'm happy to see him in play. He leans back on his tail, and power kicks a guy twenty feet backward and into a column. After a little happy dance hop, he bounces off to box with the next guy.

Dillan is cutting the air with his dual daggers, deflecting everything that comes at him. As he cartwheels over one opponent, he catches another with his New Rock combat boots and stomps them into the concrete.

"Incoming!" I dive to tackle Anyx out of the way of another arrow, and the tip glances off my shoulder and hits one of Anca's guys.

Friendly fire!

Anyx and I roll for a moment, then I release him and gain some distance. Alpha shifters don't appreciate being tackled or held down and he's liable to turn into a lion and bite my head off.

Without waiting to see if I'm right about that, I continue through the crowd, heading for our budding archer.

A shamrock shuriken whistles past my head, and I smile. "Patty's in the *hoooouse!*" I turn back to find him standing on a stack of skids by a steel support beam whipping pink hearts, yellow moons, orange stars, and green clovers.

I bark a laugh and keep pushing forward.

I love my friends.

An orange star thwacks the brute of a man between Anca and me, and he goes down cursing.

"Thanks, Patty!" I wave over my head. I have Anca in my

sights, and I'm closing fast. *"Bestial Strength."* Spinning Birga in my hand, I go in hard.

Anca is rapid-firing arrows at me, and I'm smacking them out of the air with Birga as fast as I can. When I get through the last of her offenses, I spin my spear and give her the line-drive treatment.

If her head were a baseball, I would've hit it outta the park.

She goes down like a rock, and I grab the bow. "Winner, winner, chicken dinner."

The strike comes from my side and knocks me flying. I've got the bow though, and there's no way I'm giving it up. When the little birdies stop spinning over my head, I roll to my knees to see what the name of that semi-truck was that ran me over.

"Garnet? What the hell, dude?"

Garnet has Anca in his arms and is cradling her against his chest. "You hurt my beloved, Lady Druid. You will pay for that."

His lion lets out a long, threatening growl and he flashes out.

I push up to my feet and look around. "What happened? Did anyone see Garnet get cracked in the head?"

Anyx jogs over to pick up a spent arrow. When he sniffs the blood on its tip, his lion's growl rumbles deep in my chest. "It wasn't a crack to the head, Fi. She shot Garnet with one of Cupid's arrows."

Well, shit.

When the dust settles and we take inventory, it seems the only two things we have to put in the loss column are the structural damage to the Enercare Centre's skylights and the loss of Garnet.

That's a huge loss—tactically and personally.

Anyx calls Thaos and a couple of the other Moon Called guild soldiers to take care of cleanup, arresting our opponents, and mitigating fallout. Eva takes charge of escorting the dead to wherever they need to go. Patty mounts Dart to fly home with him, and Sloan *poofs* me, Emmet, and Dillan back to our house.

The moment we arrive, I round on Dillan. "Fess up. How much of the reaper revelation wasn't a surprise to you? I swear I'm gonna throat-punch you if you knew and didn't tell us even after I gave you the briefing about the mass death hanging over our heads."

"Simmer down, sista," Dillan snaps, stomping toward me. "I didn't know she was a reaper. Hell, I didn't know reapers were angels. When Eva told me she was an angel, I figured she was one of the harp-strumming, cloud-hopping kind. Do you honestly think I'd keep something like that a secret? Where the fuck do you think my loyalty is?"

"I'm not questioning your loyalty, dumbass, just your common sense. It's not unprecedented you'd omit something about your girlfriend because you don't want the family to weigh in. Remember Jessie? What about Alexa? Don't get me started about the Brittanys. What's with you and Brittanys anyway?"

He leans back and points at me. "Oh, are we dragging up old relationship mistakes, baby girl? How do I crush thee, let me count the ways?"

"All right, you two." Emmet steps between us and scowls. "To your corners until the bell rings. Fi is upset about Garnet, and Dillan is upset about whatever he's upset about—there's no way to know what's pissing him off at any given moment."

"Fuck you, Emmet."

"Harsh, bro. I call it as I see it."

"And side with Fi. You always side with Fi."

"Fuck you, D."

"No. Fuck you. You guys need to learn that I'm the big brother and shut the hell up. You don't get to mouth off to me."

"Hey." Calum stomps in from the back door in his uniform. "I trump the big brother card on all of you assholes, so shut the hell up. What did I miss? Is this about the call for backup earlier? Is everyone all right?"

"We're fine," Emmet snaps.

"Fuckin' A," Dillan growls.

"Just peachy," I chime in.

Calum crosses his arms and straightens. "Excellent. I'm glad everyone is on the same page. Now, let's hear it. What's all the hubbub, bubs?"

The three of us cross our arms as well and glare at one another. We might be mad as bulls in a bronco chute, but snitches get stitches.

Calum chuckles and grins at Sloan. "Moving right along. How did things go in the field today? You all look a little rumpled from battle."

I unlock my jaw enough to fill him in. "We confirmed Anca Romanov stole the bow and that her family of criminals currently have a strong presence in the city. We also found out Evangeline is a reaper and lied about it."

"I didn't lie." Evangeline bounces into the kitchen. "Angels don't lie. That's a big no-no in my world. I told you I was an angel."

"But not that you're a reaper."

"Does my designation matter?"

"No. It doesn't," Dillan snaps. "Fi's upset because Garnet got lovestruck by Cupid's arrow and is off in the city somewhere sexing the enemy."

"No," I shout, not wanting to consider that. "I'm upset because there's a mass gathering of reapers in Toronto, and I've spent the past two days trying to figure out what the source of the problem is and why they're here. If I'd known Evangeline is a reaper, I would've asked her and saved two days of tracking down dead ends when the lives of hundreds or maybe thousands of innocents are at risk."

The room turns to look at Evangeline, but she doesn't offer

anything up.

"Really? You've got nothing?" I say.

"Oh, I'm sorry, was there a question put to me?"

"Not in any way you'd recognize as a polite or civilized inquiry," Dillan snaps.

I fight the urge to stomp my foot and growl at my brother. He's so stubborn and annoying sometimes.

Yeah, I know…pot-kettle and all that.

Getting a grip, I draw a deep breath and start from the top. "Evangeline, I've been tasked to find out what pending mass death event is hanging over the city. Being a reaper, could you please tell me what's going on?"

"No, sorry, I can't." Evangeline's smile is as bright and shiny as ever. "That's not how it works."

"That's very *not* helpful. Awesome."

Dillan scowls at me. "Go pour yourself a drink and while you're at it, get that broomstick out of your ass. Maybe then you'll stop being such a witch."

I middle finger that comment and stride off toward the bar. Sloan joins me, grabs the bottle, and clasps my arm. A split second later, we're standing in our bedroom, and he points at the café table in front of the window. "Sit, luv. I think a little distance from the situation will be a good thing."

"You're putting me on a timeout?"

"If that's the way ye want to look at it, aye, I am." He half-fills the tumbler in my hand and sits opposite me. "Draw a deep breath, take a long swallow, and center yourself. I'll wait."

I do as told, and after a few minutes of deep breathing and deep drinking, my jagged edges start to wear down. "All right, I'm calm. Impart upon me your wisdom so we can go back downstairs and figure out what to do next."

Sloan reaches across the table, and I surrender my glass. He swirls the amber liquid at the bottom of my glass and up-ends what's left into his mouth. When he sets the glass on the little table, he takes my hands and leans forward on his elbows.

"Ye recovered the bow, ye have a lead on how to find information about the reapers, and ye know who the enemy is. I understand how upset ye are about Garnet and somehow in yer chaotic mind, I expect ye've now convinced yerself that yer the ruination of his life, and Myra's and Imari's happiness—but yer not."

"Of course, I am."

"No. Yer not. We'll talk to Eros, we'll find Garnet, and we'll fix it like always."

I like the story he's spinning. The problem is I don't believe it. "I told Anyx I need to tell Myra. How do I explain to her the love of her life and shifter mate is currently under the passionate thrall of a Romanian crime queen and is likely sexing her up and making crazy lion love to her as we speak?"

"Well, the first thing ye do is leave that last bit of speculation off. Keep it simple. Garnet was struck by one of Cupid's arrows in the battle and is currently under the enemy's influence. Assure her we'll do whatever it takes to get him back and tell her not to panic. Garnet loves her to the depths of his bound soul. I doubt very much even Eros's dominion can negate that love."

I text Nikon and Dionysus the good news about the bow and invite them to come over. "All right. Let's go downstairs and talk to Eros. You're right. We don't know what we're dealing with yet. There's no way a stupid enchanted arrow will erase what Garnet and Myra went through to be together. I'm probably making myself sick over nothing."

"That's right. Garnet will fight this and reclaim his life with his family. Ye'll see. It'll be fine."

CHAPTER ELEVEN

"Your friend is screwed. There's no fighting it," Eros says absently. "The man who loved his wife and child is gone. My power overwrites free will."

"You smarmy piece of—" Nikon grabs me around the waist as I lunge. I didn't mean to throw myself at the god of love, but he doesn't even care that his dominion just ruined three lives.

"Whoa, okay." Nikon swings me in the air to set my feet down, facing away from his friend. "Eros could've worded that better, granted, but beating the crap out of him doesn't help anyone, especially Myra and Imari."

I peg Nikon with a look and try to breathe. "What do I say to them? How do I explain the man who left them this morning is gone forever?"

"Ye don't say anything of the sort." Patty comes in from the back door and reaches up to clasp my hand. "We'll get Garnet back despite the damage done."

"Are you saying I'm wrong, leprechaun?"

Patty glares at Eros and laughs. "Och, little boy, if ye'd seen half the things I have in life, ye'd not be so big in yer britches.

Gods are so conceited they're ignorant about the world around them, so arrogant, they think their shite don't stink."

I hope he's right.

Man, I like that version of things better than Eros'.

Patting Nikon's wrist, I signal for him to let me go. "I'm good, Greek, honest."

After Nikon releases me, I turn to Eros and force a smile. "You have your bow back, you've said there's nothing you can do to help us with the fallout of what happened, so I'm sure you're anxious to return to Mount Olympus or wherever it is you hail from."

Eros chuckles. "If I didn't know better, I'd think I'm getting shown the door."

"See," Dillan says to Emmet, "I told you he couldn't possibly be as stupid as he acts. He got his dismissal on the first try."

Emmet grins and waggles his brow. "Will he take the out and leave? Inquiring minds want to know."

Eros scowls around the room, and his gaze ends up on Nikon and Dionysus. "Then I guess we take our leave. Where to next, gentlemen?"

Nikon shakes his head. "You're flying solo for the moment, my friend. I want to stay and help Garnet and his family. They're good people, and we played a part in this mess by losing track of your bow in the first place."

Eros shrugs, unaffected. "Okay, how long will it take? Dionysus and I can go back to the loft and invite some randoms over for a good time. When can we expect you?"

Dionysus meets my gaze, and his expression softens to a genuine smile. "I think my days of inviting random people over have come to a close. I'm staying to help Fi and my Cumhaill family figure out how to fix what's going wrong in our city. It'll take however long it takes."

Eros lifts his bow and reaches behind his head. It magically secures to his back within his reach. "Toronto isn't your city, *adelphos*. This isn't even your time."

"Even still. I'm staying."

Nikon drapes a heavy arm across the back of my shoulders and leans in to kiss the side of my head. "It's time to stop watching life pass by while we bemoan lives of endless privilege. There are troubled times ahead, and there is strength in unity. If you ever want to stick your neck out for the cause, we'll be here."

Eros sweeps his hands out to his sides and takes a bow. "Then I bid you all a fond farewell. Until we meet again, folks."

When he snaps out, the tension in the room lessens.

"I can't say I'll miss him," I say.

"Me either," Emmet says. "Besides, the position of Greek god has already been filled in our circle. We don't need to collect doubles and certainly not inferior ones."

"Did that asshat even say thank you for us nearly dying to recover his bow?" Dillan asks.

"No, he didn't," Patty snaps.

I shrug. "I mentioned his lack of gratitude once before. He responded that he's the god of love. He doesn't need help from people beneath him, and he definitely doesn't need to placate us for offering it."

Dillan makes a face. "Sorry, Greeks. That guy is squad captain of all douche canoes."

Nikon doesn't take offense to that. He shrugs and accepts the beer Emmet offers. "He helped me get through a lot of years when Hecate's curse bound me. Maybe our friendship is real, or maybe it was based on me having no other options, but it is what it is."

I can understand that. For centuries, the witch cut Nikon off from making loving, lasting relationships. If Eros helped him through that time in his life, I'm grateful.

I accept the beer Emmet passes me, and while everyone mingles and chats about the day's events, I head over to where

Dillan is standing with Evangeline. "Hey there… Dillan told me earlier that I was being a witch."

"Because you were," Dillan says.

"Fine. I was." I meet Evangeline's gaze and ignore Dillan's hostility. "Something you'll learn about me is that I care for the people in my life very deeply. When they hurt, I hurt. I took that out on you. That was shitty."

"True story," Dillan says.

He's not going to make this easy on me. Oh, well. I have my big girl panties on today, s'all good.

"What happened this afternoon with Garnet wasn't your fault. You being a reaper and us not knowing wasn't your fault. Me biting off Dillan's head about it wasn't your fault or his. I apologize to you both. I hope you can forgive me."

Evangeline smiles so wide her cheeks dimple. "Forgiveness is very important in my circles. Done. You're forgiven. Thank you for the apology. I suppose I owe you one myself."

"You do? How so?"

"I've studied the human plane for centuries but being here is different. I miss social cues. I didn't realize I omitted something about myself you would find important. Being a reaper is my duty. It's not who I am."

"You don't have to apologize for that," Dillan says.

"No, of course, you don't. I didn't ask, and you didn't mention it. I shouldn't have lost my temper."

"No, you shouldn't have," Dillan adds.

"Geez, D, stop riding me. I'm trying here. When I flew off the handle, I was burning adrenaline from the fight and felt blindsided about Garnet and doubly blindsided about Eva being a reaper. I spouted off. End. Of."

Eva lifts her finger and bops the end of Dillan's nose. "Enough scowls and growls for one day, sweetie. Your sister and I have made amends. In the future, simply tell me plainly what I need to do better."

"There is no better." Dillan squeezes her hand. "You're amazing the way you are. I didn't ask for details about your life because it changes nothing for me. You're the woman I fell in love with, and that's good enough. The rest is all white noise."

Uh...exsqueeze me?

Dillan is admitting he's in love?

I glance around and find the same look of wide-eyed shock on Calum's and Emmet's faces too.

This is big—huge!

I gather my thoughts on that and get back to the problem at hand—or at least one of them. "Eva, in the spirit of communication, I'd like to talk about the gathering of reapers in Toronto. You mentioned you don't know anything about it. Can you explain to me how I find out what's causing the upcoming event?"

"I can try. As I mentioned, that's not how it works. Some of us do the regular escorts for a given region and others respond to a call for a mass event. I'm one of the former and am unaware of any mass gathering. Who told you there were others?"

"Garnet held an emergency meeting and announced it. I don't know how he found out. Does that matter?"

"I suppose not. Leave it with me. I'll get back to you as soon as I can." She turns to Dillan and kisses his cheek. "It was fun fighting with you today. Thanks for the invite."

"You were amazing. You can fight with Clan Cumhaill any time."

"You're sweet. Are you coming over later?"

Dillan checks his watch. "I promised Tad I'd help him with house repairs for an hour or two across the road. When I finish there, I can grab a bucket of chicken and come to your place."

"And some of those honey biscuits?"

"You know it."

"Sounds perfect. I'll see you soon." Eva waves goodbye and

practically bounces as she makes her way to the back door, her curls springing up and down with every step.

When the door *clicks* shut, I turn to Dillan and raise my palms. "You want to free shot?"

He rolls his eyes and steps in to hug me. "No, you dope. Just don't say anything mean about Eva. She's honestly the sweetest person I've ever met. I don't want anyone here to make her feel bad for who she is."

"I get that, and I'm sorry, but seeing her battling with a scythe and kicking the snot out of hired thugs threw me off my game. Are we okay?"

"Yeah. We're good." He eases back from our hug and turns to Emmet. "Are we good?"

Emmet nods and holds out his knuckles for a bump. "Yeah. We're good."

"Now that everyone's good," Sloan says. "I need to take Fi to Africa to speak to Myra, and someone needs to check on Dart and make sure he's all right. He ate quite a few men this afternoon. I wouldn't be surprised if he's overdone it and has a bellyache."

Emmet chuckles. "I'll check in with Dart. If he needs an antacid, I'll take care of him."

I laugh at the thought of Emmet giving Dart a dragon-sized Alka-Seltzer. Plop, plop, fizz, fizz. "Yeah, you take care of that, Em. Or keep him company and Sloan can whip him up a remedy when we get back."

"On it."

Sloan *poofs* us to a schmancy, high-income part of mid-town and the two of us take form in the blind spot on Garnet's driveway. With some strategic landscaping, the Alpha of the Toronto Moon Called made it so not only his visitors but the members of his pride can arrive by any number of teleportation modes and remain unseen.

We step outside the shadows of the manicured hedge and through the elaborate brick arbor. If I weren't a welcome guest of Garnet's, I would pass straight under the arbor and continue along the walkway toward his lovely Toronto home.

Because Sloan and I are empowered, and on the approved guest list, we're transported to Garnet's private compound in the African savanna as we step through the arbor.

Usually, the temperature change is drastic and often uncomfortable. Today it's a hot July afternoon in Toronto, and it's not that much hotter in Africa.

"Fi, a wonderful surprise." Myra climbs out of the oasis pool and grabs her wrap. The ash nymph is closing in on two hundred years old but looks like a fit and feisty middle-aged woman. "Did you two come for a swim?"

"Auntie Fi!" Imari shouts, waving from atop the giant blow-up swan in the middle of the pool. "Did you bring Jackson and Meggie to play?"

"Not this time, sweetie. I came to talk to your mommy for a minute, but I'll bring the kids over to play soon. We'll make a plan."

"Okay. Real soon, right?"

"Yep. Real soon."

I smile at Sloan, and he knows without me asking that I need him to step away and let me talk to Myra alone. "Imari," he says, assuming lifeguard duty. "I hear yer learning to dive. Do ye want to show me?"

While the two of them strike up a conversation, I tilt my head toward the shade of the covered porch of the house and gain some distance. Moon Called have heightened hearing, and while Myra is an ash nymph, Imari is a bear shifter, and I don't want her to overhear.

When the two of us are far enough that I'm sure we can speak privately, I take Myra's hand and tug her to sit on the outdoor sofa beside me. Forcing breath into my lead lungs, I pray the right words come out of my mouth.

"I have to tell you something, but I don't want you to freak out. Whatever happened, we'll find a way to undo it. Keep that in mind."

Myra frowns. "What's happened, Fi?"

"There was a battle this afternoon. I was tracking the thief of Eros's enchanted bow, and it went sideways. The woman who stole it is part of the Romanov cartel, and she unleashed a dozen of her men on me. I called for backup, and among others, Garnet responded to help."

Myra closes her eyes and swallows. "Is he dead?"

"No. As far as I know, he's perfectly healthy."

"Is he captured?"

"Sort of."

She pauses and searches my expression. "What do you mean sort of, Fi? How can he be sort of captured?"

I adjust my position on my seat so we're face-to-face. "During the fight, the woman started targeting us and shooting arrows. One of the enchanted arrows pierced Garnet, and he got whammied by the whole Cupid thing. At the moment—and this is only temporary—he switched sides and thinks he's protecting the woman he loves."

I swallow and wait for that to sink in.

I'm not sure what I expect Myra to say or do, but the resolute calm nothingness I see in front of me isn't on the list. "Thank you for telling me. What do we do now to correct the problem?"

"Well, I know who she is and have a good idea where her family is rooting their illegal business. Anyx and I will coordinate an investigation to find her and take her down. At the same time, Sloan, Dionysus, Patty, and Merlin will all work on how to break Cupid's spell and bring Garnet home to you."

Myra shivers, and I don't think it has anything to do with the fact that she is fresh from the pool. "For now, I'll tell Imari her daddy had to go out of town for work. That will buy us a few days. Find him, Fi. Find him, fix him, and bring him home to us."

"I will. I promise. Somehow I will fix this."

Myra nods. "I know you will. You always do."

I watch as Imari points her hands over her head and bellyflops across the surface of the pool. The smack of impact makes Myra and I wince, but the little bear doesn't seem to notice. "Do you want Sloan and I to stay for a while?"

Myra shakes her head. "No. You go. Find my husband and bring him home to me.

CHAPTER TWELVE

S loan and I leave the compound in Africa and make our way back to the chaos of life in Toronto. Standing on the rich, black asphalt of Garnet's driveway, I watch the heat of the day rise from the ground in waves of distortion and stop Sloan to brainstorm. "Obvi, our priority is to get Garnet back and fixed so he can resume his life. How do you envision we get that ball rolling?"

"I think Xavier is our first stop. He has the most invested in bringing down the Romanovs both personally and professionally. I wouldn't be surprised if he's already taken steps to that end."

I pull out my phone and call up Xavier's contact. "I'll ask if he'll meet with us. Maybe between the three of us, we can come up with a plan that doesn't result in dragging Toronto into a vampire war."

"We can hope."

After I hit "Send," I scan my messages to see if anything urgent happened while we were out of range.

No news is good news on that front.

"Where do ye want to go, *a ghra*?"

"Let's go to Casa Loma. We can walk the grounds until I hear back from Xavier. Today's been a lot, and I could use a minute with you just being two people in love on a nice summer day."

"That I can do, luv."

Sloan *poofs* us into the shadows of the carriage house opposite the beautiful stone castle. The grounds are public, so I take his hand, and the two of us strike off on a stroll.

After the chaos of the day, my mind is full of too many things to sort through all at once. Instead of trying, I lean into him and hug his arm as we walk silently across the manicured grass.

"This is nice." I breathe deeply. The sweet scent of summer blooms is heavy in the warm summer air. "It hurts my heart to think of an arrow point erasing Garnet's and Myra's love. If anything like that ever happens to me, I want you to know I would never want that. I love you, and I love who I am when I'm with you."

Sloan sets his hand over mine where it rests on his arm. "I know ye do, *a ghra*. How could ye not? I'm fan-feckin'-tastic."

I burst out laughing. Just like that, Sloan Mackenzie has pulled me out of the depths. "I think that's my line. Get some original material, Mackenzie."

He chuckles, his smile betraying how pleased he is with himself for cheering me up. "Ye may have used that line on me once or twice. It seemed only fitting to return the favor."

"Well played, hotness. Well played."

My phone vibrates in my back pocket, and I pull it free. "Xavier is asking where to meet. I'll let them know we're here and see what he says."

I finish the text and send it. A moment later, Xavier is striding across the grounds to join us.

The man is intense.

Bearing down on us as he is, my mind burps up panicked flashes from the night he almost bit through my neck: me racing through Karuna's mansion to find a panic room locked and inaccessible...smashing through the upstairs window with no other means of escape...being tackled and pinned as his canines descended and he punctured my body armor to gain access to my throat.

I lock my anxiety down and take comfort in my shield lying inert and unresponsive against my back.

This man is not that man.

"Fiona. Sloan. What can I do for you?"

Xavier is all business. The fleeting moments when I wondered if we were more than acquaintances have been few and far between. Sloan's right. For the most part, when the vampire king is nice to me, it's because he feels guilty about mistreating me in one way or another.

"Before we get into the why, how is Benjamin?"

He stops next to an old oak and shifts his position to have the wide trunk at his back. "Inconsolable at the moment but thank you for asking. Vampires feel and see things on a heightened scale. The loss of Laurel as his companion will take time from which to recover."

"Please let him know I'm closing in on Anca and will find out for certain if she's responsible for Laurel's murder."

"Oh, she is. I've spent the past two days tracking down the security footage to prove it."

"That must serve as some comfort, to know for certain who was responsible."

"Not yet, but it will."

The threat is thick in his tone, and I don't doubt that Anca Romanov is living on borrowed time. "Will there be any kind of memorial for Laurel? I'd like to attend if that's possible. I miss her too."

"That's kind of you to say. I'll mention it to Karuna and the other ladies. They're taking care of things. Now, why did you ask to see me?"

"I have news—some of it good, some of it not so good—but either way, you need to know. This afternoon, there was an altercation between Anca Romanov and a dozen of her men and Team Trouble."

His head tilts to the side as a slight smile curls the edges of his mouth. "I'm surprised you tracked her down before I did. I have some of my best men on it."

I start from the beginning, filling Xavier in on Eros' missing bow and how we used its magical signature to track it to the Enercare Centre.

"She got away?"

"She had help. Unbeknownst to us, one of the arrows struck Garnet during the fight, and he's currently under Anca's love spell. We weren't ready when he turned on us and flashed her away."

"Garnet has been turned?"

"Not willingly. My point is we suffered a significant loss by having Garnet compromised. More than the personal implications of him believing he's in love with Anca, there are political and safety implications as well. He knows everything about how we run the city, our procedures, and the locations of all the sect leaders and their operations."

By the scowl on Xavier's face, he doesn't like that any more than I do. "So, the man with the keys to our lives might hand them over to our enemy."

"I don't want to think that, but it's a possibility. Knowing Garnet, even with his conscious mind altered, he knows not to expose sensitive information."

"Are you willing to bet the lives of your family members on that? I'm not."

No, I'm not, and he can read that from me. "Let's work together to take the Romanov family down and boot them out of our city. In the process, we can seek out Garnet and remove him from their camp. Even if we can't break the stupid Cupid spell, if he's locked in the cell of the Batcave, he can't hurt himself or others."

Xavier arches a brow and an eerie light flashes in his eyes. "We get to take Garnet on? I admit that sounds appealing."

I wave away his challenge. "That's all you got out of what I said? It was more about uniting forces and taking down our common enemy and less about seeing who's king of the hill."

"Still, there's a fundamental point you've overlooked in your plan."

"There is? What's that?"

"What happens when the heads of the other sects learn Garnet has gone rogue? As much as I hate to say it, the only thing keeping some of the more violent sects in line is the threat of Garnet's retaliation. The man plays at being civilized, but he's a brutal animal. He's respected, yes, but he's also hated and feared."

"Then we make sure the other sects don't find out. My family won't say anything, and Myra and the Moon Called certainly won't broadcast it, so if you keep it quiet, we shouldn't have a problem."

Xavier smiles. "There's that naïve optimism people hate you for."

Whatevs. I don't care if I'm the only one in the room that still believes in the Easter Bunny. I know he's real. I have one of his psychedelic poops in my pocket.

Sloan stiffens beside me as the air blurs with the arrival of another vampire. It's the Pinky Blinders edition of Xavier's siring line.

"'Allo, Oli. What's new with you since you last slammed me up against a wall?"

Oli—whose actual name is Oscar—is standing at a respectful distance and doesn't engage. He clasps his hands behind his back and waits until Xavier turns and gives the man his attention. "Yes, Oscar? What is it?"

Oscar strides forward and hands him the tablet he held behind his back. "We thought you should see this right away. A video has gone viral on the city chat boards, Witchipedia, and Faebook."

"What is it about?"

"It's a call for an uprising in the city."

Xavier accepts the tablet, steps in beside Sloan and me, and holds the screen so we can all see.

I take one look at the weird grin on Garnet's face and my innies twist and tighten.

"You were saying, Lady Druid?"

I sigh. "Even if the lion is out of the bag on Garnet's current situation, do you think it'll cause a citywide uprising?"

Oscar chuckles. "You haven't seen it yet, little girl. Garnet Grant not only approves an uprising; he grants free rein for the city's empowered folks to do whatever they want without repercussion. Do you expect them to pass on the opportunity?"

My mind stalls out on that as Xavier hits "Play." In horror, the three of us watch Garnet tank everything we worked so hard for over the past six months.

"Do you want to murder the gnome next door for having bad taste in music? Have at it.

"Are you tired of keeping your tail tucked in your trousers when you go to the grocery store? Don't bother. Fly your preternatural freak flag with honor.

"Have you been harboring a grudge against another sect? Then out those blades and see who's the last man standing."

My brain is pounding a steady rhythm against the backs of my eyelids by the time the video ends. "Are you freaking kidding me?"

Sloan frowns. "I doubt very much this was Garnet's idea. Creatin' citywide havoc sounds like an excellent way fer the Romanovs to move into a seat of power. I would wager they stole the bow for this exact purpose."

"Well, how do we veto Garnet's hall pass?"

Xavier looks at me and frowns. "I'm not sure we can. Garnet took all reason out of our hands."

———

"Hello the house." I shout first upstairs, then down. When nothing comes back to me but silence, I toss my purse on the counter and grab my phone from my pocket. "Since when is there no one home?"

"It's a freak occurrence, that's fer sure." Sloan goes to the refrigerator and pulls out containers. "Perhaps they're across the road at Tad's place. Yer brothers were keen to help him settle in, and we asked the companions to make Aurora feel at home."

"That makes sense." I finish texting the call for an emergency family meeting and rush over to see the choices for a quick meal. "We better carb load. I feel a lot of hand-to-hand coming on."

"Ominous," Emmet says, poofing into the living room with Ciara, Calum, Kevin, and Tad. "Why text us, 'The end is nigh.'? Are you playing Chicken Little in the school play?"

I fork a pile of leftover chicken fettuccine and point at the laptop open on the kitchen table. "Check it out yourself. Garnet posted a video an hour ago on the fae channels. You tell me if I'm being dramatic."

I slide my plate into the microwave and top it with the splash guard. After setting my time and getting things rolling, I grab a glass and fill it with water from the fridge's door. By the time my early supper is *beeping*, the construction crew from across the road has finished watching the video.

Cue the cricket choir.

I set my plate on a placemat on the island and eat standing up. "We believe Garnet is lighting the city on fire so his criminal girl crush and her family can take root in our underworld."

Emmet blinks. "Is that crazy or romantic?"

"Can something be cromantic?" Kevin asks.

"Having been in more than one romantic relationship that tipped the scales of cray-cray, I vote yes."

Tad laughs. "I've had more than a couple of cromantic relationships myself in that case."

"There's nothing romantic about it." I point my fork at them. "Garnet belongs with Myra. The arrow brainwashed him. We need to figure out how to reverse the effects and get him back."

The microwave *beeps* to indicate Sloan's plate is hot and ready, and he steps in to retrieve it. "I think yer underestimatin' how complex it'll be to free Garnet from the love spell. Yer first goal should be to gather the Guild Governors and release yer own video about how ye won't tolerate wild abandon in the streets."

"Not everyone will listen," Calum says.

"No, but it will move some of the chaotic neutral members of the communities back on our side."

I swallow another bite of creamy goodness as Nikon snaps in to join us with Dionysus.

"I assume you hitting the panic button has something to do with Garnet's video?" Nikon asks.

"So, you've seen it?"

"Andromeda showed it to me. She's meeting Maxwell at the Batcave to woman the phones. She figures people will soon be calling in to request help."

"I hope she's wrong, but I've already heard once today how much people hate my naïve optimism."

"Centaur shit." Dionysus scowls on my behalf. "People love your naïve optimism."

Sloan finishes his meal beside me and pulls out his phone. "Dillan is at Eva's. He says they can be on their way now and drive home or if it's a super emergency I'll need to get them."

"Well, considering we don't know where Eva lives and we don't have a plan yet, tell him driving home works. We'll see them soon."

Da and Aiden come in the back door, both in uniform. One of

the best parts about Maxwell setting up SITFU as a multiple-agency task force is the "get out of beat duty free" card they get to play when the shit hits.

If the empowered world is going to hell and I need them, my brothers and father can leave their shift duty and flip over to help me while still on the clock.

"Welcome home, boys. Anyone who's hungry should grab a plate. We have a long night ahead of us, and there's no telling when we'll have time to stop for something to eat."

"Why, *mo chroi?* What's happened?"

While I answer my dad's question, I grab a couple of cookies out of the package and abandon the kitchen to the invading horde.

When I finish, Da scratches the back of his head and frowns. "I know I've been at the front of the line to criticize the man, but Garnet has proven his devotion to the city time and again. I might not approve of his methods most times, but he's dealing with a different set of rules for a different kind of community. It's a shame this happened. I'm sorry, baby girl."

"We'll get him back." I swallow my cookie. "We have to. I promised Myra we wouldn't stop until we find him, fix him, and bring him home."

"No. That's right," Da says. "We won't."

Finished with my meal, I brush cookie crumbs off my hand and get us started. "Sloan, I'm putting you and Dionysus on magical research. Find a way to get Garnet back. Patty says he'll stay on it and ask around in his circles. Merlin is working on it too. Coordinate with them and if you come up with something, let me know."

Sloan doesn't look like he approves. "It might be wiser to have more bodies in battle, luv. We can help capture and contain Garnet, then worry about breakin' the spell once he's secure."

"I thought about that, and we might go that way, but for now, let's get started on all fronts. We can shift gears on the fly if we need to. Both of you can portal, so you can join us in the blink when we're ready to move."

"Ye promise ye won't go after Anca and Garnet without tellin' us first?"

"Cross my heart, hotness. We'll need all the help we can get, I'm sure."

"Och, I'm sure," Da says. "If we're talkin' about a magical revolt, we've got our work cut out for us."

"So, where do we start?" Calum asks.

I study the group and check the time on my phone. "I called an emergency Lakeshore Guild meeting for twenty minutes from now. Nikon and I will create a video to veto Garnet's. Xavier assured me he'll help in any way he can, so maybe with him looking stern and dangerous in the background, the message might seem more imposing."

Da frowns. "I'm sure it will. Keep in mind, Xavier will help because resolving this takes the Romanovs off the board and frees him to be the uncontested king vampire once again."

I wave that away. "I get that, but I don't care about motives at the moment. We're solidly focused on the finish line right now."

"Your comment about stern-looking men in the background is a good one," Nikon says. "We should see if Anyx and Thaos will stand in the background looking threatening too. The two of them are Garnet's top two enforcers, and if they're behind you, it might give people pause."

Da nods. "A smart idea, son. Also, ye'll need to discredit Garnet's video somehow and make people doubt what they think they saw."

Emmet tosses his crust onto the pizza box and grabs the last slice of last night's snack. "We'll say the video was an AI computer simulation and wasn't real. People are so used to the world of technology being able to do anything that they probably won't question it."

Okay. I can work with that. "The Romanovs are new in town.

The other members of the empowered community won't know if they're high-tech or not."

Da selects a pear from the fruit bowl and takes a bite. "All ye need to do is create doubt. If people worry they'll be held accountable and punished for any offense they make, they might back down and reconsider."

"Let's hope." I slot my plate in the dishwasher and reclaim my water. "Emmet, do you think you can get the original video removed from the empowered social media sites? The original, I mean. I know there's not much to be done about downloads or reposts."

"You said Maxwell's at the Batcave, yeah?"

I glance at Nikon to confirm. "Yeah."

"I have a few ideas. If Maxwell's there, I'm sure he can help me getter done."

"Excellent. The sooner, the better. Sloan, can you take him over right now?"

"I can." Tad steps forward. "I probably can help them with the computer hacking too. I've been known to trespass behind a few firewalls when bored."

"I'll go too," Ciara says. "I can help Andromeda on the phones if it gets crazy."

"Awesome, thanks."

The three of them *poof* out before Dillan and Evangeline arrive. We catch them up on what happened and our plans to fix it.

"It's time for Nikon and me to go." I kiss Sloan's cheek and start across the room toward Nikon. "Oh, but before I leave, what did you find out about the reapers gathering? It feels sort of self-evident now, but is this the beginning of the mass death event?"

Eva offers me an apologetic smile. "I haven't got a definitive answer. The way it works is more like a calling than a playbook of what's coming. When a mass death is pending, we simply know where to go and await the call to action. Everything is compartmentalized, and everyone keeps to themselves."

I see in her expression that she wishes she could be more helpful and that's some consolation.

You don't know what you don't know.

"Okay, so we'll proceed as if this *is* the event. The rest of you should stay in contact with the Batcave and respond to the distress calls as they come in."

"I'd like to come with you, Fi," Eva says. "I have a feeling that's where I need to be."

Calum frowns. "I don't like the sound of that."

Dillan's brow pinches tight too. "Do you mean that's where you need to be to help Fi or in the capacity of a reaper? If it's the second one, I'm sorry, babe, but there is no way we'll let you reap Fi's soul."

Eva giggles. "No, silly. I'm not here to reap your sister. I thought if she's facing vampires, I can help her. Reapers can't take lives, but if her foes are vampires, they don't have souls and are already dead. I can fight the undead without any penalty points."

"We haven't confirmed they're vampires." I point out the flaw in her plan. "So, then what? You'll stand back and let me get my butt kicked?"

Eva smiles. "You're hilarious."

I'm glad she thinks so. I was serious. By her tone and smile, she thinks that's enough information. Not by a long shot. Unfortunately, I don't have time to worm more info out of her.

"That's fine. You and Dillan can come with us if you want to. S'all good."

Nikon takes my hand and hers, and we snap out.

CHAPTER THIRTEEN

No offense to Eva, but she's now become the strangest of all Dillan's girlfriends. That's a category brimming with competition and steeped in colorful history. He fell in love with a sunshiny reaper. If I had more time to think, I'm sure there's lots to say, jokes to make, and a million different ways to torment Dillan.

I don't.

Right now, the immediate problems at hand consume all my mental bandwidth. One, unite the Guild Governors and get a video out to stop the chaos. Two, find Anca Romanov and stop her from torpedoing my city. Three, recover Garnet, get him away from Anca, and break him free from the love spell.

After those are taken care of, I'll revisit the idea of Dillan falling for a reaper. Was she allowed to get involved with a human? Doesn't that cross some kind of professional boundary or something?

It just seems weird.

She's an angel and ended up sexing my brother the first night they met. Did she play him? I don't want to see him get hurt.

Dillan's a big boy. He's smart, and he's capable of protecting his heart.

From what I've seen between him and Eva, they adore each other. Maybe I'm overthinking it.

Not my circus. Not my monkeys.

Nikon gestures toward the conference room. "I know that look, Fi. We have enough things to worry about without taking on more. We need to follow the bouncing ball and not get distracted."

"Right you are, Greek. Let's do this." I draw a deep breath, lift my head, and stride into the Lakeshore Guild's meeting chamber. With my shoulders back, I project far more confidence than I feel and hope I'm pulling it off.

We need a win on this.

I can't let Garnet down. I *won't* let Garnet down.

At a monthly guild meeting, there is upward of forty people who attend. An emergency meeting only requires the highest power-holders to show up, and the others can come if they choose. That usually means twenty or twenty-five people around the table.

Today there are nine.

I'm not sure if the failure to show is because I was the one who called the meeting or because the others have seen Garnet's video and don't want to get involved. Or maybe they've watched Garnet's video and are currently on a criminal rampage throughout the Toronto streets.

Whatever the reason, I didn't get the turnout I wanted.

"Thanks for coming." I raise a hand to get their attention. "I'll get right to the point. I'm sure by now everyone has seen the video that went viral this afternoon. I'm here to explain what happened and tell you what we're doing about it."

"You're telling *us* what we're doing about it?" Andreas Markdale snaps. "Who died and put you in charge, Druid? You've been on the council for what now, all of ten minutes?"

"And you, five." I match his snark. "But you inheriting your seat from your batshit cousin is neither here nor there. I'm not leading the charge because I have delusions of grandeur. I'm here because I know the most about the situation we're facing."

"Which is what, exactly?" Suede asks.

"This afternoon, during a battle, Anca Romanov infected Garnet with a powerful spell that currently has him brainwashed. Thus, the video. Inciting riots in the street isn't something Garnet wants nor do we. We're here to put a stop to it before it gets out of hand and the mass death event is upon us."

Nikon and I explain the video we want to produce and how a united front of Guild Governors will set a good example. Since we only have nine people, we'll narrow the field of view and do our best with what we've got.

Nikon sets up the camera, and Suede and I get everyone into the frame. By the time Anyx and Thaos arrive, we're ready to film.

"You know what to do." Nikon leaves Dillan and Eva in charge of starting things.

Dillan does…Eva definitely does not.

Dillan sets himself up behind the camera, and when Nikon comes around and assumes his place at my side, I glance over my shoulders and ensure everyone is ready. "No bunny ears, people. Lives depend on others taking this seriously."

When my brother pushes the button and gives us the thumbs-up, I glance at the statement Nikon and I prepared to get this home video started. "Good afternoon, empowered citizens of Toronto. I am Fiona Cumhaill, Guild Governor of the Toronto Druids. I come to you today with the most urgent of messages…"

"How did it turn out?" I ask Dillan once he's watched the playback. "Do you think it'll do the job?"

"Yeah, it's good. I think the part about people staying inside to keep their heads down while we deal with those responsible for turmoil is especially convincing."

"Good." Xavier tugs the cuffs of his dress shirt below the sleeves of his jacket. "Now we get back to taking down the Romanovs."

There's too much anticipation in his tone, but I understand why. They violated one of his homes, murdered one of the people under his protection, and one of his family members is reeling in the wake of the loss.

Nikon finishes chatting with a few of the other Guild Governors and joins us, smiling. "We uploaded our counter-video on the same fae platforms as Garnet's and the views are climbing."

"Can you check in with Andromeda and see what we're facing in the streets? I'd be interested to know how many calls have come in and what kind of situations we're dealing with."

"I can do that." Nikon pulls out his phone and heads toward the hall.

"How can we help?" Suede comes up to me with Zxata.

"Send word through your elven and nymph channels to lock down and wait this out. We're expecting this to get worse before it gets better, and the fewer people involved, the easier it will be to get control of things."

"We can do that." Zxata steps close. "What really happened to Garnet? I find it hard to believe that a newly made vampire has the power or friends powerful enough to cast a spell on Garnet. The man in that video wasn't my brother-in-law. That's one hell of a spell."

I glance over my shoulder to ensure our conversation is private. In a voice barely above a whisper, I tell the two what we're facing.

"Myra must be devastated," Zxata says.

"I'm sure she is, but she's not showing it so far. When I left her a few hours ago, she seemed angrier than upset. She told me to get out there and fix it and bring her husband home to her."

"That sounds like my sister. All right, I'll make those calls to keep my nymph community in line. Then I'll head to the compound to spend time with her and Imari. Send word when you know more."

"I promise."

Zxata strides off, says something private to Anyx in passing, and takes his leave.

"What can I do?" Suede asks.

"Beyond what I've mentioned, I don't think there's much any of us can do. Team Trouble is tracking down the Romanovs. We've got people handling the phones, people in the streets, and now people consoling Myra. I don't know that there's anything more to be done except wait for our opportunity to confront the people behind it and try to capture a possessed lion."

"Maybe I can help you there." She leans in. "Most people that go after Moon Called either attack the man or the animal. Both are incredibly powerful and hard to take down."

"Yeah, I'm not looking forward to it."

"I wouldn't either, but what few people consider is how much energy it takes for one of them to shift. If you disrupt their energy, it fritzes out their shift and throws them off in human form as well. It's the best way to take down a species so powerful."

"Disrupt their energy how?"

"Electrocution."

"Seriously? You want me to rescue Garnet by electrocuting him? That seems a little counterproductive, doesn't it?"

Suede checks that our conversation isn't being listened to and continues. "It's not ideal, and maybe it's the last resort, but I thought you should know. If he's coming at you and you have no other choice, electricity is your best defense."

"Does it have any lasting effects?"

"It can scramble them up pretty badly. Maybe it doesn't have to. If you had something where you could control the energy output, perhaps you could tone it down a bit so it doesn't fry him."

"So, what do you suggest I use?"

"A Taser might do it. The setting would have to be high enough to scramble him, but not so high that you cause lasting damage."

"Any idea what setting that would be?"

"No, none."

I run my fingers through my hair. The pressure of the headache behind my eyes threatens to shoot my eyeballs across the room. "Thanks. That's good information and something we can consider as a last resort."

"Be careful, Fi. I know you and Garnet are close, but the man he is right now isn't your mentor or friend—he's lethal, and he considers you his enemy."

I think about that as I scan the room.

Xavier has his back to the room and his phone at his ear. By his body language, it's obvious the caller is telling him something important, and he's not too pleased to hear it.

"Thanks again for your help," I say to Suede. "Excuse me. Many fires to put out."

"Good luck, Fi. You've got this."

Ha! If only that were true.

I wait in the wings until Xavier ends his call. When he slides his cell into the breast pocket of his suit jacket, I approach. "I couldn't help but notice your call seemed to set you off. Have you got a lead for us to follow?"

He meets my gaze, but his expression tells me nothing. "As much as I appreciate the power of joining forces, this is where our partnership ends, Lady Druid. I've claimed a Vow of Vengeance against the Romanovs for the offense of killing Laurel. I'm well within my rights to track them down and exterminate them."

"I'm familiar with the Vow of Vengeance. If you remember, the hobgoblin king declared one against me during my first week as a druid. While I realize it might be within your rights to exterminate those who cause you and yours a personal loss, you haven't presented your proof to the governors that Anca killed Laurel."

"Are you calling me a liar, Fi?"

"No, but there is a burden of proof."

"Not in the empowered world, there's not."

"If you kill the wrong person, *they'll* have the right to make a Vow of Vengeance claim against you. And on and on we go in dizzying circles."

"Nice try, Fi, but I gave Benjamin my word that I would find those responsible and make them pay."

"Fine. Laurel was my friend too. Take me with you, and we'll punish the Romanovs together."

"Or I can leave you here and take care of it myself."

"Or you can take me with you, and I could focus on retrieving Garnet."

"Or I can leave you here and retrieve him myself."

I make a face. "Is that what this is about? You're still itching to hit Garnet head-on to flex your manly muscles and see where you stand?"

Xavier arches a brow and stiffens. "Be careful, Lady Druid. I give you quite a bit of leeway because I know you can't help yourself, but I still expect you to speak to me with a modicum of respect."

"Oh, I respect your power and you being lethal but even powerful people need to be held accountable. I'm trying to stop slaughter in our city. If I get a little snarky, it's because you aren't cooperating."

"Despite being a vampire, I feel no need to encourage excessive bloodshed. I *am* on your side. I want the city to survive this incursion. I may disagree with some of my rivals in the streets, but I'm not about to take up the call to arms at Garnet's urging. To disagree without bloodshed is the cornerstone of civilization."

"Agreed. So, where are we going?"

He offers me a patient smile. "I'm not sure where *you* are going, but I'm off to settle the score."

Before I have a chance to argue, Xavier strides out the open door. I follow, but all I see is a blur of a man rounding the corner at the far end of the hall as Xavier's vamp speed-runs and leaves me in his dust.

"Fi, you better get in here," Nikon calls. "You're going to want to see this."

I return to the conference room and join the others. Both Nikon and Suede have their phones up and are watching a live feed of Garnet dragging a man kicking and screaming down the street and into an alley.

"Cat crap on a cracker." I move in closer so I can get a better look at the violent scene. Garnet is in a rage, his mane of ebony hair spiked up like Vlad the Impaler. "Does anybody recognize where they are?"

At best this live stream depicts Garnet as a deranged thug. At worst, if the man he's dragging turns up dead or beaten, it's evidence of Garnet's involvement.

"Anything? Look at the architecture, the storefronts, are there any street signs?"

There aren't.

Dillan is leaning in and frowning. "An industrial section. Could be the waterfront, or fashion district, or the Danforth, or any other area in the city."

Dillan's right. Nothing tells us where he is, and the city is too big to go out wandering to try to find him. Anca is setting up Garnet as a monster, and there's no way for me to find him and stop it.

I extend one hand in front of Nikon and the other back to Dillan and Eva. "Flash us to the Batcave, Greek. We need to regroup with the others. If you don't mind, can you drop off Eva and me and take Dillan home to get his Taser?"

Dillan makes a face at me. "My Taser? Is that your idea of crowd control?"

I shake my head. "No. It's my idea of lion taming. I just hope it doesn't come to that."

CHAPTER FOURTEEN

Nikon snaps us to the tenth floor of the Acropolis, and the four of us make our way inside. Emmet and Tad are working at one of the computer terminals while Ciara and Andromeda are talking on the phones.

"Have there been a lot of calls for help?" I ask.

Emmet stands and comes over to welcome us. "Yeah, unfortunately, they've been nonstop for the past hour. We managed to get Garnet's video down half an hour ago, only for it to be replaced by another one that features him as a murderous caveman."

"We've almost got that one shutdown too," Tad says, "but it's a live stream so we had to change gears a bit to get it done."

"Can you use the live feed to find him?"

Emmet looks at me and glances at Tad. "Do you mean can we triangulate a location based on the streaming?"

"Yeah. What can you do to help me find him?"

Maxwell comes out of his office looking grim. "I'm trying to keep the incidents covered by your family and the list of enforcers Garnet gave me as a backup, but we're running thin.

This is about to spill over into non-magical society. I need more responders."

I scowl at the live feed on the monitor wall. "If we can find Garnet, I bet we find either Anca Romanov or some of her men."

"Well, somebody is shooting the video of Garnet," Emmet says. "It's more likely one of the Romanians than an onlooker. Who in their right mind wants to piss off Garnet when he looks like that?"

"Excellent point."

"Back to the triangulation," Tad says. "Who do we have in the field? More importantly, do we have their cell phone numbers listed somewhere?"

"Well, we have all the cell phone numbers of the people in our family for sure," I say. "I'm not sure who's on Garnet's list of backups, but Anyx likely can get hold of them so I'm guessing the answer is yes. Why do you ask?"

"Because I can track the streaming signal to the closest cell tower, but if I had two other signals in the same area, I could triangulate the actual location."

"Down to how big an area?"

"A city block? Half that maybe."

"Well, that's a fuck ton closer than where we are now." Emmet pulls out his phone. "I'll give you the ones we know and get you started. Are you ready?"

Tad opens a new screen on the computer and adjusts the keyboard. "Ready."

While they work on that, I go over to check on Eva. She's standing off to the side and has a strange look on her face. Strange, meaning that she isn't smiling.

"Eva? Are you okay? You look sad or distracted."

"I don't like it when your family is all spread out and in danger. I haven't figured out yet how I'm supposed to feel when you all lead such dangerous lives. I feel the pull to protect Dillan's heart, but it's pulling me in different directions. It's disturbing."

"That's how love works, and it's how I feel every day. Da and my brothers are police officers and go to work every day knowing they might not come home that night. I think it's part of the reason why we're all so close. We live each day thankful we're all there to share it."

"Dillan told me you lost a brother last year."

"Brendan, yeah. He didn't make it home from an undercover assignment."

"How do I make sure Dillan doesn't suffer that loss again?"

I take her hands in mine and squeeze them. The signature of her power tingles up my arms and into my core. "The first thing you need to do is realize each of us is well-trained and aware of the dangers around us. I might not be a cop, but Da and my brothers raised me like one. We're street-smart, and our druid powers and training makes us more prepared than most for danger."

"You could still get hurt."

"I don't think there's any way to ensure none of us get hurt—we get hurt all the time. Let's focus on no one dying and have faith we can take care of ourselves for the most part."

She takes strength from that suggestion. "Faith is something I have a lot of."

"Good, then unless there is an incredibly dangerous situation like tonight, I think you do your best to be there for Dillan, and we'll all do our best to keep each other safe when things get dangerous."

"What should I do tonight?"

"If reaper duties haven't called you, stay with us. Da, Aiden, and Calum are helping people, and when we leave here, Dillan, Emmet, and I will be taking on the people behind all this murder and mayhem. It won't hurt to have an angel on our side."

"Thanks, Fi. That's very helpful. Having feelings for a mortal is very unsettling."

AUBURN TEMPEST & MICHAEL ANDERLE

"I'm sure it is. The important thing is that you both try to keep each other happy and healthy. The rest will work itself out."

By the time Nikon snaps back with Dillan, Tad and Maxwell have two points of reference and are positioning Anyx and Thaos in the area to capture a third ping point they can use.

"What are the odds this will work?" I ask.

Tad cranks his head around and gives me a look. "I wouldn't be bustin' my balls fer it not to work. Just be ready when it does. We're closin' in now."

All righty then.

I text Sloan and ask that he, Merlin, and Dionysus join us here at the Acropolis.

The three of them snap straight into the room with us, and I blink. "Apparently, the god of wine and orgies doesn't have the same portal restrictions as everyone else. You can materialize right here."

Dionysus winks at me. "Oh, Jane, there are so many things I can do which other men can't."

I chuckle and catch them up on what they've missed over the past couple of hours.

"And ye think Xavier went after her on his own?" Sloan asks.

"Probably not on his own, but without me. I'm quite sure he took his vampire backup band, and they're getting ready to rock 'n roll."

"Och, well, there's not much to be done about that. If Anca is a vampire, Xavier is her king, and he has every right to discipline her fer an uprising. He claimed a Vow of Vengeance, so he's doubly entitled."

"If she's human and simply a criminal, we can't have the vampires attacking her."

"How do we find out if someone is or isn't a vampire?" Ciara asks.

"*Cosmo* questionnaire?" Emmet suggests. "They might have a 'How To Know If Your Neighbor Is A Vampire?' edition."

"We check the basement for a coffin," Dillan says.

"See if they sparkle in direct sunlight," Nikon adds.

"Not helpful, boys." I rack my brain.

"What about yer fae vision?" Ciara asks. "Ye mentioned once it's like seein' things in infrared only different, right? Surely humans look different than empowered folks."

I sigh and shake my head. "No. My fae sight shows me the alignment of a person's true nature, but Anca and her men could be evil humans or vampires. That doesn't really tell me anything."

"Ciara's not far off with her idea," Sloan says. "Vampires are undead, so their body temperature won't register the same way as a human. If we use thermal imaging, we'll know fer sure and be able to respond accordingly."

"Good one, Sloan and Ciara." Emmet high-fives his lady. "Maxwell, do we have heat vision goggles lying around here somewhere?"

Maxwell straightens from where he's looking at the computer terminal and points toward the armory in the back room. "Garnet has this place stocked and ready for the empowered Armageddon. The keys for the supply cabinets are hanging on the hook inside my office door."

"What about Tasers?" I ask. "If you see any of those, bring them out too. As much as I don't want to scramble Garnet's shifter mojo, if it's a choice between any of you or evil Garnet, we need to be armed."

Emmet and Dillan stride off to assess what we have in stock. Sloan, Eva, and I move over to watch Tad and Maxwell work on the triangulation.

"How long until we know where he is?"

"Almost there, Fi." Tad raises a hand-held mic to his mouth. "Anyx, flash one intersection to the east."

As we watch, a blue dot on the screen disappears and reappears on the city map one street over. I'm not sure what it triggers, but when he materializes, a line appears connecting three points and shades the enclosed triangle in red.

"Ladies and germs, ye have yer search area. Yer welcome."

I wrap my arms around Tad's shoulders from behind and hug him. "Yay you, McNiff. Great job."

"Score." Emmet returns from the back, arms raised to show us what they found. Dangling in his hands are four masks. He also holds four Tasers. Dillan comes out behind them with four more of each. "It's like a tactical playground back there. So many fun toys to look at. It was hard to stay on topic."

Dillan chuckles. "Impossible, really. We might've pocketed a few extra delights."

"I didn't hear that," Maxwell says. "As far as I know, you only borrowed the infrared goggles and the Tasers."

"If you say so," Emmet says.

I laugh at my brothers and squeeze Tad's shoulder. "Do you want to stay here and handle the computers or join the fight?"

Tad grins. "Maxwell can run the computers. It's the belly of the beast time, bitches."

Our group materializes down by the docks south of Lakeshore Avenue. Once we orient ourselves, we fan out to get the lay of the land. The summer sky is bleeding pink across the horizon. It won't be long before night falls. With Lake Ontario to the south, there's only east, west, or north.

"Along the water in this area, there aren't any of the brick buildings and alleyways we saw in the live stream of Garnet caveman video. I say we head north to the first street and start our search there."

No one objects, so we strike off.

"Tad, you stay with Nikon, Merlin, Ciara, and Emmet. Sloan, you're with Dillan, Eva, Dionysus, and me. That way, there's a wayfarer and a Greek in each group if we get into big trouble and need to portal out."

"Sounds good." Dillan pulls up his hood and takes Eva's hand. "Keep it right and tight, everyone."

"Ready and steady, bro," Emmet says.

"Safe home, everyone," I add.

When we get to the next street, our group goes right, and the other group takes the left. Summer nights along the Lakeshore are busy, especially during the week when everyone is taking their time to get home.

"It's nice that people want to have a drink on the patio after work, but at moments like this, it's also a giant pain in the ass—"

Someone bolts into the shadows across the road and my shield flares. "Did you guys see that?"

"I did." Sloan holds up his hand to signal the cars that we're going to run across the road.

"Was it Garnet? A vampire? A streaker?"

"I didn't see." Dionysus cranes his neck. "Was it a streaker? I'm hoping for a streaker."

Dillan laughs and takes off like a shot. "Game on."

I point at where I saw the runner and beat feet after him or maybe her. It's dark enough now that forms are getting lost in the shadows, and I can't be sure what I saw other than someone moving in them.

The rhythmic *thud* of footsteps around me is comforting. Whatever we're facing, we're not alone.

We weave through the maze of back alley obstacles, sensing the movement ahead of us more than seeing it. A flash of silver up ahead makes the hair on the back of my neck stand on end.

There's no telling what's lost in the shadows. A knife? A sword? A—

"Flying pot!" Dillan shouts.

I duck as a stainless steel pot sails through the air and narrowly misses my head.

"Not human," Dillan says to my right.

I glance over and smile. He has the infrared goggles on. "Definitely not warm enough to be living."

As we run, I point up at the rooflines of the surrounding buildings. "Tarzan, you take the high road."

"Yes, ma'am."

"Eva, aerial support would be good. Let us know if you see anything we should be wary of."

"Sure thing. Don't get dead, anyone." With a grace born of her station, she transforms into a stunning white dove and takes to the air.

Sloan, Dillan, and I barrel through another back alley and spook a scavenging raccoon. The rotund bandit hisses and charges us in a flurry of hostile chatter.

"Dude, chill." Dillan sidesteps to keep from being attacked. "We're playing through, buddy."

The three of us continue the chase, hurdling over broken skids, our boots propelling us around graffiti-covered dumpsters. We get a couple more glimpses of our runner, but they're too quick to know who we're chasing.

Is it Xavier or one of his men?

Maybe it's Anca or one of her men?

Sloan vaults over an anorexic bush and signals Dillan and me to flank left and cover the next building. We peel off and change course.

Dillan and I end up back on the docks with nothing but open space on our right and a dilapidated, two-story warehouse on our left. As we round the side and end up at the back, we almost crash into Sloan coming from the other direction.

I stop myself before we collide and bend over to catch my breath. "That was one helluva sprint. Where the hell did he go?"

Dillan cranks the doorknob as Sloan leans down to eyeball the corner of a window almost entirely covered with cardboard on the inside.

"I think there's only one option, luv."

Eva lands beside us and takes her human form. "The man you were chasing went inside."

"Then that's where we're heading too."

Eva grabs my arm to stop me from stepping away. "I should tell you, four of my reaper brothers and sisters are also here. Something lethal is about to happen."

Sloan frowns. "Dillan, call in the others. Fi, we wait until they arrive. There's no need to take chances and tempt fate. Only fools rush in."

I chuckle. "Wise men say, only fools rush in."

Dillan curls his lip and finishes with the text. "Thank you. Thank you very much."

Sloan shakes his head. "Could the two of ye stay on point, please? Fer once, let's take things seriously."

I sober and offer him a sweet and serious smile.

I get his need for caution, but maybe the reapers are here for someone else. Maybe we're totes in the clear here, and he's worried about nothing.

"I'm not worried about nothin'." He arches a brow at me. "I know that look, Cumhaill. Yer convincin' yerself I'm overly cautious, and I'm not."

I cross my arms and huff. "Maybe you don't know me as well as you think you do, Mackenzie."

Dillan snorts. "Yeah, he does. You were totally convincing yourself we should go in without backup. It was written all over your face, baby girl."

"Hmph, whatevs." I step closer to the building and put my back flat against the spalling brick. Bits of clay detritus crumble onto the ground beside my boots, and I stare at the lake's darkness and the distant lights on the islands in the harbor.

Ending up here, in the heart of warehouse-landia makes sense. It's super isolated with direct access to the water. No nosy neighbors to notice when boats filled with drugs or kidnapped women dock. And it's close to the Eastern European empowered communities.

The other team flashes in and in two shakes, we're surrounding the building and preparing to enter. When Emmet texts the countdown from the front of the building, we're good to go from the back.

Three... Two... One...

CHAPTER FIFTEEN

D illan takes the lead as we force our entry and move in. The place is pitch dark. The only light to guide us is fighting its way through grimy skylights above. As rundown and nondescript as the warehouse is outside, it's even more underwhelming inside.

Dillan adjusts his hood so we can see his eyes and signals for us to follow him.

I release Bruin as a scout and blink into the dark void, waiting for my vision to adjust. It's taking too long, so I release my fae vision and move to my version of night sight.

Somewhere ahead of us, the other group is entering the front of the building and working their way toward us. I've never tested the maximum range I can reach Nikon's mind but focus on him anyway.

How are things on your end, Greek?

So far so good. See you soon.

Tucked behind Sloan, I miss what causes him and Dillan to stop the advance. One second, we're in motion, moving at a quick clip. The next second, I almost crash into the back of them.

Almost.

It would be so much easier if I could speak to everyone the way I can with Nikon, Bruin, and Dart. I suppose that's greedy. Fionn and the goddess blessed me with so many gifts that I should be content with what I have.

Still, it would be awesome.

Dillan flashes a few hand signals, and I nod. He wants to move forward and check something while we hold position.

It's not often when I fall back and let others venture into unknown danger first, but Dillan is a special case. With his Cloak of Knowledge on and his hood up, he can sense things as well as I can with my shield.

He slips into the darkness, and my anxiety knots my bowels. Trusting him to check things out is different than watching him get swallowed by the shadows.

That just sucks.

I fight the urge to follow, and Sloan squeezes my hand. "He'll be fine, *a ghra*," he whispers. "Give him a chance to do his thing."

I glance over to check in with Eva. She doesn't look nervous at all. She's scanning the metal beam structures above with a smile on her face as if she's looking up at the sun on a summer morning.

I wonder what she would look like if the world crashed down around her and someone took us hostage or shot us. Would she still be smiling?

Something tells me she would.

Then I see them…four people standing on the top of the steel crossbeams fifty feet above our heads.

Reapers.

A shiver runs down my spine, and I send them a mental message. We won't have any trouble as long as they stay up there and keep their eyes and hands off my family and friends.

A *crash* and clamor ahead end our caution.

Sloan and I take off at the same time. I launch into the lead with Birga raised and my ears and eyes open.

It's a massive interior, chock full of nooks and places for the enemy to hide. With vampires on the ground and reapers in the rafters, I keep a sharp eye on my surroundings. Maybe the vampire we're chasing isn't on the ground.

Sloan says vampires can drop from incredible heights and not feel the impact.

That's not comforting in a building with metal beams and catwalks lost in the darkness above. It's bad enough there are reapers up there.

Sloan and I move through the warehouse as one—silent as the night outside. As we cut through the space, he secures the left while I scan the right. There's nothing remarkable in the surroundings.

Stacked wooden skids. Forklifts. Storage racks.

The rubber soles of our boots whisper over the painted concrete as we secure the loading area and continue toward the front of the building.

It seems to be a storage facility with offices at the front, shipping at the back, and a huge warehouse in between. Whether this is a property belonging to the Romanovs or somewhere they—and we—broke into, I have no idea.

We're halfway through the belly of the warehouse when the whimpering of women catches my attention.

Sloan hears it too and stops our advance.

The pervasive darkness would give him nothing to go by but dull, gray silhouettes. I, however, can see everything and adjust my grip on Birga, easing forward step by step.

What the fuckety-fuck?

On the side wall of the warehouse runs a long row of wood and metal cages. They're stacked three high and extend the length of the warehouse.

Inside each three-by-three cubicle, a woman is bound and either sitting curled up or lying on her side. The tattered rags and hopeless gazes they wear are heartbreaking. Seriously. What the hell?

Many of them look near death.

I glance back up into the rafters and understand now. The reapers aren't here for us.

That's so sad.

Movement deeper in the shadows has me bringing Birga up, ready to defend. There's no need.

Dillan jogs up to join me. "What the fuck have we stumbled into?"

"I have no idea." I reach out to Nikon and try to warn him. *We've got a nightmare of whacked back here, Greek. Watch yourselves.*

Can you elaborate on that, Red?

With the hair on the nape of my neck doing an Irish jig, I try to put it into words. *I think we found the holding cells for the Romanov's sex trafficking castoffs. These women don't look like they made the cut. They certainly won't be catching the eye of any big spenders anytime soon. I'm not sure they'll even survive. That's why Eva's reaper siblings are here, I'm sure.*

Okay, we finished searching the offices. We're coming back to help. Emmet found the power panel. He's turning things on now.

I replace the glamor on my eyes so I don't scare the captives. When the lights *hum* to life above, I can't decide if it's better or worse to see what we're dealing with. What kind of monsters are these people?

The air around me stirs as Bruin returns from his intel gathering. The fact that he merges back with me instead of staying out on his own is telling.

Nothing?

Sorry, Red. I searched the place, and the guy ye followed here is gone.

Gone where?

There's a metal grate in the floor in the center of the warehouse. It opens into a tunnel below. My guess is yer vampire lured ye here and used that to escape.

Well, that's disappointing.

I thought about followin', but with the state of things, I figured I'd stay close. There's death here, and I don't like the feel of it.

I'm with you. The sooner we leave, the better.

"Help is here, ladies." Dillan examines the locks on the cages. "If you're still with us, I need you to let us know so we can get you out of here."

When no one responds, it takes a minute to figure out why. "They came from remote villages in Romania. English might be the problem. Anyone know how to speak Romanian?"

Eva grins and waves a hand. "I speak every language spoken and written. Would you like me to repeat what Dillan just said?"

"Yeah, babe." Dillan frowns at the locks on the cage doors. "That would be a big help."

While Eva talks to the girls, I step in to speak to my scowling brother. "What's wrong?"

"The cage doors are wired to avoid tampering and being opened. I haven't followed the leads anywhere yet, but I'm guessing the Romanovs rigged this place to blow."

"Blow if it's tampered with or at the whim of whoever set the bombs?"

"I don't know yet." He steps along the run of cages toward the front wall. "If you, Sloan, and Eva take over with the rescuing, I'll see what I can figure out. Whatever you do, though, don't open those cages."

Right. Rescue the women but don't open the cages.

I study the situation for a second and come up with the answer. "Hotness, if you, Tad, Nikon, and Dionysus reach through the cages, can you *poof* these women to the Batcave? Andy and Maxwell can get them food and take care of them in the safehouse until we get back."

"Fi, these women aren't empowered. If we portal them, we'll be intentionally exposing our world."

"I know, but you can clear their memory of the portaling, can't you?"

Sloan doesn't look happy with the prospect but nods. "I can. Although I don't relish the idea of sifting through their most recent memories."

"I'm sorry about that. Do you have another idea? Their captors wired the cages to blow up, and reapers are looming. I'd like to get out of here."

He follows my gesture to the rafters above and winces. "Aye, I'm not surprised. Many of the women look near to death."

"Then odds are they won't remember what happens next in any case."

Nikon and the other group join us and catch the tail end of the conversation. "Why not bust them free?"

"The whole containment area is rigged. Dillan's tracking the wiring but thinks we're in the core of Bomb City. So, getting the women who are still alive on the quick is the best idea."

Emmet scowls at the wiring, following the line of cages in the same direction Dillan did. "Seriously?"

"Yep. Ciara, if you could go on the first run and explain to Andy and Maxwell what we're dealing with, that would be great. We need to scan their memories before turning them over to the proper authorities, but they can get cleaned up, rest, and eat in the meantime."

"Got it."

"Okay, boys, have at it."

While Sloan, Nikon, Tad, and Dionysus go cage to cage, reaching through the grid of the metal caging and transporting the women still alive back to the Acropolis building, Emmet, Eva, and I go to find Dillan.

"Marco," Emmet calls.

Nothing comes back to us, so we go on a hunt.

I'm tracing the wires running along the doors of the cages as we walk. Halfway to the wall where the offices begin, the wires merge and run up the exterior wall. From there, zip ties bundle them, and they go up the wall and along metal beams that run overhead.

"Em? What do you think those are?"

Thirty feet above our heads, the bundled cables start feeding into a linked series of long, metal tubes. They're like metal link sausages, but I'm guessing more lethal.

Emmet follows my pointed finger and curses.

"Marco," he tries again with more force.

"Polo." Dillan's response comes from around the next set of storage racks.

The three of us round the wall of boxes and jog forward to catch up with Dillan. "D. We gotta book it. This place is lousy with pipe bombs."

"Yeah, I noticed that. They've rigged them to trip like falling dominoes. It looks like they trigger on contact, but there could also be a remote."

I swallow, but my mouth remains dry. "The boys are working on evacuating the women. I say we don't touch anything and get the hell out of here. Maxwell can send the bomb squad back to take care of things and make sure no one gets hurt."

"Sounds good to me."

The four of us backpedal and check on the evacuation's progress. Nikon, Tad, Dionysus, and Sloan are flashing in and out at a dizzying rate. They appear, race to the next trapped woman, reach in, assess her status, and disappear.

And so on. And so on...

The growl of an angry lion rumbles through the sound system. "You shouldn't have come, Lady Druid."

"Garnet." I spin, looking up to find the speakers.

"I warned you that you'd pay for challenging my beloved. You need to stop meddling in our business."

"Where is that coming from?"

Emmet points toward the front of the building. "In the mechanical room where I found the light breakers, there was also a microphone and an intercom setup."

"Can you show me?"

"No," Dillan snaps. "Fi, we gotta go, *now*. If there's a remote trigger, this place can blow at any second."

"This isn't guild business, Lady Druid," Garnet says. "Let the vampires work out their territories themselves and go home."

"The man makes a good point," Dillan says.

"I'm not leaving Garnet." I return Birga to her resting place and pull the Taser out of my purse. "I promised Myra I'd bring her husband home. You three go. I'm right behind you."

Emmet snorts. "Not fucking likely."

Dillan curses. "If you get us killed, I'm going to be pissed."

"I don't want that...I really don't, but Garnet deserves a chance to get home too. Text the team and tell them to finish the evac and stay away. We'll get Garnet and get out ourselves."

I take off, running toward the front of the warehouse with the Taser in my hand. Hopefully, I can reason with Garnet. If not, we'll fight him. As a last resort, I'll use the Taser and scramble his molecules.

"Em? Where's the mechanical room?"

I fall back a little and let Emmet lead the way. Once he's in front, the four of us weave the maze of cubicles and half-walls. We're rushing but careful. If Garnet's in here, there might be others too.

We round the last corner and arrive at the office with the intercom system. Emmet bursts through the door first, and I'm hot on his heels with Dillan and Eva close on our six.

"You're out of your league, Lady Druid. You should've gotten free when you had the chance."

As Garnet's voice fades, I scowl at the untouched intercom system. "Damn it."

"It's a recording." Emmet violently shakes the mouse and wakes the computer. "He's not here. He's never been here."

"Smart boy." The monitor on the computer opens to an image of Anca Romanov smiling at us with Garnet standing behind her, stroking her hair. "Yet still, you meddle in my business."

I scoff. "Kidnapping and selling women isn't a business. It's inhumane."

"What does humanity matter when I'm not human? My family evolved past humanity months ago. Romanovs are invincible now."

"No. You're new to the empowered world, and you're pissing off a lot of powerful people. In this world, when you overstep your bounds, you don't get a slap on the wrist and go to jail. In the empowered world, you get dead."

"Then we understand each other. You overstepped. Now it's time you get dead." Anca types a few keystrokes on the computer she's facing, and a loud *hum* brings metal screens down on all the windows.

Dillan leans out the office door and curses. "Every window is locking down."

"Why?" Emmet asks. "What does that do?"

Anca smiles. "Ensures justice is served. I investigated Galina's death. Three people were responsible: the alpha lion, the lady druid, and the king of vampires. By the end of tonight, I'll have revenge on all three."

When the window screens stop descending and *click* into place, Anca lifts a small, black cylinder in her palm. With an evil grin spreading across her mouth, she presses her thumb over the red button.

The high-pitched whine that follows doesn't come from her or her computer. It's in the warehouse.

"That can't be good," Em says.

Anca smiles. "Depends on who weighs in. I think it's good. With the doors and windows sealed, the lockdown activates inhibitors to block intruders from portaling in and out. You're trapped, and thirty seconds from now, you're dead."

Dillan grabs the monitor and smashes it on the floor. "I hate that bitch."

"Hey, Google, set a timer for twenty-five seconds." I race past my brothers and head for the door. After yanking and cranking the front doors, I throw a chair against the steel screens covering the window. "Think, think, think, think...how do we get—*Oh!* Follow me."

I bolt as fast as my legs can propel me and release my bear. "Bruin! We need that trap door open to the grate tunnel."

We beat feet, racing as fast as we can back into the warehouse and around the first rack of shelves.

"Here, Red!" My bear's grunt and the *creak* and *screech* of bending metal guide me to where Bruin is ripping a grate out of the floor.

The thundering of boots behind me is music to my ears, but before I drop into the two-foot-square opening, I check that Em, Dillan, and Eva are all with me.

They are.

I pause at the opening, shove Emmet down the hole, and am about to do the same to Dillan when the timer goes off on my phone and the world around us bursts into high-velocity shrapnel.

Dillan shoves me through the opening in the floor and turns to grab Eva.

I'm falling then and lose track of my brother.

The moment I crash into Emmet's arms, I scramble to regain my footing and turn back. The *ping* and crash of metal debris are deafening. I wince at the bombardment a split second before being knocked back onto my ass with Dillan on top of me.

He lets out a pained groan, and I struggle to get out from under him. The movement sends a wave of excruciating pain burning through me.

I gasp and cry out. "Crap, that hurts."

"What hurts?" Emmet asks.

"I think Dillan broke my ass."

"D, are you alive?" Emmet asks. "If so, we need to get you off Fi."

He groans again, and my bruised or possibly broken tailbone seems less important. I stop struggling to get out from underneath him and run my hands over his back and shoulders, feeling for metal missiles shredding his muscles.

"Faery Fire." I call the power of light to my palm and throw the ball of blue flame toward the ceiling of the tunnel. "Em, check him and see—"

"Eva!" Dillan comes to in a rush and launches to his feet, crushing me into the tunnel's floor as he gets to his feet.

I cry out and roll to my side, pain exploding from everywhere at once. Resting with my cheek in the cold dirt, I close my eyes and fight not to pass out.

"Nonononono..." Dillan drops to his knees. "What did you do? Babe. What did you do?"

I open my eyes and pivot enough so I can see. Eva is down, and for the first time, she's not smiling.

CHAPTER SIXTEEN

"What did *I* do?" Evangeline pushes onto her hands and knees and sits back on her heels. She brushes the dirt from her palms and shakes out a span of bronze feathers behind her that I can't believe are real. "What part of me being immortal don't you understand? When it comes to the last line of defense, that's me, not you."

"When a building is about to explode, and the woman I love is standing in the middle of the detonation zone, I can't save myself. I'm not wired that way."

"Only by saving *you* can I be part of your life."

"I get it. Sorry not sorry."

She rolls her eyes at him and looks at me. "And I'm told you're all this stubborn?"

"Guilty as charged," I grumble, still stuck on the ground and unable to move. "The good news is we're all alive...if not slightly broken."

"Broken?" Dillan looks at me and seems to realize I didn't get up when the rest of them did. He drops to his knees and looks me over. "Shit. Did you get hit by the bomb, baby girl?"

"You da bomb, my brother." I chuckle at my joke. "You da bomb."

Dillan shakes his head. "Are you concussed? English, please."

"I broke your fall when you crashed into the tunnel. It sounds silly, but I think you broke my ass."

"It's been cracked for years, and I had nothing to do with that."

I laugh, but it hurts so I cut that out. "Em, I'm not going anywhere until you heal my tailbone. I could probably get up and walk, but if we come against an opposing force, I'll never be able to defend myself. Get your healing mojo flowing. You're up."

Emmet nods and shifts to kneel behind me on the ground. "Sloan and I have been working on some mid-level healing spells. He says I'm getting pretty good."

"Excellent. I look forward to being your guinea pig. Make it stop hurting."

"Hey," Dillan says while Emmet is casting his healing spell. "Where's Bruin?"

Oh…I don't know. I was so distracted between Dillan and my broken butt that I lost track. "He dematerialized after he got the grate open."

"Maybe he's checking things out down the tunnel and gathering us intel," Dillan says.

"I wouldn't be surprised. He has quite a strategic mind, my bear."

"He does. Quick thinking on us using this tunnel to avoid the bomb. How'd you know it was here?"

"That was Bruin too."

I close my eyes and relax as the healing warmth of Emmet's power soothes the searing ache in my butt. When he finishes, he stands, brushes off his pant legs, and extends his hand. "Any chance you feel well enough to get out of here? I'm sure Ciara and Sloan are both losing their minds right about now."

"Any luck with the cell signal?" I ask.

Dillan has been playing with his phone for the past few minutes, trying to get word to the other team. "Nothing. Our best bet is to get out of this tunnel and make our way to the street so we can call them."

I roll onto my back and wait a few seconds to see if anything still hurts. Nope. S'all good. "Where do you think the tunnel ends?"

Emmet snorts. "I hope it's somewhere the world isn't exploding with pipe bombs."

I clasp hands with him and let him help me to my feet. "I can get behind that."

As it turns out, the tunnel is a recently dug extension leading back to a centuries-old brick passage that seems to stretch on forever. By the old, iron torch sconces set in regular intervals and the worn brick pathways, I'd say people once used these tunnels quite frequently.

We're far enough away from the warehouse that the danger has faded, and my mind has begun to wander. "Who do you think made this tunnel and why?"

Dillan swings the torch we lit to scan the brick passage. "My guess would be bootlegging from the harbor during Prohibition. There are tunnels like these in different parts of the city. Running so close to the docks, this one could've been very useful back in the day."

Imagining bootleggers smuggling alcohol from the harbor is a welcome distraction. I'm trying not to dwell on the fact that Garnet is actively working against us.

When Anca talked about her plan to kill me, there wasn't a glint of concern in those amethyst eyes. Even knowing Eros' magical taint possesses him, part of me believed our connection was strong enough that part of him would still be there for me.

Guess not.

We walk for ten minutes before we get to the first intersection. "Left or right? Anybody feeling lucky?"

Dillan hands me the torch, pulls his hood up, and shakes out his hands as if limbering up. He takes a minute to stare down the brick pathway to the left. Then he assesses the pathway to the right. When he's done, he pulls the hood back so we can see his eyes and smiles. "I've got nothing."

I chuckle. "It's the thought that counts."

"Bear, hunter, ninja?" Emmet asks.

"Sure." I hand Dillan the torch, stride over to my brother, and take my position standing back-to-back. "If I win, we'll go right. If Em wins, we'll go left."

"On three," Dillan says. "One…two…three."

With each number Dillan counts off, Emmet and I take one step away from each other. On the count of three, we leap around and take our form.

I choose bear. Emmet chooses ninja.

"Bears eat ninjas." I chuckle. "So sorry. You're dead. Right it is."

Emmet laughs. "What happened to hunter, Fi? You always chose hunter when we were kids. Ninja kills the hunters."

"I guess I'm a bear girl now." My hair lifts as the scent of evergreens and outdoors swirl around me. "Speaking of which, Bruin is back."

The air stirs with my mythical beast's power signature, and a moment later he materializes in all his furry glory. I walk over, wrap my arms around his massively boxy head, and snuggle into the side of his neck. "Great job ripping that grate open, buddy. You saved our bacon on that one."

"Glad to be of service. I'm rather fond of yer bacon, Red. I prefer it not fried and crispy."

I chuckle and ease back, scrubbing my knuckles over his ears as I retreat. "Where have you been? Have you got intel for us?"

"I do. The first thing I did was go out through the warehouse and wait fer Sloan and the others to arrive. I knew they'd be panicked."

"So, you told them we were fine?" Emmet asks.

"I told them what I knew. The four of ye got into an underground tunnel before the bombs went off and the building collapsed."

"Where are they now?" Dillan asks.

"Waiting fer direction on where to meet up."

"We're trying to find a way back to the street. We thought that way unless you have information to the contrary."

"Och, well, I have information, but I don't know if it's to the contrary."

"What does that mean?"

"It means the direction yer plannin' to take will land ye right in a nest of vampires."

"Romanov vampires or Xavier's men?"

"Based on them speakin' Romanian, I'll go out on a limb and say the first one."

"Well, all right then," I say, jazzed we're out to deal with that fiasco. "That's good intel, Bear."

Dillan holds up a finger to pause my celebration. "When you say a nest of vampires, how many were there?"

"I'd say a dozen, maybe fifteen."

Dillan arches a brow at me and frowns. "We're good, Fi, but we're not strong enough to take on fifteen vampires with only Bruin and the four of us. If they were Barghest, sure, but not vampires."

As much as I hate to admit it, Dillan's right.

"I guess the ninja wins after all. What do we face if we go down this tunnel instead?"

"Och, that tunnel takes ye to the abandoned subway tunnels and into the home base of the hobgoblins."

"Seriously?" I roll my eyes. "The last time I was in their

subway tunnels, they tried to kill me and shot and nearly killed Liam."

"Neither option is ideal," Emmet says, "but there's a chance we could talk to the hobgoblins and not end up shredded."

"You don't think they're going to want to kill me after they found every adult male in their Toronto community brutally hacked up by my battle beast?"

Evangeline glances over at Bruin wide-eyed.

"In his defense, they did buy me from a despicable man and try to kill my best friend and me."

Dillan waves that away. "The point is, you've got no friends in either camp."

"You do burn a lot of bridges, Fi," Emmet says.

I chuff. "You say that as if any of it was my choice. Life throws shit in my fan blades most days. I'm the one dodging and trying to duck the chunks."

"Colorful," Dillan says. "Still, it doesn't help. We need a way out of here. C'mon, people, think. What are our options? What do we do next?"

"I have idea," someone says from the shadows down the warehouse tunnel the way we came. "Get down on knees and link fingers behind heads."

We spin toward the bodiless accent escaping the darkness as half a dozen vampires with semi-automatic weapons step into view.

Well, that's not good.

Movement to our right brings another group of vampires from the tunnel we were about to take. "Yuri said surrender. Do it. *Now.*"

I consider making a run for the hobgoblin tunnel for the briefest moment but then reality sets in. Vampires are really freaking fast, and so are bullets from rapid-fire assault weapons.

Bruin swirls around me. *What do you want me to do, Red? I can take out a few, but vampires are hard to kill, and the three of you aren't.*

155

No. We can't fight. Not yet anyway. Stay and see where they lock us down. Once we're prisoners, find Sloan and the others.

The thundering boom of weapons fire makes me duck. Bits of rock and dirt rain down from the tunnel ceiling and the echo rings in my ears.

Dillan curses and moves Eva closer to me. I'm not sure if he's protecting her or positioning her to protect me. In any event, we drop to our knees and lace our fingers at the backs of our heads as ordered.

"Mistress said gather bodies in warehouse. Imagine surprise when no bodies in rubble."

"Life is all about surprises," I say. "We're happy to make your life richer. You're welcome."

Strong hands grip my arms and pull them in front of me. One vampire holds me still while another wraps a piece of iron rebar around my wrists. Most people use plastic cable ties. Apparently, vampires use metal rods.

Overkill much?

The four of us are pulled to our feet and shoved into motion down the tunnel to the right. It seems far less triumphant now than it did five minutes ago when I battled Emmet and won.

"So, have you told your mistress the good news?" I say. "She gets to try to kill us again. If at first you don't succeed, amirite?"

Dillan scowls at me. "Is this you helping?"

I shrug. "If you can't beat them, join them. It's a thing."

"Not when the 'them' are trying to kill us, it's not."

My mind is already whirling, wondering how to get out of this. I have my dragon band portal but getting the four of us together is logistically unlikely. If I were capturing four skilled opponents, I wouldn't allow them close enough together to interact.

If things get bad enough, there's always Dart's instinct to intervene. Being underground, I'm not sure how he would find us. Then there's Bruin. As he said, he can take out a few, but they heavily outnumber us, which might lead to not all of us getting out safely.

That doesn't work for me.

Clan Cumhaill lives under the musketeer principle—all for one and one for all.

Always. End. Of.

I'm still thinking through our options when the tunnel opens, and we arrive at an open loading dock. The underground garage is full of workers moving pallets of wrapped crates into the backs of six white cube trucks with a splotchy blue logo. The cargo is impossible to discern, but whatever it is, I'd bet it falls on the wrong side of the law.

Drugs. Guns. Sex trade workers being kidnapped and transported from Europe. That was what Maxwell dug up on the Romanovs, and they seem to be living up to their reputation.

"Get in truck," Yuri snaps.

They outnumbered us before. Now it's worse.

There's no sense making a stand here, and we all know it. It's awkward climbing into the back of a truck with my hands bound and the muzzle of a gun pressed between my shoulder blades, but I get there.

Eva is next, and the man inside the truck pushes us to sit on a small wooden bench secured to the wall. "Stay."

We do as told, and I wait for my brothers to climb in too.

They don't.

Yuri stops them from climbing in and points at another truck. "You two, there."

"Like fuck," Dillan snaps. "There's no way you're taking the girls without us. We're a package deal."

I scream as the butt of Yuri's gun comes across Dillan's face. He crumples to the ground, and I launch to my feet, only to get knocked back on my ass.

Eva's on her feet too, but I grasp her wrist and shake my head.

"Not yet. It's not time to fight." She doesn't look convinced but trusts my instincts.

"Sit. Stay," our captor says.

If I weren't preoccupied with Dillan being knocked out cold on the ground, I'd say something witty about us not being obedient canines, but I am...so, I don't.

"You two, there," Yuri repeats, pointing his gun at Emmet and gesturing at the next truck.

Emmet looks like a deer caught in the headlights. "Don't fight them, Em. Take care of Dillan. We'll be fine, I swear."

Emmet doesn't look as confident as I am, but I nod and give him a reassuring smile. "We've got this. Love you lots. Take care of Dillan. Safe home."

Before Yuri gets angry again and takes it out on Emmet, I shoo him into action. "Go. Seriously, go."

Emmet struggles a moment, trying to pick up Dillan but with his wrists bound, it's no use. Yuri whistles and has two workers come over and toss Dillan into the back of the next truck.

Being separated from them is worse than torture. My heart is hammering, and my lungs are too tight to draw air. *Bruin. Stay with Emmet and Dillan. Keep them safe and get them free when you get the chance.*

What about you?

I have Eva and my dragon band and Dart if things get hairy. Seriously. I need you to keep them safe. Emmet's not the most offensive player and Dillan's unconscious.

I don't like it, Red.

I know, but I need you to trust me. Watch over them and once Dillan is awake, get them to freedom.

On it. Don't die, Red.

I'll try my darndest.

CHAPTER SEVENTEEN

Alone and locked in the back of a cube truck, Evangeline and I sit close together on the rickety wooden bench tied to the wall with bungee cords. When the motor revs and we rock into motion, I turn to Eva.

"Now, turn into a dove and follow my brothers. Dillan needs you. The moment you can get to them and get them free from captivity, do that. Bruin will be there to help you."

"What about you? If I go and your bear is there, who's helping you?"

"I'll be fine. I've dealt with situations like this alone before. Worst case scenario, I can press my pendant and call for help. Go...before we lose what truck they're in."

Only she doesn't go.

She looks me straight in the eye and shakes her head. "No. Dillan would want me to stay with you. If you sent your bear for him, I'll stay with you."

I groan as the truck shifts gears and continues to move. "You love Dillan and want to keep him safe." I plead to her sense of worry.

She doesn't move. "I'm sure Dillan would want me to stay with you until I know you're safe."

"And you called us stubborn." I draw a deep breath and try to stay focused on weighing the pros and cons of the situation.

Pro. If they take me to Anca, I might have a chance to find Garnet.

Con. Between the race to the grate and being captured, I've lost my Taser.

Pro. Eva and I are fighting fit and able to take care of ourselves. Both of us have unexpected ways to escape if things go to hell.

Con. That's only if we're well enough to escape. Vampires are fast and can kill us in a split second...well, me anyway. Eva is immortal.

"Do you think Bruin will be able to keep Dillan and Emmet safe?" Eva asks.

"He'll ensure they survive. He's good that way."

"When Dillan wakes, he will be very angry."

I chuckle. "That's an understatement. Dillan's blood runs the hottest of all of us. That translates to him having a foul temper at times, but it also means he's wildly protective of those he loves. Those vampires don't know what's coming for them."

Eva's expression softens but she's not smiling. "I know the feeling."

"Oh? How so?"

"I didn't know what was coming for me when Dillan came into my life either. I'm not supposed to form attachments to humans. I serve a purpose. I'm a reaper. Death won't be pleased I've deviated from the rules of my designation."

"Well, love sneaks up on people. Like you said, being a reaper is what you do. It's not who you are."

She shakes her head, her blonde corkscrew curls swinging beside her full cheeks. "He's not going to see it that way. Believe it or not, he's not that forgiving."

"Death isn't forgiving? I'm honestly not surprised."

"It's likely too late now anyway. My siblings at the warehouse will report to him I was in the presence of your family and not in any official capacity. I will be held accountable for the violation."

"What will that mean?"

"I'm not certain...reapers don't deviate from their tasks. I never considered doing anything of the sort and don't know what the repercussions will be."

"Then we'll make sure it all turns out. After losing Brendan last October, our family is more determined than ever not to lose anyone else. You can help us, and we'll help you. Dillan loves you. That means you're one of us. You now have the full support of Clan Cumhaill behind you for whatever comes."

"Thanks, Fi."

I feel the pull of driving uphill and the shift in position as we level out on the street level. That much is good news. It'll be easier for people to find us if we're not locked in some unknown tunnel below ground. After a brief pause, the vehicle turns right, and the engine's rumble pulls us into motion once again.

"There's something you should know that I doubt Dillan told you. If we ever get into a bad situation, I have a portal band on this arm that transports me to the dragon lair where Dart's mother and siblings live."

"*If* we get into a bad situation? Don't you consider this bad?"

"No. Not yet. It's sticky, yes, but not bad."

"They blocked transport in the warehouse. What if it doesn't work?"

"It might be possible someone powerful could block the portal, but so far I've never been stopped from using it to escape."

"You can only use it if you're conscious and able," she says. "If you're badly injured, or your wrists or arms are bound so you can't make the connection with the band, you can't activate the portal, correct?"

"That's right."

"Well, it's something, but it's not everything."

"No, but if I get the chance, I need to get Garnet away from Anca. If I tell you to leave, I need you to turn into a dove and fly away or portal or do whatever you need to vacate quickly. It'll be split-second timing, and I'll need to know you're safe."

The truck stops, and the bumps and jostles of our ride end. The springs at the front of the truck *squeak* and *squawk* as men get out.

"Bestial Strength." I call forward the extra muscle I'll need to take on vampires with my bare hands. Before they open the back door, I shift on the bench and reach over to the iron rod wrapped around Eva's wrists.

Gripping them the best I can with my wrists bound, I flex my fingers and untwist her binding enough to loosen it.

Once I finish that, I press my fists together and force my wrists apart enough to pull my hands free when the opportunity to escape or fight arises. The metal is stiff and strong, and I wince at the pain of bruising.

Strength doesn't mean pain-free.

Unfortunately.

"My priority is to find and secure Garnet and if not him, we need to take out Anca. If neither option is available to us, and all we're looking at is execution, we portal out and regroup at the Batcave."

Eva nods. "Don't worry about me. I'm immortal."

"True, but you're also the first woman Dillan has ever loved. I can't let anything happen to you. We both escape or neither of us. You have to promise to get out if I tell you it's time."

She looks like she might argue the point but nods. "All right, if it keeps you safe and frees us to find Dillan and Emmet."

"It will."

The metallic *clank* of the door latch sounds. The noisy rumble of the door rising on the metal tracks echoes in the box, and a moment later we're staring into the dark gaze of a vampire.

"Time to meet with mistress."

I hide my smile and get to my feet. "Lead the way."

I can't tell where we are as we make our way from the back of the truck into another parking garage and an elevator. The vampires must be under strict orders not to let me escape because they're pressed close to me on all sides like we're at a rave and they're hoping to get lucky.

Has love-crazed Garnet ratted me out and told them something? Eros said his power trumps free will, but I didn't succumb to his seduction. I was determined enough to steer my ship.

Garnet is as determined as me—isn't he?

A sickening dread snakes my insides. Maybe it wasn't me who thwarted the seduction at all. Perhaps my shield protected me. Garnet might've succumbed to Eros's power. In which case, maybe he's told Anca everything she needs to know to wreck our city.

Dammit. I prefer to go into a situation like this being underestimated and well-informed. If Garnet has been chatty, it could make things difficult.

We enter the elevator in a tight group, and the doors rumble on their mechanical tracks and bump closed behind me. I shift to face front, brushing against the bodies of too many strange men for my liking.

"Dudes, I'm not your scratching post. Back off."

My comment makes no impact, and no one acknowledges my request. I keep an eye on the floors we're passing as we rise, anticipating what scenario we might find when the elevator doors open.

The important part is that Yuri said he's taking me to Anca. Whatever she has in store, I'm ready for it: threats of bodily harm, enacting bodily harm, or chatting it out in a game of cat and mouse.

I'd prefer that last one but am ready for anything.

When the doors open, my vampire guard parts like the undead sea and—

Garnet grabs the front of my shirt and yanks me off my feet. He throws me thirty feet into the penthouse apartment. I forget the sharp pain at the nape of my neck as I flip from shock to instinct.

"Feline Finesse." Shifting in the air, I right myself in flight and land in a crouch on the balls of my feet.

The searing pain at the sides of my neck soon makes sense. Garnet is smiling with my Team Trouble pendant hanging in his fisted hand.

"That was rude, Puss. A little warning next time, eh? If you wanted the necklace, you could've asked."

I straighten, rising to stand in the middle of what seems to be a vampire cocktail party. A dozen men in dark suits are milling around with drinks in hand and don't seem at all put off by the druid shotput routine.

They seem quite entertained.

I scan the faces of the partygoers. There are the snazzily dressed men and the arm candy. The ladies in the room are all in slinky black lingerie, and all carry the same haunted looks as the women in the warehouse. These must be the ladies who made the first cut.

"Wow, I think we're grossly underdressed, Eva." I scan the room and smile at the angel standing by the elevator doors. "You know what? If you give us twenty minutes, we can pop home, change, and come back wearing something more party-appropriate."

A feminine chuckle rings through the air and draws my attention to the woman in the floor-length, red silk sheath. She's all hips and legs as she swaggers into the doorway, entering from another part of the penthouse. Her long dark hair hangs smoothed and straightened to curl around the ample mounds of her breasts, and she painted her lips to match her gown.

She's fifty shades of starlet stunning.

"Wow, you really clean up, girlfriend. That color looks baller on you."

"Blood red." Anca steps down the three shallow stairs from the raised entrance to the bedrooms. "Agreed. My new life suits me well. Shame on you and your city for not being more welcoming to our family. It didn't have to be like this, Lady Druid."

I swallow and scan the curious grins of the onlookers. "I don't think there was much chance of it going any other way. Toronto has a certain flow to it. You came here intending to make an impression. You did that. It was your mistake to make a bad impression."

I try to make sense of the scenery out the window. The easiest way to pinpoint where I am in Toronto is to find the CN Tower or the lake. Either one makes orienting yourself easier if you're familiar with the Toronto skyline...and I am.

The sun has long set, and I'm not facing the CN Tower because it's lit up and colored at night. I don't see the lake either. The neighborhood outside stretches on without end, streetlights, and lit office buildings for as far as I can see.

Unfortunate. I thought the penthouse of the Toronto downtown building would have a skyline view.

"Tell me, Fiona, when you woke this morning did you have any sense it was your last day on Earth?"

"It didn't occur to me, no."

"And now? How do you feel?"

"Pretty good. I'm not dead yet."

Anca lifts her hand like a lady of the 50s, and one of her guards reaches out to steady her as she descends the three stairs.

She navigates the space with loose hips and a sultry smile and all the men in the room notice.

Especially Garnet.

His amethyst gaze is locked, and part of me doesn't care that it's not his fault. I'm offended on Myra's behalf.

"In truth, I didn't expect you to survive the warehouse blast." Anca wags a manicured finger at me. "Also truth, I didn't expect Galina to fall to you and your friends. She was a force—a true leader. She had a vision for Toronto, and it never occurred to us she could fail."

"We have a governing body in Toronto. If your family wants to start up a business, there are procedures. Meeting with the Lakeshore Guild is one of them. Meeting with Xavier, King of the Toronto Seethes, would be the second. Instead of recognizing that, your cousin attacked those two governing bodies. Her death was an unfortunate result."

"We are vampires. We are powerful. We are family with deep ties and many friends. We are not junior players in adult games. We make rules."

Anca's accent gets stronger when she's upset. Good to know. "It's important that if you think so, you should reconsider. If you continue with that opinion of yourself, your time in Toronto will likely be short and end in the same way Galina's did."

Anca scoffs and turns to a silver-haired man with dark, hooded eyes. "You see, Uncle? No respect."

I recognize him then, and yeah, it's a little unnerving. Facing the niece of the crime syndicate devil is much less intimidating than facing the devil himself.

I don't use that moniker lightly.

For a man to build the foundation of his business around kidnapping, enslaving, and selling women to other men either short-term or as a final transaction is not only greedy and despicable—it's evil.

He meets my gaze and lifts his drink to toast me. "I see by fear in your eyes. You know who I am."

"Andrei Romanov, criminal kingpin of Romania. Brother to Anton Romanov, trader of women, smuggler of drugs and guns, and killer of all who stand in your way. Yes, I know who you are."

Andrei's dark brow arches and he seems impressed that I know as much as I do. "I know you. Youngest of five. Family of pigs. The one who kills my Galina."

I shake my head. "Your intel is wrong. Galina poisoned Xavier to attack me. At the time someone killed her, I was on the back lawn pinned with the vampire king draining me."

I turn my head and sweep my hair back for him to see the scars. "I didn't kill your daughter, and neither did Xavier."

"Maybe not you, but Galina's men say you have a pet bear who kills on your behalf."

"A pet bear? No. I have no pets."

The deep rumble of a lion's growl fills the air. "Not her pet. Her bonded battle beast."

I scowl at Garnet. "Hey. Snitches end up in ditches, Lion."

Anca smiles and winks at Garnet. "Thank you, pet."

"Bring battle beast here to meet," Andrei says, handing his glass to the man beside him.

"I can't. He's a mythical being. He doesn't have a phone, and he didn't come with me."

"Lies," Garnet growls. "Bruin is always with her. He lives within her."

I turn and scowl. "Seriously, boss, you're pissing me off. Not always, and you know it. I sent him on another more important matter. He's not here."

"I don't believe you," Anca says. "Make her release the bear."

Before I have time to convince her otherwise, Garnet lunges. He takes three running steps, launches into the air, and clears a sofa with a couple of people lounging on it. Diving at me, he shifts mid-air, and I'm frantic to free my hands. *Tough as Bark.*

I brace for impact and grip Garnet's front paws, letting his powerful momentum take me into a back roll.

My *Bestial Strength* is still activated, so I'm not at a total loss to protect myself.

The most difficult thing is that he's trying to hurt me and I'm trying *not* to hurt him. Well, not unless I could electrocute him a little.

Just a little.

The two of us crash through a glass coffee table as elegant partygoers scatter like cockroaches. I absorb the impact of the floor, bring up my knees and use his weight and the positions of my boots to leverage a solid two-footed thrust. I launch him over my head in the wildest game of helicopter ever.

He lets out a feral growl, his cat flailing in the air as he smashes through the glass door and slides across the balcony. His claws gouge deep tracks in the concrete as he slows his momentum and changes direction to attack me once again.

"Eva, now! Time to leave."

"All right."

I flip my gaze back for a split second and catch sight of Evangeline's beautiful white dove soaring out the patio door and into the night.

Garnet's lion is on top of me.

I grunt, grapple around his neck, and close my arms, gripping my dragon band. "Got you."

CHAPTER EIGHTEEN

From one moment to the next, my world shifts as the portal magic transports me to the dragons' lair in Ireland. I'm relieved I was able to portal. Garnet's reaction is equal and opposite.

I lose my hold on the raging lion in the transfer, and the moment his paws find purchase against the lair's stone floor, he roars and throws me violently against the cave wall.

The impact rattles my skull.

I fall to my knees, but I'm quick to get back on my feet because my dragon brood is closing in. They've heard the intruder's growl, and now a dozen adolescent dragons are racing to see who's trying to kill their human mother.

"It's fine guys. It might not look like it, but Garnet is a dear friend. He's under the influence of a magic spell."

"Fi!" Patty runs into the main cavern. "Ye brought him here?"

"Not my first choice." I brace for impact as the massive lion with an ebony mane knocks me flying back, his mouth clamped around my neck. "Vampires had me."

My shield is on fire, and as much as I understand the danger, it's hard to reconcile my instincts with my reality. Garnet is my friend. Surely somewhere inside his mind and soul, he realizes that.

I reach back with my right and power through, delivering an uppercut to the side of his head with everything I have. My fist connects solidly with the orbital bone of his cheek and twists him around with a blow you'd see in a prizefight.

I take advantage of the moment his brains are rattled and cast a scattered glance toward Patty. "Feel like jumping in here? If you can't stop a raging lion, I hear a Taser or electrocution will knock him on his ass."

I don't want to hurt Garnet, but if we don't get him under control, my dragon children will step in. I'm not sure how I know this. I just do. I sense their intention, and while they're trying to be obedient, they don't like seeing me attacked.

Also…they want to fight.

Part of me believed that when faced with hurting me, the Garnet I know would come through.

Not so much.

As dangerous as it is to keep engaging with him, I'm afraid if I get too far from him one of the dragons will take the opportunity to step in.

If Garnet hurts one of the Queen's babies, all hope of him getting out of here unscathed is lost. The Queen of Wyrms is many things but forgiving of those who would harm her children isn't one of them.

"He's my friend, kids. Remember that."

Another frontal assault and Garnet clamps his powerful jaws around my wrist, swinging me off-balance and onto the floor as he shakes his head.

I can't help the scream that peals from my throat. Then the world explodes into a flurry of scales and wings and bolts of fire.

Singed fur burns my nostrils, but the distraction of being attacked on all fronts is enough for Garnet to release my arm and give me the chance to reposition.

Scarlet and Green Guy are right there with me, and I'm thankful they fall back once I'm on my feet. They're exercising more control than I thought.

I'm proud of them.

"Garnet, it's me, Puss. Stop this. You need to snap out of it so I can take you home to Myra and Imari."

I study the golden glow of his eyes the whole time I'm speaking. There's no recognition, no glimmer of the man I know, the boss, the husband, the father.

We wrestle for a few more aggressive challenges. Then Patty rounds Green Guy's massive hind leg. There's a glimmer of silver as he raises his hand and runs at us.

I don't have time to see what he has, but I trust him. Not wanting him to get hurt, I double my efforts and secure Garnet's head. Turning him so he doesn't see what's coming, I fight against his resistance.

With the heightened hearing of his shifter side, no doubt he can hear the approach, but it's too late.

The moment Patty leans in, Garnet stiffens.

I pray we did the right thing.

It probably would be smart to let go and back off, but I'm afraid he'll retaliate against Patty. The voltage going through Garnet hits me, and my arms lock as much from electrocution as defiant will.

It's only the brutal strike of Scarlet's head that breaks me from the tangled mess. I soar through the air but don't have the motor function to get my arms up or land with any kind of grace.

Thankfully my armor is still in place.

I crash spectacularly and lay breathless, staring up at the cavern ceiling. It smells like my hair is on fire, which is gross, but I suppose it could be worse.

With a groan, I roll to my hands and knees and push up, pausing for a moment to check my balance.

Garnet has fallen still. Well, not exactly still...he's lying

AUBURN TEMPEST & MICHAEL ANDERLE

unconscious with his form flipping from lion to man to lion in rapid succession.

Suede warned me this was a brutal last resort. My pulse races at triple time. What if I've killed my best friend's husband or left him in a state where he'll never be the same again?

As the thought slams into my mind, I know what Myra would say if she were here. *You did what you had to do. Garnet would never have been able to live with himself if he killed you.*

I'd say, *That doesn't make it suck any less.*

"Are ye all right, Red?" Patty asks.

I've bent at the waist with my hands propped against my knees to keep from falling over. "I will be. I need to get him back to the Batcave. We have a cell there that can contain even the deadliest members of the empowered community. Once he's in there, Sloan and the others can work on breaking Eros' spell."

"Ye better take this, just in case." Patty steps in, places a gentle hand on my side, and hands me the cattle prod he used on Garnet. "I wasn't sure what voltage to use on a lion. I hope I didn't make things worse."

"Me too, but I wouldn't have known any better. Thanks, Patty."

"Och, ye don't need to thank me, Red. Just get him back to where you need to. If ye could do it before Her Graciousness gets back from her outing with the wyverns, all the better. She won't like it much that you brought a stranger here, but I'll explain. I doubt Garnet will remember this."

"I apologize for bringing him here. I do. I'll have Sloan double-check his memories to make sure nothing of the lair's secrecy is compromised."

"That's all we can ask. Now, off ye go. The man appears to be in one fine mess. I'm sure his people will want to care fer him."

Speaking of people caring for one of their own, I straighten and look at my dragon kids. "A great job, guys. Thank you for your help. And thank you for not hurting him. It probably looked a lot worse than it was, but I appreciate how well you followed my instructions and how well everything turned out. I'm proud of you."

I take a moment to hug Scarlet and Green Guy and pat a few of the others. "Thanks, guys. Love you all." With that said, I kneel next to Garnet and grab my dragon band, focusing on being back at the Batcave.

The moment we materialize, I remember I don't have my security pendant. I get up from where I'm crouched beside Garnet and bang my palm against the glass door. My claddagh band *clacks* against the glass and brings Andy running to the door.

"Fi! What's happened?" She looks at Garnet and curses in what I guess is ancient Greek.

"Help me get him inside. Then I need you to call Anyx or Thaos."

Andromeda holds the first door open while Maxwell runs out from his office to get the second. Between *Bestial Strength* and the adrenaline from the fight, I manage to drag Garnet inside myself.

"I need to get him into the empowered holding cell."

"I've got him, Fi." Anyx catches the door behind me and is quick to lift Garnet and throw him over his shoulder. Jogging with him in a fireman's hold, the golden lion makes a beeline for the back room.

I follow in a rush and my mind fritzes out on the scene inside. Right. I forgot about all the women rescued from the warehouse. The Batcave safe house is usually empty, but tonight it's filled and overflowing with cots and women.

Anyx makes quick work of securing Garnet and locks things up tight. When he comes to me, I'm blinking back the hot sting of tears. "I'm so sorry." I hand him the cattle prod. "I didn't know what else to do, and he was kicking my ass, and I needed to get him here. I didn't want to scramble his eggs."

Anyx takes the cattle prod from me and checks the setting. He frowns but then shakes his head. "He should be fine. He's stronger than most. It'll likely be fine."

I'm not sure if he's trying to convince himself or me, but I'm not going to question it. I want him to be right.

I *need* him to be right.

"I have to go. The vampires took Emmet and Dillan, and Sloan doesn't know where we are. Eva flew off, and I don't know how to find her, and Anca and Andrei are having a cocktail party on the seventy-fifth floor of some building. I have to go."

Anyx lifts his nose and sniffs the air. "You can go in a minute. First, I want you to lower your armor and let me have a look at whatever is bleeding. Come out to the office. Andromeda, can you please grab the first aid kit?"

I wave that away. "I'm fine."

"I'm sure you believe that, but you took on vampires and the Alpha of the Toronto Moon Called. You're running on adrenaline and worry. Let me look you over. You'll be no good to anyone if you drop in the street because you're hurt and go into shock."

"Druids don't go into shock," I say absently, scanning the poor women who were locked in those cages. "What I need is to contact Sloan and find out about Emmet and Dillan."

Firm hands turn me and get me moving. Anyx leads me out to the front office as Andromeda runs for her phone. He points at the chairs around the conference table, and I don't have the energy to fight.

I release *Tough as Bark* and plunk into the closest chair. "I don't mean to be a pain in the butt, but vampires have my brothers, and I can't sit here while they're in danger."

"I promise I'll be very quick. You look dead on your feet. Just close your eyes for two minutes, and you'll be on your way."

I do as told and sink back in my chair. My eyes are only closed for a brief second when Anyx touches the gouge on my neck, and it hits me. "Maxwell, cancel the security access for my pendant. Garnet ripped it off my neck and gave it to Anca. I don't know if she knows about the Batcave or not, but better safe than sorry."

"Consider it done." Maxwell turns on his heel and jogs back into his office.

Anyx touches something on my wrist, and I screech and pull back my arm. "Fuckety-fuck, dude. That hurts."

Anyx offers me a patient smile and lifts my hand so I see the damage done. Oh, that. Between forcing free of the rebar and Garnet... It looks like bloody hamburger. "You're not fine, Fi. I take it that Garnet got hold of this arm and tried to shake you like a rag doll?"

"That sounds familiar."

Andromeda rushes back with the first aid kit. Right behind her, Sloan and the other team come running.

"*A ghra*," Sloan says, the words more breath than voice. "Ye made it back. Are ye all right?"

"For a girl who took on an alpha lion in a rage, she is doing remarkably well," Anyx says while cleaning the lacerations on my wrists.

"Only a few holes to fill," I say. "Anca has Dillan and Emmet. We have to find them."

"We will, luv," Sloan says, "but first, it seems ye need a bit of tendin' to."

Anyx chuffs. "I swear, if it were anyone else, we'd be racing to stop blood loss. Garnet is a beast in battle."

"Ye got Garnet, then?" Sloan says.

"Mostly me, with an assist by Patty and a few dragons. I promised Patty you'd make sure Garnet doesn't remember anything about the lair."

"I will. As soon as we get control of what's happenin'." Sloan eases in beside me and kneels. "If ye don't mind, lion, I'll take it from here."

The moment Sloan takes hold of my wrist, the familiar signature of his healing power tingles under my skin. I didn't realize how much it hurt until now, but removing the pain is exquisite.

It clears my mind, and I get back to what's important. "Emmet and Dillan...we have to find them."

"Where did ye last see them?" Ciara asks.

"In an underground garage. Dillan was knocked unconscious. They split us up. I sent Bruin with them to help them."

"Ye sent Bruin?" Sloan snaps. "He's *yer* battle beast, Fi. He's supposed to be keeping ye safe."

"My brothers needed him more. I had Eva."

"Where is she?" Sloan's tone is clipped.

I blink, unsure what to tell him. "When the shit hit, I told her to escape. She flew out into the night, and I used the dragon portal to try to get control of Garnet. I don't know where she is exactly, but I do know she was safe and free of the vampires."

"Well, that's something," Ciara says. "Maybe she has a way to find Dillan and went to help them."

"Yeah, maybe."

I lean to the side and find the rest of Team Trouble all looking safe and whole. "It's good to see everyone. Quite a night, eh?"

"Ye called it, Fi," Tad says. "Ye told us to carb up because it was goin' to be a long one."

Sloan releases my arm, and I twist it in the air. Good as new. Next, he rises on his knees a little higher and reaches for my neck. "Why must everyone that attacks ye go for yer neck? First Xavier. Now Garnet."

I shrug. "You tell me I have a lovely neck all the time. Irresistible, I think you've said."

Sloan arches an ebony brow. "That's an entirely different matter, and ye know it."

I chuckle. "Yeah, but I made you smile."

Sloan finishes with my first aid treatment and pulls me to my feet. "I suppose it's futile to suggest ye go home and rest while we search fer yer brothers, aye?"

"You suppose right." I lean into him for the strength of his hug and draw a deep breath. "Maxwell? Can I ask you a question about the software available to us?"

He steps over to join us and offers me a smile. "Of course, what would you like to know?"

"I was watching *Blindspot* the other night, and Patterson was able to reconstruct where Kurt and Jane were being held prisoner by them describing the buildings and scenery outside the window. She erected a three-dimensional map of the city that reverse-engineered a location based on what they saw. Do we have anything that does that?"

He looks at me and frowns. "Is that a television show?"

"Yeah, why? Isn't that a thing?"

He shakes his head. "Not a thing we have, sorry. We have a map of the city, but nothing as high-tech as that."

"Poop. That would've been so cool."

Sloan chuckles, and I know he's directing it at me. "Are ye trying to recreate where Anca held ye at her cocktail party last night?"

"Yeah, I thought we might be able to get back there. With any luck, she's cocky enough to think I can't figure out where I was."

"Then why don't we go old-school? Tell us what ye remember, and we'll try to figure out where ye were."

I close my eyes and try to recall all I can. "Yuri and other vampires took Eva and me to the penthouse of a condo building. Downtown. Seventy-five floors. Not facing the CN Tower or the lake. Garnet and I broke the glass doors on the balcony during our fight."

I try to go through everything else that might help, but that's all I've got.

Sloan winks. "If we can combine that information, maybe we

can find Anca and force her to tell us where her men took yer brothers."

"On it." Tad races toward the main computer with Ciara on his heels. "We'll find them, Fi."

"So, it's true then." Da rushes in from the elevators. "The vampire bitch has yer brothers."

Something unexplainable happens to me when the world goes to hell and Da races in. It doesn't matter that I'm twenty-four. In that instant, when his blue eyes meet mine, and I feel his strength reaching out to me, I'm eight years old again and he's scooping me up to tell me everything is going to be all right.

He pulls me against his chest and cups the back of my head. "Hush now, baby girl. Yer all right."

Hot tears streak down my cheeks and I gasp for breath. "I'm sorry, Da. I tried to keep everyone safe, but there were so many vampires. I thought not fighting was smarter because they outnumbered us and knocked Dillan out, but then they took them…"

"Och, *mo chroi*, I don't doubt that. Yer instincts are sound. Don't cry, my wee girl. We'll get yer brothers back. I promise ye that." He hugs me tighter, and I'm a little crushed, but I won't complain. One day soon, he'll move to Ireland, and he won't be here to hold me together when things go badly.

I soak up another moment of Da's strength, then ease back and accept the tissue Sloan offers me. "All right then, *a ghra?*"

"Better." I ease back and give Da a nod that I've pulled it together. "While Tad looks for Anca's penthouse, someone look up a company called Cuceri. It was the name on the side of the white cube trucks. It had this splotchy blue logo and that word in dark purple."

"On it." Calum strikes off with Nikon.

I accept Sloan's open arms and hug him. "While they do that, can you look at Garnet? I'm not sure how we heal him or if he needs time, but I feel horrible about electrocuting him."

"Don't feel that way, Fi." Anyx waves away my concern. "I've seen worse transition dysphoria. You have enough to worry about. By morning, he'll be human again. That's when the real struggle will begin."

"We'll figure out how to break the love spell and bring him back to us. I promise, luv," Sloan says.

"Don't promise me. It's not my life that hangs in the balance. It's Myra's."

"Does Myra know ye got Garnet back?"

I look at Anyx for the answer to that one. "I told her we have him and that he's secured for the night in the cell. I asked that she not come until morning to give us a chance to work with him."

I chuckle. "I bet that went over well."

Anyx grunts. "The point is, she knows he's here and will be here bright and early to see her mate."

I sigh and wrap my arm tighter around Sloan's back. "Let's hope it's her mate she finds when she arrives."

CHAPTER NINETEEN

It's close to midnight by the time I abandon my hopes to get through to Garnet. Sloan and I return to the main room to see what we've found out about Anca and her organization. Calum flags us over and points at the monitor wall. They found the company logo I described and have dug up some new information as well.

"Cuceri is a local startup company that registered for a business license last year," Calum says. "It says in their company application they offer a one-stop-shop for all things involved in high-end events."

"Including women for the guests," I say. "Talk about anticipating the needs of your clients."

Calum nods. "The word cuceri means conquer in Romanian, which seems a little aggressive for an events company but there's no law against that."

"What about their business locations?" I ask. "Do any of them have an underground garage that can connect to the old bootleg tunnels?"

"Dionysus and Nikon are checking that out now. I've given

them the six addresses, and they're snapping there and finding out what they can."

"What about the penthouse? Did we find out anything about where that is?"

Tad straightens and spins in his chair. "Seventy-five was a good number. Based on the description of what you saw out the window, the proximity to the tunnel where they took you hostage, and the description of the underground garage, I'm ninety-nine percent confident ye were at One Bloor Condominiums."

"Who's available to check it out with me?"

"Give me two minutes to call in a team," Anyx says, "and we'll portal whoever wants to go."

Da nods. "That's good of you, Lion. Thank you."

I draw a deep breath and break off to the bathroom. I freshen up, wash my hands, and splash some cold water on my face. Staring at the reflection in the mirror, I give myself a once-over. "It's going to be fine. You're going to bust in there, take prisoners, and find Dillan and Emmet. Damn straight you are. Watch out, Anca Romanov. Clan Cumhaill is gunning for you."

I get back out there, and everyone is milling around, ready to go. Anyx, Thaos, and five other heavily muscled military men are speaking to Da and the others.

They see me, the energy in the room shifts, and the adrenaline notches up.

"Time to crash a party, boys and girls. Who's with me?" I hold my hand out in front of me, and my friends and family start stacking hands.

We all make contact, and Anyx and Thaos each touch someone in the circle.

"Three…two…one."

As we portal to the penthouse, I have two scenarios in mind. The first is we catch Anca and her uncle off-guard by returning, and they're still here entertaining and thinking themselves invincible. The second is we arrive, the penthouse is empty, and they've already cleared out and left us nothing to find.

Neither of those is what we find.

We materialize in the center of the living room, and I scan the debris.

"Wow, what a battle zone," Calum says. "Geez, Fi, you said you battled Garnet, but you didn't say the two of you leveled the place."

"Because we didn't. Garnet and I shattered this glass table and those patio doors. I'll claim responsibility for those. The rest of this mess wasn't us."

"No, it wasn't." Anyx points at a fancy crest stenciled on the living room wall. "That's Xavier's emblem. He's been here since you left with Garnet."

"And trashed the place." I use my foot to kick over a chunk of the sofa and watch as Calum, Tad, and Ciara climb the kindling pile of what used to be some lovely pieces of furniture.

Da picks up a fridge door and tosses it on the heap. "The question is whether or not the Romanov vampires were still here when Xavier arrived."

I step deeper into the room, shuffling through the shattered glass littering the expensive area rug. "It's hard to tell without blood. I don't know if their guests were vampires, but the ladies forced to entertain certainly would've bled."

"Xavier wouldn't allow innocent women to be harmed in a skirmish no matter how angry he is," Anyx says. "That much I'm sure of."

"So then, did Xavier's people get here and have a tantrum to prove a point, or were the Romanovs still here and taken care of?"

Da scowls at the scene. "I don't know if we'll find the answer to that, Fi."

I need the answer to that.

If Xavier killed Anca and she's the one who knows where Emmet and Dillan are, we have a real problem.

I pull out my phone and call Xavier's contact information to my screen. Normally I text him and allow him time to return my message. Not tonight.

I dial him directly and press the phone to my ear.

"It's late, Lady Druid, and I'm rather busy at the moment." I hear the whimper and cries of women in the background, and my anxiety ratchets.

"Yes, I hear that. Listen, I'm standing in the middle of the penthouse at One Bloor. It seems you arrived shortly after I left with Garnet."

"The coffee table and glass doors were you I take it?"

"Wrestling a lion is hard work."

"I bet that's true. Where is our Grand Governor now?"

"We have him in the Batcave while we work on removing the effects of Anca's thrall."

"I wish you nothing but success with that, honestly."

"Thanks, but that's not actually why I called. Earlier tonight, Anca and her goons took two of my brothers prisoner. They're my priority. I don't care what your revenge plans are for the Romanovs, but I need to find my brothers before you kill Anca."

"I can appreciate that, Fi, and I give you my word, I won't do anything that endangers your family. In truth, my teams are dismantling the Romanovs as we speak. If we find your brothers in any of our raids, we will, of course, set them free for you."

"Are you aware Andrei Romanov is in town, and he too has embraced being undead? He blames us for Galina's death and has come calling."

"You are a wealth of information tonight, Lady Druid. Thank you."

I roll my neck from side to side, the strain of my evening pulling in painful ways. "I'm not sharing from the goodness of my heart, Xavier. I'm no less protective of my family than you are of yours. Please don't do anything that will endanger them."

"You have my word."

"Please call me, day or night, if you hear anything about Dillan and Emmet."

"You will be the first to know. Be at ease, Lady Druid. If your brothers are here to find, my men will come across them within the next few hours. Now, I really must go. Good night, Fiona. My best to your family in this troubled time."

When the call ends, I stare at the blank screen and sigh. "It's a strange world where I put my hopes in the vampires to protect my family."

"Strange world, indeed." Sloan scans the scene. "I don't know that there's much more to do right now. Maybe we go home and get a few hours of rest."

I shake my head. "No. Xavier's raiding all the Romanov buildings they're aware of. He said we'll know something within the next few hours. I say we go back to the Batcave, keep digging, and wait to hear."

"All right," Sloan says. "Who's going back to the Acropolis?"

"Red, wake up." I jump at the squeeze of my shoulder, only for Nikon to stop me from leaping off the couch and killing myself. "Sorry. There's no way to wake you up that doesn't set you off when you're worried."

I fall back onto the cushy leather three-seater and draw a deep breath. "Not your fault. I'm a little wound up with the boys missing. Have we heard anything?"

"Yeah, that's why I woke you. Evangeline showed up at your

house a few minutes ago. Kev invited her in but says she's agitated and he doesn't understand what she's going on about."

"Is it about Dillan and Emmet?" I ask, sitting up and grabbing my boots.

"Yeah. Sloan *poofed* your dad and Calum straight there so they don't miss anything, and I said I'd wake you and get you there right away."

I stand, and Nikon steadies me.

"Ready, Freddy?"

I lean in and hug his arm, still half-asleep and half-ready to battle. "Ready. Thanks, Nikky. I heart you big. You know that, right?"

"I do, and I send that right back atcha, babe."

We take form in the kitchen of my house and look around. There are voices in the back yard, and I rush out to find the fam jam standing on the back lawn.

Eva's wings are out, and she's pacing, rambling about duty and expectation and being disloyal…

"What's going on?"

Calum turns to me and rakes rough fingers through his hair. "Your guess is as good as mine. Apparently, I don't speak panicked reaper."

Da is trying to calm Eva down, and I rush in to help. "Eva. It's good to see you."

She meets my gaze, and the angel seems to anchor herself. "Fi, thank the stars you're safe. I flew and flew, trying to find them. There are so many white trucks. I tried for ages."

"It's all right. We've been trying for hours too and haven't found them."

"I did find them, but then Death pulled me back, and he turned me all around and was very angry. Then I couldn't find them, and I came back to the place, and they weren't there."

"Okay, back to the part about when you did find them. When was that?"

"I don't know. Time moves differently for members of the Choir, and different still in the celestial city."

"Okay, so you found them before Death called you back. Were they alive and well?"

"Yes. I saw them through a window in the roof. Your bear had a pile of bodies between him and the door, and Dillan and Emmet were behind him."

"Fucking A, Bruin," Calum says. "He must be keeping everyone at bay."

"That's great news." I draw my first deep breath in hours. "Okay, so you found them and were looking down through the window in the ceiling. What kind of place were they in? Was it a warehouse like where we found the ladies in cages or living space like the penthouse where the vampires took us to their party?"

"Neither. There were cages, but there weren't people in them. There were animals."

"Awesome. What kind of animals?" My phone buzzes in my pocket. I don't want to lose Eva's focus, so I take it out and toss it to Sloan to check what it says. "What kind of animals? Were they little animals like Daisy and Doc or bigger animals like Bruin and Manx?"

"Big and small," she says. "They were swimming animals in water boxes and shelled animals with sun lamps and dirt."

"Was it a pet store?" Calum asks. "A place where humans could go buy the fish to take home?"

Her face screws up. "I don't think so. One of the boxes of water had a shark in it. I recognized it from when Dillan and I watched *Shark Week*."

"An aquarium or an exotic fish store then..."

"Big Al's Exotic Fish Emporium," Dillan says as he steps into the back yard looking beaten and battered. "Then Xavier's men busted in and ended our confinement."

"Dillan!" I gasp, rushing with the others to hug first him and knuckle-bump Emmet because Ciara is hogging the hugs. "Ohmygoodness we were so worried. Are you all right?"

Emmet nods. "Bruin made sure we stayed that way. Honestly, I don't know what would've happened without him. He's the hero of the hour."

Dillan chuckles. "I think the Romanovs had some big idea they were going to torture us for intel, but once they locked us down with a concrete wall at our backs, Bruin appeared and kept mowing down anyone they sent in to get us."

"Not that we didn't help," Emmet says. "We were great moral support."

Bruin chuckles, tossing his head as he laughs. He lumbers in behind us and plops his massive butt into the grass. "The ugliest cheerleaders ye ever saw, amirite?"

I rush over and throw my arms around his neck. "You did it. I knew you would. Thank you, thank you, thank you."

"My pleasure, Red. I'm glad to see yer face here safe and sound. I was worried."

I kiss his black nose and scrub his fuzzy ears. "I'm good. Perfect now that you three are home."

Sloan comes over and squeezes my shoulder. "The text ye received was from Xavier, luv. He's checkin' to ensure ye received yer very special delivery as he put it."

I take the phone and respond to the text. I send him a THANK YOU in all caps and a few hearts and some party horns and some happy crying emojis. I don't think Xavier is an emoji kinda guy, but a simple thank you doesn't seem like enough.

The responding text makes me laugh out loud.

He sends me a cocky winky face with finger guns. I can't imagine the king of vampires breaking out the finger guns, but I appreciate the effort more than he knows.

"Quite a night, kids," Da says. "If someone would be so kind as to portal me to the pub, I'd very much like to hug my bride, down a dram or two, and fall into bed."

"A great idea," Sloan says. "I'll take ye, Niall."

Nikon waves that away. "No. You get Fi to bed. She looks like she's going to drop. I'm happy to take Niall home on my way. Welcome home, boys. Glad you're not dead, my friends."

After another round of hugs, we break, and everyone retreats to their beds. I barely get my boots off at the door before Sloan *poofs* me upstairs and helps me into King Henry. He says he'll only be a moment behind me, but I'm out long before he makes it to bed.

CHAPTER TWENTY

"Auntie Fi. Whys you still sleeping? It's lunchtime." I follow the curious question back from the depths of dreamland and pry open one eye. Jackson is sitting on top of me—pressing on my bladder—with a crooked smile on his face.

"Hey, buddy."

"Uncle Sloan says to tell you there's a sammich with your name on it downstairs, but I looked... there's no name. I think he's trickin' me."

I chuckle, which does me no favors with the small human weighing on my bladder situation. "He's not tricking you, buddy. It's something adults say. It means he's saving a sandwich for me if I want to come down and eat it."

"Do you wants to?"

I run my fingers over his forehead and brush his bangs out of his eyes. When the world gets too complicated and dangerous, it's amazing what a simple smile from a monkey can do to wipe the slate clean. "Yep. I sure do. Can you tell him I'll be down in two minutes? I need to pee and brush my teeth."

"Okeedoodle." He flops to the side, rolls onto his stomach, and swings his feet through King Henry's heavy tapestry curtains.

While little feet run for the stairs, I scoot out of bed and hurry to my dresser. I grab a fresh outfit, take it into the bathroom, and am ready to roll a few minutes later.

Normally I don't sleep so late, but by the time we got Dillan and Emmet home last night, it was close to four in the morning.

I'm an eight-hour sleeper.

There's nothing to be done about it, and I don't mess with it unless there's no other choice. Last night I sent a text to Myra and told her I would check in once I was alive today.

"Good mornin', *a ghra*." Sloan smiles as I join them in the kitchen. "How are ye feelin'?"

"Good. Hungry, actually. A little monkey told me there's a sandwich down here with my name on it." I wave at Jackson. He's sitting with Kevin and Meg on the couch watching cartoons.

Sloan turns to the toaster oven and pulls out the plate he's warming. He sets it on the hot pad on the breakfast bar, and I climb up on one of the stools. "Before ye ask, Garnet is doin' better physically, Dionysus is speakin' with Eros about what we can do to break the spell, and both Dillan and Emmet have gotten up fer the day and seem to be sufferin' no ill effects from their shared ordeal."

I chuckle. "Thanks for the update. I needed that."

"I thought ye might."

"What about Myra? Did you hear anything about how her visit went with Garnet this morning?"

Sloan sighs. "From what Anyx said when I called, not well, I'm afraid."

That hurts my heart. "All right. I'll call her when we have our plan for the day."

"Good idea." Sloan passes a damp cloth over the counter. "What would ye like to drink, luv?"

"What flavor of coffees do we have?"

"All yer favorites, I believe."

"Perfect, then hazelnut vanilla, please."

Sloan makes me a coffee, and I take my first bite of the toasted turkey club. As the bacon and Swiss flavor combo melt on my tongue, I melt a little as well.

As often as I tease Sloan about being an anal perfectionist, there are definite advantages.

"I take it by the feminine groans of ecstasy ye like yer sandwich?"

"I love it...and you. Thank you for your attention to detail. Has everyone else already eaten?"

Sloan slides me a mug filled with hazelnut bliss. "The wee ones finished their lunch and are having grapes on the couch while they watch their program."

"I didn't know we had the kids this morning."

"Kinu had to run out unexpectedly, and Aiden went with her. Emmet and Ciara are over with Dillan watchin' the twins, and we've got the monkeys."

"Is everything all right?"

"Yes and no. A woodland elf was out fer a walk in the Don this mornin' and found a selkie toddler. She reported her to Andromeda's call-in line. With Garnet unable to respond, Andy asked Kinu to handle it."

"Is the child lost or abandoned or orphaned?"

"Yet to be determined."

"Oh, that's sad."

"It is, indeed. Hopefully, with Kinu on the case, it'll all work out."

I take another bite of my sandwich and think. There are so many ways exposure can bite us in the butt. The vulnerable sector of the fae world is simply trying to live undiscovered among human citizens.

"Have you ever wondered if it would be better if the world was aware of the fae? Then they wouldn't have to be afraid of exposure all the time."

"No. Then they would be afraid of prejudice and violence against them and their children because they're different. People fear what they don't understand. Myths and tales have painted many of the fae folk in a light that isn't only unfavorable but often cruel and dangerous. There's safety in their existence remainin' a secret."

I finish my sandwich and cradle my mug in my palms. The coffee is still hot, so I blow across the rim of the mug to cool it. "I guess so. I wish everyone could accept everyone else without judgment. Live and let live, you know?"

"Och, that would be lovely, *a ghra*. Though I don't know how realistic it is."

"I might've been told I'm a dreamer once or twice."

"Lead by example, luv. Be the change ye want to see in the world. I don't think yer a dreamer as much as yer faith in justice, and the rightness in the world is stronger than most. There's nothin' wrong with that."

I sip my coffee and let the sweet succulence of the hazelnut and vanilla warm me. "So, what's our plan for today?"

"I cleared the decks. It's yer call."

"Then I say we check in at the Batcave, call Myra, and focus on helping Garnet."

"Sounds like a solid plan."

"Auntie Fi?" Jackson taps my thigh. "Can we go to the grove and visit your dragon? Mommy and Daddy say I can't bother him without you there."

"Sure, buddy. I could use a few minutes in the grove. Let's take my coffee out, and we'll see if we have any treats for our fae friends."

"I think Emmet and Ciara took the snacks when they were out there checking on Pip and her pregnancy this morning," Sloan says.

"How did that go?"

"Well, I think. From what he said, she and Nilm are both optimistic about things now that she's not so sick and her mood has improved. They figure it'll be another few weeks and the babes will arrive."

"That's great news. All right, then we'll visit. Does Meggie want to—"

"Flopsy?" Meggie toddles over to join us.

"Yeah, babe, we're going out to the grove. Let's go visit with Flopsy and Mopsy."

When Sloan and I relieve Kevin from kid duty, he runs upstairs to shower and get dressed, and we take the kids to the grove.

"Auntie Fi?" Jackson Superman jumps off the edge of the deck to roll on the grass. "When I grows up, can I be a dragon rider too? I wants to have a dragon."

"If you and a dragon meet and form a special bond of friendship, sure, I don't see why not."

"How old do I have to be to have a dragon?"

"I don't know, buddy. I'm kinda new to the whole thing myself."

"But not yet, right? Daddy says I'm not big enough yet. He says I've gots to be patient because I gots to grow big and tall first."

"Yeah, he's right about that. You'll have to be patient because it won't be for a few years yet."

He runs ahead and waits at the base of the first trees in the yard. "Auntie Fi?"

"Yes, buddy?"

"My six birthday is soon. Will I be old enough to have a dragon then?"

I laugh. His fifth birthday just past so his sixth is a long way off, but hey, I'm not going to burst that bubble. "No, sweetie, not six. Maybe sixteen. You should probably learn to drive a car before you fly a dragon. Let's say sixteen."

"Is that soon?"

Sloan chuckles and sets Meg down to find our Ostara rabbits. "Not soon enough, sham, I'm sure."

No. Likely not.

Still, it's cool to think about Jackson and Meg growing up to be the next generation of dragon riders. I make a mental note for the next time we're all in Ireland. I'll invite the dragons to Gran's and Granda's to get to know the family.

If the big-baddies are coming, they might think twice if we have a dragon fleet within our druid army.

Sloan and I visit in the grove with the kids for half an hour, and I try to remain present and in the moment. Jackson tells Dart all about his plans to grow up and be a dragon rider. Once again, Dart surprises me with his maturity. He's patient with my nephew and also perfectly encouraging.

"Before the summer is over, you should ask your father if you might come to watch Auntie Fi and I practice one night at the druid circle."

Jackson looks from Dart to me and lights up. "Am I allowed to watch?"

"We practice in the night *waaay* after bedtime. You might have to take an afternoon nap with Meggie so you don't get too tired."

"Only babies take naps. I don't need a nap. I'm big."

I shrug. "Everybody needs a nap sometimes, buddy. My point is, if you have a nap, I bet Mommy and Daddy will let you stay up late and watch us fly one night."

He bites his bottom lip and looks torn. "I won't have to nap every day, will I?"

"No. Only the times you want to come to the druid circle for dragon training."

"Okay."

"Mommy and Daddy still have to say it's okay, and you have

to promise to keep it a secret. Dart is a very special secret. I don't even talk about him to other adults who don't know him."

"But we can talk about him with Mommy and Daddy, right?"

"Yes. With anyone in our family."

Kevin comes out to get the kids when he's finished getting ready, and Sloan and I take that as our cue to get back to the chaotic reality of our lives.

"Where to first, *a ghra?*" Sloan asks. The two of us stand in the shade of our backyard grove.

I consider that. "Dionysus texted me earlier that Eros is at his loft for a bit. He's taking another run at him to appeal to his better nature to help us with Garnet."

"*If* Eros has a better nature—which I'm not confident he does —he said there was no way to break the spell that he knew of."

I chuckle. "Did he though? What I got from him was a lot of bravado. 'My power trumps everything. You won't be able to break it. I'm a god, after all.'"

Sloan grins. "That's yer impression of Eros, is it?"

Everyone's a critic.

"Regardless...Patty didn't share that opinion. He's seen and done a lot in his lifetime. If he says Eros is full of himself and doesn't know what he's talking about, I'm with him."

"Believin' Patty is right and provin' him right are two different things. Whether Eros is egotistical or simply out of touch with the abilities of people in the empowered realm, I don't see how he'll be any help."

"Maybe not, but what else have we got? You and Merlin didn't get anywhere, did you?"

"Not really, no." He frowns and casts an absent glance at the back of the houses. "Let's go to the Batcave first. I'd like to see Garnet again and specifically Garnet when Myra is there."

"Okay, yeah. I want to see Myra anyway."

With that, Sloan takes my hand and *poofs* us to the tenth floor of the Acropolis.

Sloan lets us in when we arrive because I don't have a security pendant thanks to lovestruck Garnet. Whatevs. We're in, and that's what matters.

The first thing I notice once we get inside is that it's quieter than it was last night.

The second thing is that we have a visitor.

The man walking toward me is close to seven feet tall with glowing gold eyes and blue ink covering his bald head, face, and neck. He's a djinn and not just any djinn. He's one I recognize.

A subtle surge of Sloan's energy tingles up my arm from our joined hands. A moment later, the flutter in my mind battens down the hatches of my brain.

So protective, my guy.

The first time I felt that sensation was at the Rockin' Ramen Restaurant when we were investigating the bizarre appearance of a unicorn in downtown Toronto. It turned out fine, and I have no doubt it's fine now.

"Dantarion Jann, how are you?" I meet him with my hand extended.

"I am well, Lady Druid, thank you. I am also pleased to be called upon. After five months, we thought you'd ignored our offer to help with your team."

"Not at all." Maxwell joins us from his office. "It took me months to learn about the empowered community and sort through the protocols we would need to put into place. Then we found ourselves dealing with an uprising of evil-minded people. It's taken me longer to reach out than it should've, but your application has always remained at the top of the pile."

"That's good to know." Dan nods.

"So, you said called upon? What do we have you doing today?"

"I was asked to interview each of the ladies rescued from the vampire warehouse. Mr. Maxwell expressed the need to clear their minds of any empowered memories and soften the trauma of what they've been through."

"Oh, wonderful. How did that go?"

"It went well, and when I finished, members of your team arranged a transport. The lovelies are in the human care system for victims of such crimes."

I glance at Maxwell, and he fills in the blanks. "Andromeda and Zuzanna arranged for several officers from the Special Victims Unit to escort the ladies to a trafficking shelter. It was a ladies-only trip, and all seemed to be in order when they left."

"I'm relieved. Thanks for the help, Dan."

"It was my pleasure. I hope to be involved in more operations moving forward."

"I'm sure you will," Maxwell says. "Come into my office. I'll get you to give me a description of what you did and your findings. Once we have your paperwork filled out, you'll be on your way."

We say our goodbyes, then Sloan and I head back to the containment area to check Garnet.

"Fi! There you are. How are you?" Myra rises from the leather chair that's been pulled in here from the main meeting room. She has it situated against the two-inch-thick reinforced glass wall that separates her from a pacing lion with a flowing, ebony mane.

"I'm fine. It's Garnet I'm worried about."

Myra looks me over. "Well, I'm worried about both of you."

"I'm fine...really."

She scoffs. "I heard you had a one-on-one fight to bring Garnet down. That's something to worry about."

"Nah, he didn't hurt me."

"I heard differently." Myra pegs me with a look that says she knows the whole story. She likely does. Being the mate of the Moon Called Alpha, all she needs to do is ask, and any of the lions within the Toronto pride will tell her anything she wants to know. "Anyx said you were banged up and bleeding when you arrived with him last night."

"I played the part of his chew toy for a few minutes, but s'all good." I hold out my arm and twist it for her to examine. "Anyx patched me up until Sloan got here and fixed me up as good as new. Honestly, it wasn't much more than a few gashes."

She seems skeptical, but that's the truth.

"Where's Imari? Is she okay?"

"She's fine. She thinks her daddy is out of town on a business trip and was excited to work in the bookstore with Uncle Zxata today."

"Fun. I bet the two of them will have a great day." I go over to the cell and press my hand against the glass. It's not as cool as regular glass, but it's just as clear and much stronger. "He looks much better today than he did last night. Seeing him flip from man to lion and back again like a faulty Christmas bulb was horrible."

Myra flinches.

My bad. "Too much sharing, sorry." I shift my attention to the angry predator sizing me up for his lunch. "Hey, Boss. How are you feeling?"

He drops his head, his tail twitches, and a long growl vibrates deep in his chest.

"Still not pleased with me, eh?"

Myra takes my hand and squeezes. "Don't mind him. He's cranky, but once he gets the stupid Cupid stuff out of his system, he'll be back to normal."

Yeah? When will that be?

I don't have the heart to tell her we have no idea how to make that happen or if it's possible.

"The important thing is he's here, and he's safe." Sloan offers her one of his award-winning smiles. "We won't give up until we find a solution."

"Thank you, sweetie." Myra leans in and accepts Sloan's hug.

She's tired. It's visible in the dark circles under her eyes as well as the hunch of her shoulders. She kisses Sloan's cheek and eases back. "What would I do without you?"

The roar of an irate lion has the three of us stumbling back. Garnet hits the glass with all his weight and the *crash* of the impact echoes throughout the space.

Dayam. He is really pissy.

I feel bad about that, but given a chance to force him away from Anca and do it differently, I wouldn't.

Garnet is right where he needs to be.

"I suppose we should go. We still have vampires to find and a love spell to break."

Myra nods. "You do that. If you find that bitch, kick her ass for me, won't you, Fi?"

"Oh, if I get the chance, you know I will."

CHAPTER TWENTY-ONE

Sloan and I return to the conference room, and I move straight to the main console. Tad is busily working on the computer, and Da and Emmet are focused on images on the monitor wall. The two are deep in conversation, and I consider not interrupting them. I ignore the impulse, eager to get caught up.

"What are we looking at?" I ask.

Da reaches out and pulls me beside him, pointing at the screens. "Yer friend Xavier went to town last night. Garnet's men turned up seven locations of destruction where we believed the Romanovs set up shop."

I scan the images, amazed at all the damage done in one night. "Yeah, he mentioned as much last night. He said his family was raiding Romanov properties but said he had no luck finding Anca and her uncle."

"The good news is he seems to have them on the run. The bad news is desperate people do desperate things. Breaking down the Romanov's plan could propel them to be even more reckless and dangerous."

"Will that trigger the mass death event?"

"There's no way to know for certain. It would be good to check in with Eva and find out what's happening on that front."

I pull out my phone and realize I don't have Eva's contact information, so I pull up Dillan's.

The phone rings half a dozen times before he picks up. "Fi, it's not a good time. Can I call you back?"

"What's wrong?"

"Eva and I are in the middle of something. Is this urgent? Do you need something?"

"Just an update on the mass death issue. Xavier cut the Romanovs down last night. We're worried it might ignite the pending violence."

"I'll ask, but she might not answer. She's getting all weird and spouting off some bullshit about duty and designation and knowing her place."

"Don't be too hard on her. Did she tell you Death called her in last night while you were missing and reamed her out?"

"No. Not a peep."

"Yeah, I think being with you and helping us has complicated her life. She's getting pressured and was pretty rattled last night when we got to her."

"This morning too. I was trying to find out what was wrong when you called."

"I'm sorry to add to the turmoil but could you ask about the mass death? It's important."

He repeats the question away from the phone and returns to speak to me. "She doesn't know the cause, but she's feeling the call and her fellow reapers are on the move. She thinks whatever has been pending is happening today."

"Oh, crappers. Any idea where or who's involved?"

There's a pause. Then he comes back to answer. "No idea who, but she says the violence is going to involve a festival. Lots of innocent civilians."

He says something away from the phone and curses. "Look, Fi. I gotta go. She's really wound up."

"Okay. Take care of her and thank her. I know she's not supposed to get involved, but I appreciate it." I end the call and relay the information. "Search on the Internet and all the Toronto bulletin boards. We're looking for a festival going on today with lots of civilians."

Tad is quick on the computer searches and throws the results onto the monitor wall. "The only festival I find is something called Toronto's Caribbean Carnival."

"Caribana?" I look at Da and Maxwell. "That's over a million people spread across the lakefront and islands."

"And a perfect place to end up with a mass death if someone breaks into the crowd with guns," Da says.

My lunch tumbles in my belly as I stare at the wall of bright costumes and smiling faces. "Maxwell, you need to call in the full team. If we're right, there isn't much time to stop what's about to happen."

Fifteen minutes later, the team has assembled. Everyone, except Dillan—we figured it was more important for him to stay with Eva as long as he's able—is called in and we're about to begin the briefing.

"Caribana is North America's largest street festival," I say, cluing in Sloan, Tad, Ciara, and Dionysus. "It draws over a million people to the multi-week events and two million to the festival's final parade during the long weekend in August."

"Thankfully, the parade isn't for another week and a half," Maxwell says. "So, wherever the violence is about to break out, we have a chance to get there without road closures and gigantic floats."

That *is* fortunate. "Maybe we can avoid another Santa Claus parade fiasco."

Da *harrumphs*. "We need to make a rule not to target Toronto parades. It's bad fer business."

"Well, hopefully, we'll figure out what's coming and contain the threat," I say.

Emmet casts the itinerary up on the screens and scowls. "It would be easier if the events weren't spread all over. There are pool parties at four different places, an event at Rebel Nightclub, a hip-hop event at Fiction, Carnival Kingdom at the fairgrounds, a DJ Trilogy at Roy Thompson Hall, an All-Star Celebrity Party at the Orchid, a rave on the *Empress* yacht in the harbor, a Wicked in White reggae event at The Pint…and the list goes on."

Da frowns. "There's no way we can cover all of those and still be effective. We need more information. Dillan, have ye got anything new?"

The group in the Batcave grows quiet, and we wait for Dillan to respond remotely over the communication system. "Nothing so far. Like she said before, reapers don't get a playbook. They feel the summons, respond to their call, transport the soul they're responsible for, and move on. There's no watercooler action in their circles."

That's unfortunate. We could use some hot gossip right about now.

On impulse, I take out my phone and text Xavier.

FYI, the reapers are on the move. If you're about to make a move on Anca or her family, please reconsider. The threat of mass death is in play.

The responding text comes back almost immediately.

It's not us. Whatever you're dealing with, my family isn't the cause. We set our revenge in motion, but it doesn't involve

**innocents, and nothing happens until tomorrow. I wish you
well in stopping the deaths. Call if I can help.**

I read his response aloud and scan the faces of my family. "I
believe him. Xavier is a lot of things, but he lives by a code, and
lying to me about killing innocents would offend his morals."

"Yer puttin' a lot of stock in the morals of a drug-dealin'
vampire, *mo chroi*," Da says.

"I know it seems like that, but my instincts are telling me to
follow his advice and keep looking."

"Even if it's not Xavier and the Toronto vampires, that doesn't
mean the mass death isn't because of the Romanian vampires,"
Aiden says.

Anyx frowns at the Caribana images on the wall. "Anca has
proven she and her family don't respect the policing system we
have in place."

"If it is the Romanians, what's the mass killing about?" I pull
an elastic out of my pocket and tie back my hair. "Feeding off
festival-goers? People in the wrong place at the wrong time?
Shits and giggles?"

"If we knew the answer, things would be a lot simpler,"
Sloan says. "Let's not blind ourselves to the chance it's something as mundane and tragic as one of the ferries sinking in the
harbor or a building collapsing with thousands of people
inside."

"Cheery," Emmet says. "You really know how to bring down a
room, Irish."

Dammit, my head is pounding. "So, we don't know who or
where or why or what. The only thing we have any clue on is
when—and that's pretty much now."

"Sounds about right," Emmet says.

"Awesomesauce. Does anyone else feel like bashing their head
against the conference table for a good time?"

The comms line crackles and Dillan whispers to us. "Guys,

we're here. Fuckety-fuck there are a lot of reapers. Gooderham and Worts…and hurry the fuck up."

Finally, somewhere to focus our frustration.

"Saddle up." Da reaches out his hand and waves everyone in. "Greek, atop one of the buildings, if ye would."

Everyone stacks hands and Nikon tops the pile. The powerful surge of the Greek's immortal snap transports us as one to the historic Distillery District to find Dillan and stop a massacre.

Our group takes form on the roof of the Cannery, one of forty historic brick buildings of the Distillery District. Established as a mill in 1831, William Gooderham and his brother-in-law James Worts built this iconic business into the largest distillery in Canada. It thrived for over a century until beer and wine became the tastes of society and the whiskey market suffered.

Since then, a group of visionary developers preserved and repurposed the entire complex as an art and entertainment outlet called the Distillery District. The thirteen acres are a popular place for shopping, shows, seasonal celebrations, movie shoots, and, of course, festivals.

"All right, boys and girls." Da stretches his neck as he gazes over the edge of the brick wall. "Somewhere in that crowd is a threat to a great many lives. We have ten streets to cover, five points of entry from different directions, plus Distillery Lane packed with dancers and pedestrians."

"All this used to be a whiskey factory?" Tad asks.

Da nods. "Aiden and Nikon, head north and make yer way back. Emmet and Ciara cover east. Tad and I will go to the west side, and Fi, Sloan, and Calum take the south. Spread out and keep an eye peeled fer Dillan and Evangeline. If ye see anythin' call us in and we'll stop whatever is about to happen."

As vague as that is, it's the best we've got.

The group breaks up, and we all head off to our assigned locations.

"Is this what police work is like?" I ask Calum as we hit the iron steps of the fire escape and head down to the crowd below. "You know there's a bomb or a bad guy in the crowd, and you have no idea who he is or what he looks like or what you're facing?"

Calum smiles at me. "Sometimes. Other times we know exactly what we're looking for and are still frantically trying to find it—a bomb, a man with a missing child, a bank robber who managed to slip into the crowd. It's a stressful job."

I descend the last of the stairs, scanning the crowd for Dillan or Anca or a guy with a flashing neon sign over his head that says, "I'm about to go postal and cull this crowd." "I much prefer knowing who's coming at me and what to expect."

"Oh, I do too, but bad guys don't take polls on what cops like. They do their thing, and we do ours the best we can. Usually, it works out."

Usually, but not always.

It didn't work out for Brendan.

I step off the last of the metal rungs and look for the opening to step into the crowd. Brendan loved the stress of not knowing what was coming at him. It played a large part in his decision to go into undercover work.

I wonder if he'd known the outcome would be his death if he would've still chosen that path. He put a lot of bad guys away... and, in the end, he defied violence and stepped between a gunman and an innocent woman and her little girl.

That's my answer.

He wouldn't have changed a thing.

Knowing him, dying so they could live was a fair trade and something he took comfort in at the end.

"Where'd ye go there, *a ghra?*"

I meet Sloan's concerned gaze and rub the sting of emotion

tingling in my nose. "Sorry, thinking about Brenny. I'm back. S'all good."

He places a warm hand at the small of my back and tugs me a little closer to his side. As we weave through the brightly colored dancers, I scan the happy faces and hope nothing happens to ruin their day.

One thing about Caribana is that it's impossible to be near any of the events and not sway your hips to the calypso music. Steel drums fill the air with a cheerful song while vibrant costumes, glittery bikinis, feathered wings, and headdresses dazzle tourists and participants.

Then there's the scent of food…

Man, the restaurants are making it difficult to focus.

"Anyone got anything?" Da asks.

It's hard to hear him over the comms, so I press a finger to my ear. "We're almost to the south exit that leads out to Distillery Lane. Nothing yet."

The other groups check in next, and no one's got eyes on the danger, the vampires, or Dillan.

We step out onto the wide cobblestone lane where a huge crowd has gathered to party. The dancers are shaking their moneymakers, and their fancy headdresses twirl eight to ten feet in the air like a living kaleidoscope.

"With all these feathers, the reapers will fit right in," Calum says. "We'll never pick them out of the crowd."

I laugh. "You haven't seen Eva with her wings out. They're stunning. I think, even among all these amazing costumes, those feathers would still draw everyone's attention if they were visible to mortals…which, of course, they're not."

Calum chuffs. "I'm still in shock that Dillan's in love with a reaper."

"Me too. Even more that he's in love at all…less that she's a reaper."

"I hear you."

Sloan shifts his palm from my back to hold my hand, and I understand why a moment later. His bone ring has activated, allowing him to see the unseen.

He must grab Calum's hand too because my brother gasps. "Holy hell, is that real?"

"Aye, I'm afraid so."

As terrifying as it is, a sea of close to forty-five reapers are standing on the sidelines like a football team waiting to take the field. The reality of the moment presses down on me.

Seeing that many of them gathered is both frightening and also breathtakingly beautiful.

The assembled angels stand shoulder-to-shoulder in every color of skin, hair, and eyes, as well as every body shape—the Children of the Choir.

Their wings reach over their heads and flare behind them like an enchanted feather backdrop. In shades of deep purple, navy, bronze, and black, they're a foreboding sight. That's before you register the subtle rays of light streaming down upon them from the heavens.

I search the faces of the assembly and find Eva standing among her siblings. Her focus is locked on the crowd before them, her familiar glowing smile nowhere in sight.

"If I could take a picture of this, Kevin would try to recreate the beauty in a work of art...well, after he craps himself...because holy shit, amirite?"

I chuckle, but there's nothing funny about it. "I guess we're in the right place." Tapping my earbud, I call the troops, watching for anything that suggests what's about to happen. "Everyone, move to protect the crowd on Distillery Lane. Whatever's about to happen, it'll start here. The reapers have gathered."

CHAPTER TWENTY-TWO

The crowd of thousands ebbs and flows with the rich array of harmony produced by the steel drums. After finding Evangeline in the crowd, standing with her siblings, I scan first near where she's standing, then where she's looking.

"There's Dillan." I point at my brother and start on a path to intercept. "Maybe he knows more about what's happening. He's been here longer. Maybe Eva got more info once she arrived."

I'm shouting over my shoulder but have no idea if Sloan and Calum hear me. As the crow flies, Dillan is only a couple of hundred feet away. In the congestion of this crowd, that might as well be across the city.

"Sloan, can you *poof* us?"

His brow creases with impressive force. "Are ye daft? There are likely five thousand people here."

"I know, but I want to talk to Dillan."

"Then ye'll need to navigate the crowd, luv. I can't help ye. It would be blatant exposure."

I knew that before I asked, but it still sucks. "Fine, help me up." I point at a stone retaining wall around a large planter and smile at the other ladies dancing above the crowd.

Sloan runs block and gets me up high enough that I'm above the heads and most of the feathers of the dancers. Pressing my fingers together, I push them under my tongue and blow a shrill whistle. It's drowned out in the music. I try again, pushing my intention across the crowd, and by some miracle, Dillan turns his head and meets my gaze.

I'm expecting him to start making his way toward me, but he doesn't move. Instead, he points toward the small parking lot at the end of the lane.

At first, I don't get the message. Then I spot the white cube van parked in one of the closest spots. "It's the Romanovs." I point at the blue splotchy Cuceri logo. "That's a truck from their fleet. We should check it out."

"That's not where the reapers are looking or where Dillan's focused," Calum says. "He knew about the van and stayed here. I think we should stay focused on the citizens and keeping them safe."

I'm torn. I lift my chin and search for Dillan, but he's not in the same spot, and I've lost him. I tap my earbud and try a different tack. "Da, in the small parking lot on the west end of the lane there's a Romanov cube van. Do we try to make it there to check it out or stay in the crowd where the reapers are?"

"Tad and I will investigate the truck. You three watch the crowd."

"Okay, be caref—oh, shit."

"Fi?" Da says. "What's wrong?"

Sloan and Calum are looking at me too. "In the crowd… Benjamin is here, and he's very not happy."

Sloan follows my extended finger and frowns. "I thought Xavier said the Toronto seethe isn't involved in anything today."

"He did. Maybe it was a lie, or maybe he doesn't know Benjamin is out here." With that in mind, I pull out my phone and text Xavier again.

**Think we found the trouble. Distillery Lane south of Good-
erham and Worts. Benjamin and Romanovs all here among
the Carnival festivities. Things are about to go to hell.**

I hit "Send," and as usual, Xavier responds almost
immediately.

On my way.

"He's coming. I don't think he knew. At least…I want to think
he didn't."

"I texted Anyx," Calum says. "He's on his way with Garnet's
pride. They'll help with the crowd and are anxious to meet Anca
and her men."

"I bet they are."

Since I have the best viewpoint, I'm the first to know when
things go off the rails. Benjamin sees something in the crowd,
and the world blurs as I try to track him in motion. "There." I
point. "Benjamin rushed behind the stage."

I barely get the words out before the horror movie screaming
starts.

Then the gunshots.

And the stampede.

"This is not a drill, folks." I'm about to jump down when Sloan
puts his arm up and holds me in place.

"Yer the only one who can see what's happening. Tell us
where to go until this crowd clears."

I'm about to tell him where to go all right when Emmet and
Ciara come out between two buildings looking lost. "Ciara and
Emmet. Fifty feet on your right, Benjamin went behind the
stage."

Shots ring out, and my head cranks around on a pivot.
"Calum! The shooters have Da and Tad pinned down, and two

vamps are grabbing girls and throwing them in the back of the Romanov truck."

"I have five vamps about to drop fang right here in the open," Aiden says.

"Veil of Privacy, *a ghra!*" Sloan shouts, running through the crowd.

"On it." Calming my mind, I cast a Veil of Privacy over the unlawful feeding on tourists while Team Trouble moves in.

More gunshots.

"What the hell is with the guns?" I shout. "Someone teach these out-of-towner assholes we don't do guns. This is Toronto! We're nice, *dammit!*"

"I am happy to teach them, Lady Druid." Xavier stands right next to me. "Don't worry. They'll get the message. Before that, where is Benjamin?"

"He tackled one of the vampires behind that stage."

Before I finish, Xavier is gone.

"Xavier and his family are here, everyone. Don't stake the wrong vamps, please."

"Baby girl, watch out! Two coming your way."

My shield flares as I hear Aiden's warning and I spin, bracing for the incoming danger. I call my armor in time but don't get my hands up fast enough to defend myself.

Damn vamps are fast.

Yuri lifts me off my feet and slams me onto the cobblestones. I land flat on my back, and if I didn't have my armor, I have no doubt bones would be broken and my skull would be fractured.

The air rushes from my lungs, and I gasp for breath, dizzy and disoriented.

I think Anca's right-hand man expects that to break me and put me out of the fight because he does nothing to protect himself or defend. He simply perches over me, glancing around at the chaos.

I'd love to call the gale force hurricane or open the ground to swallow him, but we're trying to minimize the empowered influence on the scene and things like that are hard to explain.

"Bestial Strength." As the influx of power fuels my muscles I launch my fist straight over my body and whack his sack with everything I have.

That's normal enough to blend in.

Vampire or not, if you nut-punch a guy hard enough, he'll drop like a rock.

When Yuri hits the ground, I roll onto my feet and drop a knee on his chest. "Where are Anca and Andrei? Are they here? What's this all about?"

Yuri is curled like a boiled shrimp and grunting and groaning. It might be a minute or two before he talks.

I lean in, grinding my knee into his solar plexus. With *Bestial Strength*, that's a lot of force against his chest. Even if vampires don't have to breathe, it must feel like there's a Humvee parked on top of him.

"Your mistress. Where is she? What's this attack about? What's with throwing women into the back of your truck?"

Yuri does nothing but sputter.

"Let us take care of him, Fi." Anyx taps my shoulder to take control of my prisoner. "We'll get him to talk. I think Sloan and Calum could use your help."

I straighten and follow his extended finger to where the two are triaging several of the injured attendees. "Yeah, all right."

As I rush to help them, I glimpse several reapers standing over fallen bodies. As much as we've tried, we haven't prevented the death of innocents entirely. If the reapers are actively working...

"Dammit, we failed."

Sloan glances back over his shoulder and follows the trajectory of my vision back to the fallen citizens. "Not entirely, *a ghra*. While every life here matters, this could've been much worse. We all know the potential for death and destruction we were facing."

He's right, but still... "I hate that any innocents had to die."

"Focus on the living, Fi," Calum says. "There will be time enough for self-recrimination later when we have the whole story."

I suppose he's right.

The sound of sirens draws my attention to the arrival of two ambulances pulling off Parliament Street and bumping over the curb onto the cobblestone lane. "I'll go flag down EMS."

"No, I've got that, Fi," Calum straightens. "I know the protocols and most of the responders. You stay here and apply pressure to this leg wound."

I do as Calum suggests and kneel next to a woman who is very likely in shock.

"Why?" Her gaze skitters around. "Who would do something like this? We were minding our own business celebrating."

"I know. It's awful. Thankfully, I think it's over. You're safe now."

When the EMS teams arrive, I step back and search the crowd for my peeps. Da and Aiden are speaking with the first officers at the scene. Emmet and Dillan are pushing back onlookers and establishing a perimeter. Anyx and Thaos are dragging the last of the vampires around the back of the stage.

No doubt, they'll flash them somewhere secure to interrogate them.

"Did we get Anca and Andrei?" I ask Sloan when he wraps his arms around me.

"I don't know. I hope so. If nothing else, I think we sent a clear message that the type of business the Romanovs are into isn't welcome here."

I search the post-panic destruction, and my blood runs hot on behalf of my city. This was senseless. "What was the point? They bit a few humans, they killed a few, and they tried to kidnap a few... Why?"

"My best guess is to expose vampires in Toronto? To put the

screws to the empowered community here? To retaliate for not falling at their feet? I don't know."

"Maybe you have to be disturbed to relate to something so disturbing."

"Aye, maybe so."

Dillan jogs over and doesn't look happy. "Have any of you seen Eva? She left to escort someone to their final destination and never came back. Now, all the reapers are gone, and she's nowhere I can find."

"Why are you worried?" I ask. "This is her dominion, right?"

"Yeah, but she said her boss is pissed that she broke the rules and got involved in our lives. Apparently, that's a giant no-no in reaper circles. Death wants his reapers to remain neutral. She said he considers her tainted now and she's facing termination."

"Termination from being a reaper...or another, more severe version of termination?"

Dillan pegs me with a glassy-eyed look so unfamiliar that I tear up too. He's panicked. Dillan doesn't do panic.

He's the tough, unflappable one.

"She'll be all right, D." I say it with as much conviction as I can muster. "She probably needs to check in with the Choir and report on what happened. Once that's taken care of, she'll be back. I know it."

Dillan swallows. "Yeah. You're probably right. She'll be back. She probably has reaper paperwork to take care of or something, right?"

"Right."

Dillan wipes his palms on the thighs of his jeans and sucks in a deep breath. "Irish, I need to get out of here...like right now."

"Of course. Where do you want to go?"

"My room. I need a minute."

Sloan squeezes Dillan's shoulder and leads him to the blind corner behind the stage. My heart goes out to Dillan. It's going to sting like hell if his first love gets taken away from him based on ethereal politics.

"Everything okay, Fi?" Calum jogs back from putting out fires.

"I don't know. I hope so...for Dillan's sake."

It takes another half-hour before the craziness dies down and Anyx suggests we all go home. There's no way to be sure if the existence of vampires has been exposed or not. We think we covered things up well enough to keep it from appearing on the front page of the papers in the morning but only time will tell.

"I'm beat." Sitting on the bench at the back door, I tug off my boots and toss them toward the closet. I don't have the energy to do much more. "I feel a hot bath and a rom-com marathon coming on."

Sloan chuckles. "Oh, goody."

"Hey, if you don't want to be there, I can call Dionysus. He's always game for a movie marathon."

"Honestly, I'm fine with him taking rom-com duty as long as I can cut in afterward to be your romantic hero. I have some research to do for Garnet's predicament, and I'd like to have a couple of hours to unwind with my nose in my books."

How did I ever end up with such a book nerd?

"You do you, hotness. We'll meet up later. Hopefully, you'll have great news, and we can get Garnet back to normal. Wouldn't it be nice if we could go to bed tonight with everything being right in the world?"

"It sounds so good that I might even sleep in."

I gasp and raise my fingers to my lips. "Sleep in? You? That's cray-cray."

Sloan tilts his head and gives me a look. "Go have yer bath, *a ghra*. I'll catch up with ye in a—"

A brown river otter races out of the kitchen, scurries past our feet, and descends the basement steps in a sleek wave of motion.

I blink at Sloan. "You saw that, didn't you? I'm not imagining things, am I?"

Kevin races toward the back door with a bottle in his hand. "Did you see Bizzy?"

"Is Bizzy an otter?"

"Yep. She's an otterkie."

"Oh, the selkie toddler Kinu went to assess this morning?"

"Yeah. She didn't have anyone to take her, so I volunteered. Hope you don't mind. Oh, and don't tell Calum yet. He doesn't know. Surprise. Our fostering starts now."

I point down the stairs. "Then you better get running. She got a head start on you."

Kevin laughs. "It's fine. She has a serious crush on Doc and keeps running downstairs to climb into his den to snuggle."

"Aw, that's sweet."

"Yeah. She's sad about being separated from her mom, but she's doing better. She's a funny little thing." Kevin rushes down the stairs. "I know exactly why her name is Bizzy too."

I laugh as his voice trails off and kiss Sloan's cheek. "Close your apothecary door, would you? I'd hate for a baby otterkie to get into your herbs and potions."

"As wise as ye are beautiful, *a ghra*. Now, go soak yerself pruny and make a date with another man while I try to solve the world's problems."

I burst out laughing. "Okay, I'll do that."

CHAPTER TWENTY-THREE

The next two days have Da, Andromeda, Maxwell, and me helping Anyx weather the fallout of the attack at the distillery. There's a general buzz about crazy chaos, but for the most part, it seems my privacy spell mostly masked the vampire activity.

Emmet finds three or four people on the Internet blabbing about craziness, so Dan the Djinn is sent to their homes selling chocolate-covered almonds to adjust their memories and keep things under control.

Yes, some crazy things happened—they can remember that—but nobody dropped fang and juice-boxed civilians.

No way. Never happened.

Sloan and I are ships passing in the night as he spends the same time working on the Garnet issue. I don't know how he can spend so many hours with his nose buried in books, but I guess that's one of the aftereffects of being an only child growing up in an emotionally distant home.

I try not to pry or distract him because he's the smartest person I know and with the knowledge of Patty, Merlin, and Dionysus at his disposal, he's bound to figure something out.

Dillan and I are both going stir crazy waiting to hear news, so we drive over to the Acropolis to work off some energy.

Patience isn't the most natural virtue in our family. We all score high on the activator scale, which makes it hard not to get a little rangy when the world isn't cooperating fast enough.

"You're droppin' yer guard when ye strike, Red," Bruin says from the sidelines. "Keep yer left fist higher."

I adjust my position and go again.

Dillan is lost in thought too. "If I knew whether she's in trouble or been reassigned or is still working on making things right with her boss, it would help." He sweeps his right foot, trying to catch my ankle. "Something…anything."

I hop over his leg and wipe the sweat dripping into my eye with the back of my wrist. "She told me time works differently for her and in the ethereal realm. For her, maybe it's only been a couple of hours, and she doesn't realize you're climbing the walls. She'll be back. One way or another, I'm sure she'll come back to tell you what's going on."

"One way or another." He curses and advances to take one, two, three swings at me, forcing me to retreat. "It sucks that our happiness has anything to do with Death or the Choir of Angels or anyone other than the two of us. Why does it have to be so complicated?"

I duck the incoming jab and spin out of his reach to gain some distance. "I'd say it's because you fell in love with a reaper, but I think that's self-evident."

He grunts and swings at my jaw. "Smartass."

The timer goes off, and we drop our hands and step over to the table. I grab my towel and Dillan goes for his water bottle.

I pat my face dry and wipe my forehead. "Merlin wants to work out with us and get back into top form but said we should be doing more training in the Don. He says we're working out like cops and not druids. He says we're stunting our growth."

"He knows best on that front. We might as well get the most

out of the season. We've only got another three or four months before we go back into the deep freeze. The Winter Solstice will be upon us before we know it."

"Sad but true."

I'm not ready to start worrying about the Culling, and whether or not we'll be able to diffuse things before then, so I push off all thoughts of the Winter Solstice.

"Okay, I'll post it in the chatroom. Starting tomorrow, we work out in the Don and get our druid on."

"Sounds good."

I toss my towel onto the bench and am in the process of resetting the buzzer when Sloan *poofs* in. "Hey, hotness. Long time no see."

"Miss me, do ye?"

I'd like to do a show-and-tell of how much I've missed his face over the past couple of days but put that impulse on hold. Dillan is treading water in relationship hell, and I don't want to torpedo him into the depths.

"Always. Now, let's skip the whole 'behold my genius' part of why you're here and get to the good stuff. Did you find something?"

"I think I have a solid idea. I'm meeting Myra upstairs in a few minutes. Would ye care to clean up and join me?"

"Of course." I pull the Velcro tabs on my gloves and unwrap my hands. "Do I have time for a quick shower and change?"

"Ye do. I figured ye might need to freshen up and built that into the schedule."

I chuckle and finish unwrapping my other hand. He's hilarious, thoughtful...and hilarious. "So, do we get any hints as to what this idea of yours is?"

"I want to test a theory, but I don't want to get yer hopes up yet. Let's see how things go."

"I see...playing the man of mystery. I like it. Okay, give me five."

When I'm cleaned up and changed, I find Sloan stretching his shoulders out against the gym wall. "Where's Dillan?"

"He took yer keys and headed home. He wanted to get a bite to eat and visit Eva's apartment to see if she's gotten back yet. I told him I'd see ye back."

"That's fine. The not knowing is torture for him."

Sloan chuckles. "No one knows that better than me, *a ghra*. I've been the lover left behind to worry more often than not."

"I'm sorry about that."

He leans in and brushes his nose with mine. "It's not yer fault. I'm simply sayin' I sympathize with yer brother's pain."

I take my workout clothes over and pack my bag. "Maybe he'll give her a ring with a tracker in it too."

Sloan gives me a sidelong glance and smiles. "Ye say that like ye think it's funny."

"I *do* think it's funny."

"Practical, ye mean. Yer harder to keep hold of than a grain of sand in a windstorm."

"I don't argue that." I zip up my workout bag and sling it over my shoulder. "Take me upstairs, Mackenzie. Let's fix the Lion King."

I drop my duffle on the floor by the offices and peer into the three empty rooms. Maxwell's, Andromeda's, and Zuzanna's offices are empty for once. It's is a nice change. For the moment, we've put out all the fires, and people can step away to live their lives.

The two of us head into the detention area of our SITFU home base and find Myra sitting in the leather club chair next to the glass of the supercell.

Garnet is in lion form, sitting in the back corner of the cell with his head stretched over his front paws and his fierce, golden gaze narrowed on us.

"Hey bossman, how are you feeling today?"

The rumbled growl that comes back at me answers that. Okaaay, moving on.

I shift my attention and smile at my book boss and bestie. Squeezing her tightly, I lend her all the strength I can and ease back to give her a once-over. "You're looking better. Did you get some sleep?"

"I did. The miracle of Dora's sleep potion. Swallow one little vial of purple delight and wake up eight hours later feeling a thousand times better."

"Yay, Dora. Purple delight sounds way more fun than the red vials I had to drink to fight off the evil possession of Morgana's grimoire."

"Indeed." Myra steps back and hugs Sloan next. "Thank you both so much for all your efforts to bring Garnet back to me. I'll never forget it. Nor will I be able to repay you."

"Och, I'm only sorry we didn't find anything that would help. I feel like we've failed ye."

She waves that away. "Not your fault. I learned to live without Garnet after Grant died. I can do it again if I have to."

"Wait, am I missing something?" I look between the two of them and feel like someone sucker-punched me in the boob. "I thought we were trying to fix this. Sloan said he has a theory..."

"Myra, my sweet *shona*, look at you." A hunky man with long, purple hair comes into the back with Zxata. He's tall, broad in the shoulders, and has the same cracked skin and vertically slit eyes as Myra and Zxata and all the nymphs. "Your brother told me what you're going through. I came straight here."

"You didn't need to do that, Tarylorn. You're so busy running the realm."

"Didn't need to? Nonsense. I could never be too busy for you, my love." He strides over and gives her a big hug. "How have you been?"

"Until now, quite well."

Tarylorn steps back and takes both her hands in his. "Well, the two of us picked up the pieces after the last time your lion love left you heartbroken. We can do it again. I'm here now, and everything will be fine."

"Who are you?" My mind is spinning.

Myra turns to me and blushes. "Oh, Fi, I'm so sorry. Of course, Fiona and Sloan, this is Tarylorn, the beloved prince of the nymph realm and a very dear friend."

Tarylorn chuckles and the deep tone of his voice fills the space. "A dear friend, am I?"

Myra grins. "All right, Tarylorn is my one that got away. We were together during many of the years Garnet shut me out. He was my safe harbor and my warm embrace in a difficult time."

"A difficult time?" Tarylorn frowns. "The man claimed you with the mating bond of the Moon Called and walked away. It was all I could do to hold you together some nights in the beginning."

"In the beginning," Myra repeats.

His grin widens. "Things certainly improved from that point on."

Garnet's growl grows more intense. His head is up now, and he's no longer pretending he's not listening.

"Och, well, Fi and I will leave the two of you to get caught up. Myra, once again, I'm so sorry fer yer loss. I truly regret my shortcoming in this."

Myra waves that away. "None of this is your fault, sweetie. This is the hand life dealt."

Sloan takes my hand and tilts his head toward the main conference area as he tugs me toward the door. "Let's give them a moment, shall we?"

AUBURN TEMPEST & MICHAEL ANDERLE

I'm still baffled, but I'm getting the gist of things. "Yeah, okay. Myra, we'll check in with you a bit later."

"Okay, duck. Sounds good." Myra might be speaking to me, but her attention stays solely on her ex-lover, Prince Tarylorn.

Sloan steers me out the door, and Zxata comes with us. We exit the containment area and close the door behind us. "In here, luv." Sloan lets us into a room I've never been in before. "How are things looking so far, Lion?"

Anyx adjusts a few dials on a control panel and gestures at the screen up above. We're looking at Myra and Tarylorn and behind them, Garnet's lion pacing the cell. "I think you have something here, Irish."

I blink and look between the three of them. "Am I the only person not in the loop?"

"I'm sorry about that, *a ghra*, but yer close to Garnet and he can read ye. I wanted ye to be confused so our little ruse seemed authentic."

"So, that's not Myra's ex-lover who helped her forget Garnet after they split?"

Zxata shakes his head. "Oh, no, it is. We enlisted him for the cause. He was more than happy to play the part of the man who still holds a burning passion for Myra—because he does. When Tarylorn's father, the nymph king, fell ill, he chose to rule the realm and moved behind the faery glass."

"He gave up his love?"

"No. He simply had to choose between two loves. One for Myra and the other for his people."

"The needs of the many won out," Sloan says. "It's sad, but in this instance, it works to our advantage. Even if Garnet the man has been bespelled to think he desires Anca Romanov, his animal nature claimed Myra and won't like another male sniffing around his female."

I grin. "You think the magic of Moon Called bonding will trump the magic of Eros' calling."

"I do. At least I hope it will. It's honestly the only thing I've found that has any chance of working. Eros might be arrogant, but he's right. His power in the dominion of love is incredibly strong."

I hug Sloan and turn to watch things unfold in the other room. "Myra knows what's happening?"

"Aye, she does. Her only reservation was dragging Tarylorn into the issue and worrying for his safety."

Anyx grins. "If it works, I'll escort him back to his door to the faery realm myself. Garnet won't be let out of that cell until I'm certain the prince is far enough away that his lion won't be able to slay him."

"Yikes. Yeah, let's avoid unneeded prince slaying. Talk about getting the raw end of the deal."

Sloan chuckles. "Tarylorn knows the danger and is still quite keen."

"I see why." I gesture at the two of them cozying up beside the glass cell. "They have chemistry."

Zxata nods. "That's why it'll work. There's no faking the passion the two of them share. If anything can break Anca's hold on Garnet, it's his jealousy about Tarylorn. He knows he opened the door for Myra to love someone else when he pushed her away. He can't stand the man."

"Oh...look how prowly Garnet's getting." I point at the lion pacing in the background. His gaze stays locked on the adoring couple, and if looks could kill, Tarylorn would be flatlining. "They need to turn up the heat."

Sloan chuckles. "Yer enjoying this more than I thought you would. I worried ye'd think I was being intentionally cruel to torture Garnet."

"We *are* torturing Garnet, but I think it's brilliant. His possessiveness will flip him into caveman mode and break the spell—I know it will. Look how his head is down, and his tail is twitching. C'mon, Tarylorn, lay one on her."

AUBURN TEMPEST & MICHAEL ANDERLE

As if he hears my suggestion, Tarylorn, Prince of the Nymphs, gathers Myra's jaw in his hands. With a gentle caress, he pulls her into his kiss.

Garnet roars and swats the glass.

"That's it."

The kiss is long and filled with the longing of two lovers separated by duty. It's lovely and a little sad. I didn't realize Myra's heart got broken twice.

She never mentioned Tarylorn. Then again, I never asked her about anyone other than Garnet. In my mind, seeing them together and mated, I didn't imagine there could be others.

The kiss progresses, and the two of them are swept away by the reunion. Myra's hands clutch the prince's shoulders as he backs her up to pin her against the glass.

Garnet is losing his mind, the lion pacing and scraping his claws across the other side.

Tarylorn's hands are roaming, slowly dropping from her jaw to her sides and down to brush her butt.

Another long, angry roar sounds.

I grin, clapping at the building of sexual tension. "How do we know when it works?"

"We'll know." Anyx grins. "I don't doubt that."

As beautifully as it's working, I'm starting to worry about how far Myra might have to go to get the job done. What's Garnet's last straw? Groping? Kissing?

More?

How committed are we to this experiment? How committed are they? Tarylorn looks like he's all in, but that would pose another problem. Playing the part of seducing Garnet's mate is one thing.

Doing so is quite another.

"Okay, this is starting to feel a little voyeuristic. Should we give them some privacy?"

Anyx scowls at me. "Whether or not Garnet knows that's his

mate, I do. There's no way I'll let things get out of control. I'm his beta and will always protect my alpha's interests."

"There's no need," Zxata says. "Myra knows where she belongs and knows who she loves. This is only for show, I guarantee you."

"I'm glad to hear you say that because either they're two of the best amateur actors ever, or things are truly getting hot and heavy. Look…is that the glass steaming up?"

Zxata makes a face at me and chuckles. "No, it's not steaming up. You're projecting. I know my sister. She knows where to draw the line."

"Uh-huh."

Garnet is wound tight and pacing, roaring, posturing, and smacking the glass. The thundering rattle of a five-hundred-pound lion hitting an immovable wall is hard to describe.

"I'm amazed his tantrum isn't breaking their concentration. They have focus."

Sloan looks at me and rolls his eyes. "Yer ridiculous, Cumhaill."

"No. I have eyes. Look at them and tell me I'm wrong. You can't. They're on fire."

"Then ye have to start realizin' that not everythin' ye see is real."

Whatevs. I give my full attention to the monitor screen as Myra pries her mouth from Tarylorn's and steps to the side. After turning the chair so the back is against the glass cell, she tugs her ex-lover around to the front of the seat and gives his chest a gentle push. "Sit and close your eyes."

Tarylorn sinks into the plush leather chair and lifts his muscled arms to rest on the wide frame at shoulder height. Myra is standing in front of him, facing the cell, and drops to her knees.

From where the camera is, we can see that she's not doing anything lewd in his lap, but between the height of the chair and the height of Tarylorn with his broad shoulders raised, Garnet can't.

"What a sneaky little minx," Zxata says.

Myra ducks out of view, and Tarylorn throws his head back and groans. "By the gods, *shona*, I've missed this. Yeah, that's perfect."

The lion lets out a pee-your-pants-scary roar and flips to stand as a man. He bangs his clenched fists against the glass, his face twisted in a violent rage.

"Get the fuck away from my mate, you motherfucking asshole. I'm going to slit your scrotum, pull your balls out, and shove them down your throat. That's my mate. My wife. *Mine!*"

Anyx straightens and heads toward the door. "That sounds promising. Let me go test the waters. You two stay here."

Garnet's beta leaves and two racing heartbeats later, he appears on the screen in the other room.

"Anyx, secure that motherfucker and let me out. We have a prince to flay."

"On what grounds?"

"Are you blind? He's fucking around with Myra. He's done something to her—drugged her maybe. Myra, stand up and look at me. It's me, baby…your mate. I love you. Whatever he's done, he can't erase that. No one could ever love you the way I do."

I raise my hand and high-five Sloan. Leaning forward, I tap the intercom microphone. "And that, my friends, is a wrap. Welcome back, bossman. We missed you, big guy."

CHAPTER TWENTY-FOUR

Floating on the high of a big win, Sloan, Myra, and I keep Garnet company while Zxata and Anyx escort Tarylorn to safety. Once the prince of nymphs is safely back in the fae realm, they return, and we let the big guy out. It's been trying for everyone, but most of all for Garnet.

He doesn't say much about what happened in those few days he was Anca's puppet, but the hurt and shame are clear in his eyes. He says he remembers everything. He simply didn't have the luxury of free will.

"Do ye think they'll be all right?" Sloan walks me out to the elevator corridor.

"I do. Garnet isn't one to play the part of anyone's puppet. That's a blow to his ego as a man and a leader. What's worse will be the blow to his honor as a mate. Did you know that even while they were apart, he never took another lover? Myra is his whole heart."

"He told ye that? I have a hard time imaginin' him barin' his soul to ye about his lovers."

I wave that away. "No. I saw it when I healed his pain about Grant and cleared his emotions."

"Well, that might still be the case. Maybe his matin' bond kept him behind the fine line of infidelity even with Eros' influence upon him."

I shrug. "I don't know…and honestly, I don't want to know. What happened was absolute Cupidity. It wasn't real. Myra won't hold it against him."

"Och, no, I didn't think she would. I think it'll be Garnet who flays himself."

I wrap my arms around my guy and hug him. "Enough sad talk. Let's be happy. Garnet's back and they've been through worse. They'll figure this out."

Sloan kisses the top of my head. "Aye, I'm sure that's true."

When I step back, I point up. "Next stop, eleventh floor. Greek orgies, gluttonous feasts, and drunken revelry."

Sloan laces his fingers with mine and grins. "Yes, ma'am."

The two of us take form in the open-concept loft, and I call, "Hellooo, the house. Are you here, Tarzan?"

"Jane! Stay there. We'll be out in two minutes."

His response comes from the VR room, so I'm not sure whether the delay is a game thing or an indiscretion thing. If it's the second, I'm glad they were in there and not out here in the living room.

"I wish there was a door to knock on for this apartment," I whisper.

Sloan chuckles. "This apartment isn't even part of the building. Where would the door go?"

"I don't know, but I've seen the nakedness of this loft enough for three lifetimes."

"Hello, guests." Dionysus comes out of the game room. He has black jeans on and nothing else. Yeah, the barefoot, bare-chested, post-coital swagger is a good look for him. "Welcome. What a lovely surprise."

I chuckle. "I texted twice and would've knocked, but… " I gesture around the room. "There's no door. I was saying to Sloan that maybe you should create a portal room with a doorbell, so people don't interrupt your privacy."

Dionysus chuckles. "I don't care about privacy, Jane. In my world, friends are welcome to join no matter what they interrupt."

I chuckle. "How about for our privacy then?"

He nods. "I can do that, but I still want you to feel free to enter unannounced."

"We'll see. Now, the reason we came—"

Suede walks out of the VR room next and thankfully, is fully dressed. "Hey, guys. How's Garnet?"

Dionysus gestures at the couches, so the four of us go over and sit.

"Garnet's better," I say. "We broke Eros' spell, and he's once again hopelessly in love with Myra. She took him home. I'm sure some family time will help soothe some of the rough edges."

"Oh, that's great news," Suede says.

Dionysus shakes his head and grins. "You two never cease to amaze me. I swear there's nothing you can't do once Fi digs her heels in."

I laugh. "Thank you?"

"What about the Romanov woman?" Dionysus asks. "We heard about the attack in the Distillery District from Nikon. How did that end up?"

"Between Xavier and us, we think we've decimated the Romanov syndicate. Last I heard, they slunk back to Europe with their tails between their legs."

Sloan frowns. "Well, Andrei, at least. We found footage of him boarding a freighter and leaving with a large crew shortly after the battle. Whether that was to regroup or retreat, we've yet to see."

"Then we'll hope it's the latter," Suede says.

I nod and raise my hand. "Preach."

Dionysus shifts closer to Suede and puts his arm around her.

"In the spirit of good news, I want you two to be the first to know, Suede and I are officially dating."

"Dating? Wow, that is news," I say.

"Congratulations," Sloan says. "We wish you both all the happiness the world can offer."

Dionysus grins. "I've been thinking a lot about what I want and who I am and the mistakes I've made in the past. In all the millennia, I've never had a girlfriend and decided it's time. Suede was kind enough to say yes."

Suede chuckles. "Not that I had much choice. Being with him is like getting sucked into dicksand. The deeper I get, the faster I succumb."

Dionysus nods. "That's poetic."

I scratch my head, unsure how to respond to that. "That's great. It'll be a big change for you to settle down and be a one-woman man—"

Both of them look at me and burst out laughing.

I check in with Sloan. Did I say something funny?

Dionysus gets control of his laughter and waves his finger. "Now you're talking crazy. I said we're dating, not dying. Elves and Greek gods are both hedonistic. We're still going to live life and have sexy parties and drunken fun, but we'll do it together—as a couple."

Sloan pats my knee and is quicker to respond than me. "However ye plan to share yer lives, is yer business. We're happy fer ye."

"True story. You do you and live your lives." When I stand, I step around the hippo coffee table to hug them. "I'm happy for you," I say to Suede before moving to hug Dionysus. "It takes a lot of courage to let someone into your heart. I'm proud of you, Tarzan."

Dionysus hugs me and kisses my forehead. "Thanks, Red. I'm proud of myself too."

I step back to take Sloan's hand and give them a little wave.

"We only stopped in to tell you about Garnet so you can let Eros know that all's well that ends well."

"Assuming he cares," Sloan says.

Dionysus shrugs. "He might not, but we do."

I blow them a kiss, and Sloan *poofs* us home.

The two of us materialize at the back door and take off our shoes. I'm about to take my duffle down to start the laundry when Sloan reaches for the handles. "Allow me. I've left my textbooks lyin' around in my apothecary room and need to clean up. I'll start the load."

"He's smart. He's beautiful. *Annnd* he does laundry. You are a keeper, Sloan Mackenzie."

He laughs and heads down the basement steps. "Glad ye think so."

I do.

I take the opt-out on laundry duty and head into the kitchen to see who's milling around. Kevin is making afternoon snacks and setting up a tray.

He and Calum have been running ragged for the past two days taking care of the four-year-old otterkie orphan. "How's our Bizzy girl today?"

Kevin rolls his eyes and laughs. "She's a wild one, but she's great. Calum bought one of those inflatable pools, and we're filling it up on the back deck. It's only cold hose water so far, and we can't get her out of it."

"Calum's back there with her?"

Kev picks up the serving tray by the handles and starts to walk. "Yeah. Come out and see."

I follow Kev to the back and get the door. Calum's sitting in a camp chair with Daisy on his lap and next to him are Aiden and

Jackson. All of them are watching the little river otter swish and swirl around in the blue rubber pool.

"Hey, Bizzy, Fi's here," Calum says.

Bizzy surfaces, blinks her little round eyes at me, and goes right back to diving.

"You're not swimming, Jackson?" I grab a camp chair from the storage bin and open it. "It's a hot and sunny day. Why don't you get your swimsuit?"

"It's too cold, Auntie Fi. Daddy says only polar bears and otters swim in water that cold."

I laugh and accept the blue Freezie Aiden offers me. "That's because Daddy is spoiled. When we were kids, all of us used to run through the sprinkler and Daddy refused. He said it was too cold and missed all the fun."

Aiden shakes his head and laughs. "No. I was older than the rest of you and wise enough not to do it."

"Sure, let's go with that." Calum laughs.

"Here, buddy, let me see if I can help." I hand Kev my Freezie and place my hands in the water. *"Water Warmth."*

Summoning my druid power, I connect with the natural energy of the water and warm the molecules. Keeping in mind that river water isn't too warm, I only warm it enough to take the chill off and not as warm as I'd like it if I were getting in.

Bizzy must recognize the change because she pops her head up and shifts back to a naked little girl wearing her fur pelt like one of those hooded bath towels.

"Hey, Bizzy girl," Calum says. "Fi warmed the water a little so Jackson can come in and splash with you. Is that all right?"

"Come swim." Bizzy swishes her hands in the water. "Jackson swim too."

She doesn't wait for a response. While Jackson rushes across the deck and into the other house to get changed, Bizzy wraps her pelt around herself and shifts back into an otter. Dipping under the surface, she begins another circuit of cutting through the water.

"Wow, I guess you never have to worry about her being unattended near the water," I say.

"Nope. I think swimming is an inherited skill. She's a natural."

The four of us sit there, mesmerized by the little girl. "Any word yet on what happened?" I point at the pool.

All three of them shake their heads.

"Well, she's safe and happy, and now that Garnet's back to being Garnet, I'm sure he'll figure out what happened."

"Garnet's fixed?" Calum asks. "Since when? How'd that happen?"

I fill them in and finish the story as Emmet comes outside looking like he might throw up. He stops at the edge of the pool and studiously examines the palm of his hand. "Fi? Can I talk to you privately for a minute?"

The tension on his face twists my insides, and I stand. "Yeah, sure. What's wrong?"

"Nothing. Not really. I just need to talk to you. Can we go into the grove for a minute and have a chat?"

I scan the expressions of Kev, Calum, and Aiden and they look as confused and concerned as I feel.

Okay, so they don't know either.

Drawing a deep breath, I force air through tight lungs and try not to panic. The two of us step off the deck and over into the shade of the grove. The loss of heat sends a shiver down my spine.

"What's wrong, Em? Are you okay? Is it Ciara? What's happened?"

Emmet turns to me, and the moisture building in his eyes does me in. I blink against the sting of my own eyes glassing up as my sinuses tingle with emotion. "We're fine, Fi." He swipes his palms on his shorts. "We're amazing actually. That's part of the reason we need to talk."

"What does that mean?"

He walks farther into the grove and leans his shoulder against the bark of a big elm tree. "It means she and I are going to move out. Well…across the road is more accurate. Tad's place is too big for only him, and he's still going through the loss of his family. He invited us to take one of the other rooms, and we accepted."

The finality of that knocks the wind out of me. It's not even a discussion. It's a done deal.

"But why? You have a room with us, and things have been good, haven't they?"

"They've been great…"

"Buuuut?"

He looks at me and sighs. "Ciara's not comfortable living with you and Sloan. There's history there, and she's always worried about saying the wrong thing or overstepping or upsetting the balance. She thinks it's weird living with an ex and doesn't love it."

"Sloan and I had the same conversation when you first brought her here, so I get it, but I thought things have been pretty good. We haven't been fighting, and I've really tried to include her and be supportive."

Emmet waves that away. "You've been great, Fi, better than I expected. It's not that. It's just…she practically hides in the basement or our room. Being at Tad's the past couple of days has been a huge improvement. She's been her normal, mouthy, sarcastic self and it hit me how much she's been trying not to make waves. When I thought about it, I realized you were doing the same thing."

"I want you to be happy, Em. I mean that. If Ciara Doyle is the woman of your dreams, I want the two of you to be as happy as two people can be."

Emmet nods. "I know that…so you must understand, right? You've had the same reservations. It would be easier on you too, wouldn't it?"

I blink at the moisture brimming my eyes and fight not to cry. "I love having you live with me. We've always been together. Hell, we shared a room until I was fifteen."

"I know. It'll be weird, and I'll miss seeing your face every morning at breakfast, but even if it wasn't Ciara and I found someone and got married, I'd have to move out sometime, right?"

I nod. "I suppose so."

"So, yeah, Tad asked. We talked, and I want her to feel one hundred percent comfortable being herself in our home. This is our year to make a go of it, and it's kinda my job as her partner to set it right, don't you think?"

I swallow, part of me hating everything about this and another part of me relieved that if he has to go, at least he's only moving into Tad's. They'll be close enough to be part of our lives but far enough that I don't have to be on guard all the time. Ciara isn't the only one walking on eggshells and trying to keep the peace.

"I can't say I'm not sad and disappointed—I am. It's always been you and me against the world, and I don't want that to change. I know we both have significant others now, but you're my rock, Em... You've always been my safe place."

We can't hold back the tears threatening to break free on both sides of this conversation anymore.

Emmet swipes his cheeks and steps in to wrap me in his arms. "I'll always be your safe place, Fi, and you'll always be mine. Me living across the road won't change that and us having significant others won't change that either."

It's silly to get so worked up about him moving across the road. It's just...Emmet has always been mine.

"Adulting is hard." I wipe my cheeks.

Emmet barks a laugh and wipes his. "Yeah. I've dreaded this conversation. I need you to know it's not anything against you and Irish. We love you guys, and you've been so good to us. We just need a clean slate to start our life."

I hug him again and don't step back this time. "You'll still hang out all the time and empty my fridge, right?"

"You better believe it. Leaving Sloan's cooking is as devastating as leaving you."

I laugh. "Thanks. At least I rank up there with chicken tetrazzini."

"You do. You definitely do."

I step back and draw a deep breath. "When are you moving out?"

"Right away. With Tad's wayfarer help, it's a matter of a few *poofs* back and forth to settle us. Then, Kev and Calum can use our room for Bizzy or any of the other foster kids that might come their way."

"Don't let that be a concern. We have four bedrooms. We have a spare room for foster kids without you needing to move out."

Emmet shakes his head. "Nah, it's not that. It's so Ciara can figure out who she is and what she wants to do in her new life. I want her to be happy, you know?"

I breathe in deep and exhale a long breath. "I know, Em. You're right. She needs to be able to relax and become who she's supposed to be. You're a good partner."

Em grins. "I knew you'd understand. Thanks, Fi."

I turn back toward the house and start walking. As much as I don't want to see Emmet go, he's right. It would've happened sooner or later. If he's going to make a go of it with Ciara, her needs have to come first.

And who are we kidding...I'm a bit relieved.

CHAPTER TWENTY-FIVE

The fam jam hangs out in the backyard for most of the day. The kids swim, Emmet and Ciara portal their stuff across the road, and I try not to dwell on what I'm losing but instead focus on what I have.

Sloan and I are building a life. We're in love, and it's good. Garnet is back with his family where he belongs. Toronto is safe. Everyone I love is healthy and happy—except Dillan.

Once his situation with Evangeline settles, I have a feeling everything will be good on that front too. After all, everything happens for a reason, and Dillan didn't give away his heart for the first time simply to have it ripped out and crushed.

Everything will work out.

By the time the sun has set and the pervasive heat of the day has faded, everyone disperses, and I'm left in the backyard, sitting in my camp chair, staring at the stars.

"Are ye comin' in, *a ghra?*" Sloan loads the serving tray with empty beer bottles and snack bowls and heads to the back door.

I draw a deep breath, not ready to face Emmet's empty bedroom. "I'm right behind you. Give me a few more minutes."

"Do ye want me to stay out here with ye?"

I shake that off. "No. I'm fine. I'm soaking it all in. It was a good day, wasn't it?"

He smiles. "One of the best. Yer family is wonderful. I treasure every moment we spend with them."

"Thanks, hotness."

He shifts the weight of the tray, opens the door, and leaves me to enjoy the warm July night.

I'm still sitting there, soaking it all in when my scalp tingles, and I open my eyes. The tall, dark, and dangerous male standing at the tree line of my grove makes most people nervous. Not me.

"Hey, bossman. Pull up a lawn chair and take a load off. How are you?"

Garnet strides out from the shadows and claims one of the abandoned chairs. He sits back and sighs. "I've been better, Fi, but I've also been worse."

"Yeah. I'm with you."

The two of us sit like that, not speaking for a few minutes before he breaks the silence. "I want to thank you and Sloan again for everything you did. I've been trying to wrap my head around what happened and how it all went so wrong."

I shift my gaze from the night sky to study him. There's no way the darkness in his expression is solely coming from the late hour.

Our Lion King feels haunted tonight.

"Did you come up with any life-changing epiphanies you want to share?"

He sits forward and absently grabs a Super Soaker off the grass. Turning it in his hand, he strokes the long plastic barrel and gives it a once-over. "It strikes me that if I'm this fucked up and my life is in this much of a shamble after a few days, it would've been much worse for the city, my pride, and especially my family if it had been weeks or months. I owe you big for that."

I hate the pain in his voice. I hate it even more because I know there's nothing I can do to make it better for him. "You can pay me back by doing whatever it takes to smooth things over with Myra. Put a smile back on her face again."

"That's my plan."

"Then we're good. Whatever happened while you were under Anca's influence isn't your fault. It wasn't you. I know that, and she knows that."

"Then you're better off than me because I'm fighting to believe that."

"Believe it. The real Garnet, if he had a choice, wouldn't have attacked me, wouldn't have sold me out to Anca, and certainly wouldn't have allowed that bitch to order him around like a prized pet. Those freaking arrows pack a wallop. That wasn't you."

Garnet stands up and sets the water gun on the chair. "That's generous of you. Anyx mentioned I drew blood in the struggle when you took me down. I'm sorry."

I wave that away. "Bygones. I'm sure you've wanted to sink your teeth in me many times and resisted. Consider this your free shot."

He chuckles and shakes his head. "You're a giant pain in my ass most days, true, but you're right...you're also the tiny mouse that pulls the thorns from my paws."

I smile, remembering how vehemently he rejected that analogy when I first suggested it. "I wish we'd taken her down for you."

"Me too. I don't think I'll get a full night's sleep until that bitch is beheaded and burned to a crisp."

"Something to put on your wish list for Santa."

He smiles. "I'd probably have more luck enlisting a djinn for a wish like that."

"Ha! It so happens we now have a djinn on the Team Trouble payroll."

"That might be considered an abuse of power."

I chuckle. "Yeah, maybe."

The two of us fall quiet for a moment, then Garnet gestures for me to stand. I do as asked and he shocks the hell out of me by stepping in and hugging me. "If you tell anyone I broke down and got personal with you, I'll deny it."

I laugh, returning the powerful squeeze. "I'm so freaking thankful you're back, and you're you, and I didn't fry you when I took you down."

He steps back and squeezes my shoulder. "You did what you needed to do to get the job done. I won't ever fault you for that. You and I are the same that way. We're survivors."

"Yeah, we are." I draw a deep breath, ready to face Emmet's empty room and a life where my closest brother has higher priorities than me.

As he said, that's the way it's supposed to be.

Garnet nods. "It's late. Get to bed. We have a big day tomorrow undoing the damage I caused."

"I'll be there first thing."

He chuckles. "By first thing, you mean..."

"Ten-thirty? Quarter to eleven?"

"Sounds good. See you then."

Garnet flashes off, and I think about abandoning the mess until tomorrow. I decide against it. Sheet lightning is flashing over the lake, and the smell of ozone is sharp in the breeze. If it rains, I'd rather the chairs and lawn games were tucked into the storage bin and not out getting soaked.

I finish putting the bean bags back in the sack and tuck them and the corn hole board into the bin with the water guns.

I gather the last couple of chairs and am lowering the lid to the deck bin when my shield fires to life.

"This is my night for uninvited guests. Come out and show yourself."

Anca Romanov steps around the trees over by the back gate and starts across the lawn. *"I'm* unwanted? You intruded into my business. You ruined everything."

There's no way she came here alone. I just don't know how many men she has left. I release my fae vision and scan the backyard.

Cat crap on a cracker.

Still quite a few. Six...seven...maybe more.

My mind buzzes with a million things all at once. There are vampires at my home. I don't think they can get inside and hurt the kids—our warding is extensive—but they can likely burn our homes down and force us out. Do vampires start fires? Maybe not.

Maybe they only want to talk.

By the look on Anca's face, I don't think so.

I reach out to call for help. *Bruin, we have vampire hostiles in the backyard. I need you to sound the alarm and get out here to help me.*

On my way.

Dart...there's trouble, buddy.

I know. They reek of fettered death.

Bruin's rounding up the family. Wait and see if they engage. I don't want to scare them off. If they attack, no one gets away this time. No one lives to return another day to threaten the family.

Understood.

"—Isn't that right, Lady Druid?"

My attention snaps back to the standoff in the yard. "I'm sorry, what? I wasn't listening."

"Weren't listening? Vampires surround house. We come to settle score. And you don't listen?"

"Sorry. You're not that interesting, and my mind wandered. What were you saying?"

Anca surges forward, and I call my armor forth and Birga to my hand. *"Bestial Strength."*

I launch off the deck and palm thrust her with everything I

have. The impact's force takes her off her feet and rockets her backward thirty feet to land on her ass in the cool grass.

"How dare you," she sputters and gets to her feet.

"We've been over that. You wildly overestimate your abilities within the empowered world. You force yourself into situations with the misguided belief that because your family is powerful in the human world, you're at the top of the heap as a vampire as well. You're not."

It might not be the wisest course of action to piss off a vampire gang leader here to kill me, but the conversation is giving Bruin the time he needs to round up the troops, and it's cathartic for me.

"If you're honest with yourself, you realized it. Otherwise, you wouldn't have targeted Garnet to take him out of play. You did that because you're aware he, the Lakeshore Guild, and a great many of our Toronto empowered citizens can stop you from getting your way."

I've been expecting the back door to swing open behind me, but that hasn't happened.

Did Bruin get sidetracked?

Um...hello? I'm out here chatting up a vampire crime boss. A little help?

"I target Garnet because Lion is part of Galina's death—no other reason."

"Then why seduce him? Why not kidnap him and try to take him out?"

"I don't answer to you. I am Anca Romanov."

Fi, her men are fanning out and positioning in the grove. What do you want me to do?

Hold your position, buddy. I'm waiting on Bruin and the others.

What's taking so long?

A very good question.

A gentle breeze swirls around me and lifts my hair, caressing my cheek. *There are fourteen hostiles, and I told the boys where they are. Sloan posted it, and Nikon is inviting Xavier and Garnet to join the fun. In the meantime, yer army is ready to deploy.*

Thanks, Bruin. I twirl Birga in my hand and exhale a long breath of anxiety. "Okay, so I'll be totally transparent with you. My defensive squad has assembled, and backup is coming."

Anca laughs. "Nice try, little girl."

"I'm serious. This is your chance to leave Toronto. If you agree, we'll escort you to the harbor and put you onto a freighter like the one your uncle took home. If you insist on a fight, your existence will end tonight."

Her laughter rings in the night, and I throw up a veil of privacy. "Stupid. Little. Girl."

"Don't say I didn't warn you."

Anca makes a sweeping gesture with her hand and the night explodes into a mass scramble. Bruin materializes at the back gate and attacks from the rear. Aiden and Dillan race out of the house next door as Calum and Sloan race out of ours.

"Entangle." I reach out to the growth in the grove. *"Grasping Vines."*

My vines aren't supposed to defeat Anca's men, simply to tangle their limbs and slow them down while my brothers and the fam jam crew do their thing.

The roar of lions signals Garnet's arrival with his pride, and a moment after that, Xavier blurs past.

The gang's all here.

"You meddlesome bitch." Yuri raises a submachine gun at me. "I should've killed you in tunnel."

"And miss all this?" I grip Birga and run straight at him. My attack throws him off because he hesitates for a moment before he realizes I'm about to take him down and starts firing.

My armor keeps the bullets from penetrating my flesh, but that doesn't mean the little fuckers don't still sting.

They do.

I don't let that slow me down though. I race full speed at the

Romanian, ram my spear into his chest, and try my best to get that marble spear tip straight through to the back.

It's remarkably difficult.

Still, the two of us go down in a glorious tangle of vampire agony, and I'm finally able to vent some of my hostility. I hated being his hostage. I hated running away from the fight at the penthouse. And I hated being the lookout at Caribana.

Finally, I can get my fight on.

I do.

Can I come out now?

Yeah, but don't swallow. Vampires give you a tummy ache. And don't chomp Xavier's men.

Promise.

Anca might've been itching to meet Bruin to try to avenge Galina, but she never got to see Dart when we were battling at the Enercare Centre. Here though—in our yard, with glamors in place and no exposure risk—here he can get his dragon groove on.

When he races from the trees, I'm facing the grove with Yuri impaled on the end of my spear. He doesn't see my blue boy coming and has no chance to defend.

Dart chomps my opponent's head off and spits it on the grass before going for the vamp Calum and Emmet are facing off against.

I chuckle and catch Anca's look of horror.

"Oh, didn't Garnet mention the dragon that lives in my back yard?"

I recognize her decision to retreat the moment the idea flashes across her expression. "No, you don't." I race to intercept her escape. "You refused to leave when I urged you to. That ship has sailed."

Anca's eyes flash red, and she hisses at me, her canines long and threatening. She's as feral as any wild animal, and I admit, her frantic frustration gives me a warm fuzzy feeling inside.

The two of us are about to face off when Garnet's lion arrives, and I step back.

He needs this more than I do.

I scan the scene and smile at Dillan's fighting partner. Eva is back, and she's smiling from ear to ear...and so is he.

Aw, so sweet.

A weighty *thunk* beside me has me dodging another head, and I see there are four now and Dart's trotting off to collect another. This is worse than a cat dropping dead moles on the back step.

What will I do with a collection of vampire heads? I make a face and press my hand against the ground. *"Mold Earth."* I make a small pit in the ground and work on making it a fire pit. *"Shape Stone."*

When that's taken care of, I guide the heads into the pit with my foot and Birga and start cleaning up the back yard. Vampires are only truly ended once they're beheaded and burned.

Looks like we're having a backyard bonfire.

"Here. Another for your collection." Garnet drops Anca's head into the pit and her body as well.

He's standing before me as a man, but the golden glow of his eyes and the massive claws protruding from the end of his fingers tell me his lion is still very much in the driver's seat right now.

"Dart, come here for a sec, buddy." My blue boy trots over with another head dangling from his teeth. I point at the pit, and he drops it in. "I thought you might like the honor of starting the fire."

Dart grins, inhales a deep breath, and blows a steady stream of blue fire into the pit. As the fire takes hold, the night dies down once again, and we've won the battle.

"It's over," I say to Garnet as Anca's body goes up in flame. "Now you and your lion can sleep. She'll never hold anything over you or anyone else ever again."

Garnet's attention stays locked on the flames as they consume the woman who stole his free will and tried to alter the course of his life. "I need to go. My lion is wild and needs to be set free. I'm sorry to leave you with such a mess."

"Don't worry. Go. Take care of yourself and your lion. We're fine." The words are still tumbling out of my mouth, but he's gone.

Burning vampires isn't like burning a human body on a pyre or even a massive log. Being dead and dried out already, vampires crumble into ash almost immediately. It makes cleanup quick and easy.

It also allows us to move on to more important things…like Evangeline's return.

"So, tell us." I wave to hurry her up. "What happened? Are you being recalled? Are you allowed to stay? We've been so worried."

Eva grins, claps, and squeals like a kid. "Death said my emotional connections to your brother and your family and friends have destroyed my neutrality as a reaper, and I'm no good to him or the dominion any longer."

I swallow and sweep my gaze over to Dillan. "Why are we celebrating Death kicking you out of your place in the Choir of Angels?"

"Because Death said if I'm so interested in fighting alongside your family, he's transferring me to another dominion."

"Oh? What dominion is that?"

Eva straightens and throws her shoulders back. "You are looking at the newest guardian in training."

"Guardian?"

"Yes. I'm going to be a guardian angel—*your* guardian angel, to be precise. Your family is my test case. I have a new destiny now. All I have to do is keep all of you safe until the Winter Solstice, and I'll get my wings."

"They took your wings?"

Eva blinks. "Sort of. It's less about me *getting* my wings and more about me getting the correct color of wings. All dominions of wing-bearing angels have different colors. I lost the right to have bronze wings and haven't earned the right to have gold, so for now, they're white."

She flexes her arms and a rush of power snaps in the air. Her wings appear and expand behind her. They're no longer the stunning bronze they were before, but now are the purest white I could ever imagine.

"So, we're your charges, and you have to safeguard us until December."

"Yes. When I stood before the Archangels, they said there is a dire event on the horizon, and it's my duty now to ensure your family lives long enough to face it."

I cast a glance to gauge how the others are taking that statement. "I'm not gonna lie, I kinda feel like Tessie, the prize pig. Like the Powers That Be want us fed and fattened up until the Culling."

Calum chuckles. "She said nothing about fattening us up. She said she'll keep us safe. Which, who are we kidding? We can use all the help we can get."

Dillan shrugs. "I don't give a shit what the implications are. The gist of it is, Eva can stay and if things work out, she has a new destiny and can stay indefinitely."

"Dillan's right," Sloan says. "We don't need to worry about why the Choir of Angels is chimin' in. We have months to worry about the implications."

"Absolutely," Emmet says. "It's amazing news."

I nod. "It is. We're all so excited for both of you. Congratulations, Eva, and welcome to the Cumhaill chaos."

EPILOGUE

"How are ye holdin' up, *a ghra?*"

Sloan grips my hips and steadies me despite the sway of the deck beneath my bare feet. I focus on the horizon and bite back the burn of bile. "Whoever invented sangria shuffleboard needs to die. If I have to take another penalty shot, I'll be puking over the rail."

Sloan sends me a rush of healing energy. "Then ye better keep the puck in play this round. Yer brothers are kickin' yer ass, luv. What happened to yer natural ability in all sports?"

I glare over my shoulder. "Shuffleboard on the deck of a yacht is not a sport."

He grins. "Yer brothers disagree. They argued that it has a puck and ye keep score."

"Irrelevant."

"C'mon, Fi," Emmet shouts at the other end of the board. "You're holding us up. If you don't take your turn, you'll get penalized for delay of game. That's a two shot penalty, isn't it, D?"

Dillan grins behind the bar and sets up two shot glasses. "Two shot penalty coming up."

My throat tightens at the suggestion. "Why did we agree to this?"

Sloan chuckles. "I believe yer exact words were 'It's his birthday. He gets to pick his party.'"

"Blech, I take it back. If Emmet wants to live out Jack Sparrow fantasies, he should do it on his dime."

"Yer cranky because ye've overdone it and the heat and sun are compoundin' the problem."

"How about we bail and you *poof* us home? I'll make it worth your while."

Sloan barks a laugh. "Empty promises. Yer in no shape to make it worth my while. If I portal ye home, ye'll be kneelin' at the porcelain altar fer the rest of the night, and ye'll wake up tomorrow disappointed ye missed the fun."

Stupid FOMO.

"Yeah, let me know when we get to the fun part."

"*Meeeeh*, time's up. You're out, Cumhaill. Two minutes in the penalty box for delay of game."

"Well, crap. Do me proud, Greek." I hand Nikon my shooting stick and give everyone at the other end of the board the finger as I head to the bar to accept my punishment.

"Welcome, welcome." Dillan grins from ear to ear. Eva is propped on the first stool, and the two of them have been making eyes at each other all weekend. "Come take your medicine like a good girl."

I stare at the clear liquid and my stomach protests. "I can't shoot vodka right now, D. I'm barely hanging on."

He winks at me. "Trust me, baby girl. I know when you've had enough."

I pick up the shot glass and give it a sniff. Nothing. After taking a tiny sip, I relax a little and toss it back.

"Oh, there she goes." Emmet and Kevin cheer from the playing field.

I pick up the second glass and repeat the process, swallowing the ice-cold water. "Thanks, D."

"Don't mention it…no, seriously, don't. They'll make me pay some horrible price."

"Your secret is safe with me." The boat takes a gentle course change, and the shift in motion redirects the tropical sea breeze into my face. "Oh, that's better."

Dionysus and Suede jog up from the lower deck and give me a wary look.

"Are you okay, Red?" Dionysus asks.

"Better now that I'm out of the sun and kicked out of sangria shuffleboard. Watch out. Emmet and Kevin are a freakishly talented team."

Dionysus waggles his brow. "Oh, I think I can hold my own. What's sangria made from, after all?"

I chuckle. "Yeah, go be the god of wine. I left my partner in the lurch." Leaning away from the bar, I shout, "Substitution. Tarzan is now playing the part of Jane in sangria shuffleboard."

Emmet frowns and whispers something to Kevin. They debate that for a moment and nod. "We accept the substitution. Nikon, you have a new partner. Feel free to take a moment to strategize."

I'm off the hook. Thank the gods. "Sloan, take me to our stateroom. I'm going to hurl."

"As ye wish." Sloan *poofs* us below deck and straight into the washroom.

"Bless you." I take the three steps toward the toilet and drop to my knees. "I'm so over this. Why do I let my brothers suck me into drinking like a teenaged idiot?"

Before he has time to answer, I double over, and my stomach ejects all the fluid it no longer wants.

Life becomes unpleasant for a while, and Sloan holds my hair back until my self-inflicted agony ends. When the world stops spinning, I sit back on my heels and accept the cool facecloth he offers me.

While I press that against my forehead, I fight the urge to go for another round.

"Knock, knock." Ciara's voice carries through the door of our stateroom and Sloan goes out to see what that's about.

I pull the cloth off my face and shiver. Between the loss of sun and the puking and the cold cloth, I need to be wearing more than a two-piece bathing suit.

"Hey, there," Ciara says, coming in with a glass of water and a tablet in her hand. "I brought a few extra remedy pills to the party if ye want one."

"The one you gave me the night I took on Riordan McNiff in the shot-for-shot pissing contest?"

"The very same. If yer done with yer buzz, I mean. I'm not tryin' to rush ye."

I laugh at that, accept the nausea remedy, and swallow it without a second thought. "I need to start saying no...especially when the world can fall apart at any moment."

"Speaking of which...have ye had a chance to speak to Tad in the past hour or so?"

I get up, set the facecloth on the side of the sink, and make my way out of the washroom. "Beyond shouting drunken banter from the gaming deck, no. Why? What's up with Tad?"

"The guards back home called him a bit ago. They wanted to apologize fer the error in accusin' him of killin' Riordan. It seems the bastard was seen around Dublin and word got back to them."

"Riordan's in Dublin?"

She lifts a bare shoulder. "Riordan or Mingin or whomever he is at the moment."

I grab my wrap off the end of the bed and shrug it on. "What does that mean? Was Melanippe with him? Where was he seen?"

"Och, I can't tell ye much more than I have. Tad got the call.

They said the investigation against him has been closed. He's rather upset about the entire exchange."

I nod, the buzz of my poor judgment fading fast. "Okay. Well, I suppose it was bound to happen with the Culling creeping closer every day."

"How do ye want to handle it?" Sloan asks.

I think about that for a moment. "Let me talk to Tad. Then I'll text Samuel, Quon Shen, and Ahren to see where they are and what they know. If Mingin is still possessing Riordan, we need to figure out what he and Melanippe are up to."

THANK YOU!

Thank you for reading *A Destiny Unlocked*. While the story is fresh in your mind, and as a favor to Michael and me, please click HERE and tell other readers what you thought.

A quick star rating and/or even one sentence can mean so much to readers deciding whether to try a book, series, or a new-to-them author.

Thank you.

If you loved it, continue with the Chronicles of an Urban Druid and claim your copy of book thirteen:

A United Front.

NEXT IN SERIES

The story continues with *A United Front*, available now at Amazon and Kindle Unlimited.

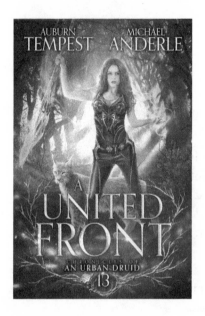

Claim your copy today!

AUTHOR NOTES - AUBURN TEMPEST

WRITTEN OCTOBER 22, 2021

Thank you for reading *A Destiny Unlocked*, and if you're reading this, the extra time and attention you've taken to turn these last few pages.

I've had some fans worry that all (almost all) of my books are free to readers because they're in the Kindle Unlimited program. They've offered me money and gift cards and felt guilty about not paying me for my stories.

Did you know when KU readers get a "free" book, authors get paid by you turning the page? Yep, Amazon tracks how many pages get viewed and pays us based on how much you read. S'all good.

You scrolling to the very end is a win-win for everyone. You get a chance to read mine and Michael's mental musings and we make a living bringing you the stories we love to tell.

So, thank you for staying with us until the end.

With book twelve live, the Chronicles of the Urban Druid

series has now become my longest-running series to date. I attribute the longevity to the encouragement of the readers wanting more, the characters being such a fun and dynamic group of goofballs, and the joy of writing the story and handing it to Michael and his LMBPN staff to finish the buff and polish. Handing it off while the story's energy is flowing is a treat and gets me back to the keyboard faster.

A huge "thanks" goes to the awesome LMBPN Team Trouble: the amazeballs JIT readers who ensure continuity, the incredibly skilled Tracey and Lynne for the edits, the organizational wizardry of Kelly, Steve, and Grace for the admin support, the stunning covers from the talented Moonchild Ljilja, the dedication to perfection of Judith for keeping the contract stuff uncomplicated, and Michael for his awesome, encouraging, Michaelness.

It really does take a village. This just happens to be a very fun village to belong to. Yay team!

Blessed be,
Auburn Tempest

AUTHOR NOTES - MICHAEL ANDERLE

WRITTEN NOVEMBER 30, 2021

Thank you for not only reading this story but these author notes as well.

This is the second set of author notes I'm writing this morning, and the more touching of the two for sure.

The first one had my collaborator tossing me under the bus. I have to admit, those wheels hurt as they roll over you! I won't be so ugly as to mention WHO did that.

Cough rhymes with "Bavid Deers" *Cough*.

So I'll throw all my appreciation to Auburn and the sweet message about how she enjoys writing the "goofball group" of characters we all have grown so fond of and the LMBPN team she works with.

Although I can't exactly say what she means by "Michaelness," even though I looked it up. There wasn't a definition.

Auburn is so easy to work with she is like that breath of fresh air when you have had a bad day. If Auburn was your first-born child, you would try to have another child fast so you didn't miss the magic that made the first child so sweet.

Of course, we all know you would have a little Beelzebub next, but that's not Auburn's fault. That's just life.

When you meet Auburn (which I suggest consider doing at the next 20Booksto50K Author event in 2022 in Las Vegas (November 2022—check it out), you will find a woman who seems to only ever smile.

I got a chance to meet her husband at this year's 20Books event, and the two of them are a great pair.

I'm honored to work with her.

There is a chance that the author-bug is a genetic trait and part of her family's DNA. I hope to find out and if so, publish another individual from her creative—if a bit over-the-top—clan.

Have a good week, or weekend and talk to you in the next story!

Ad Aeternitatem,

Michael Anderle

ABOUT AUBURN TEMPEST

Auburn Tempest is a multi-genre novelist giving life to Urban Fantasy, Paranormal, and Sci-Fi adventures. Under the pen name, JL Madore, she writes in the same genres but in full romance, sexy-steamy novels. Whether Romance or not, she loves to twist Alpha heroes and kick-ass heroines into chaotic, hilarious, fast-paced, magical situations and make them really work for their happy endings.

Auburn Tempest lives in the Greater Toronto Area, Canada with her dear, wonderful hubby of 30 years and a menagerie of family, friends, and animals.

BOOKS BY AUBURN TEMPEST

Auburn Tempest - Urban Fantasy Action/Adventure
Chronicles of an Urban Druid

Misty's Magick and Mayhem Series – Written by Carolina Mac/Contributed to by Auburn Tempest

Exemplar Hall – Co-written with Ruby Night

If you enjoy my writing and read sexy/steamy romance, my pen name for the books I write in Paranormal and Fantasy Romance is JL Madore. You can find me on Amazon HERE.

CONNECT WITH THE AUTHORS

Connect with Auburn

Amazon, Facebook, Newsletter

Web page – www.jlmadore.com

Email – AuburnTempestWrites@gmail.com

Connect with Michael Anderle and sign up for his email list here:

Website: http://lmbpn.com

Email List: http://lmbpn.com/email/

https://www.facebook.com/LMBPNPublishing

https://twitter.com/MichaelAnderle

https://www.instagram.com/lmbpn_publishing/

https://www.bookbub.com/authors/michael-anderle

OTHER LMBPN PUBLISHING BOOKS

Sign up for the LMBPN email list to be notified of new releases and special deals!

https://lmbpn.com/email/

For a complete list of books published by LMBPN please visit the following page:

https://lmbpn.com/books-by-lmbpn-publishing/

Printed in the USA
CPSIA information can be obtained
at www.ICGtesting.com
LVHW030225100923
757647LV00068B/695

9 781685 005641